A DOUBLE POINTED MURDER

A DOUBLE POINTED MURDER

THE BAIT AND STITCH COZY MYSTERY SERIES, BOOK TWO

ANN YOST

ePublishingWorks!
love what you read.

Book and cover design by eBook Prep
www.ebookprep.com

March, 2019
ISBN: 978-1-947833-55-5

ePublishing Works!
644 Shrewsbury Commons Ave
Ste 249
Shrewsbury PA 17361
United States of America

www.epublishingworks.com
Phone: 866-846-5123

For Pete, with love

FOREWORD

Now you can experience the smells and flavors of the Keweenaw Peninsula just like the ladies from Red Jacket. When you finish the story, page ahead to the recipe for Christmas tarts – *Joulutorttu* – which are not to be missed. Enjoy!

ePublishing Works!

CHAPTER 1

The body on the morgue slab reminded me of the yellow-and-black swallowtail I'd exterminated in a kill jar and mounted on a piece of foam board as part of my tenth-grade insect collection.

Maybe it was the long, streaked blond hair and the thick black eyeliner.

Or maybe it was her name: Cricket.

Or maybe it was because the smooth epidermis just below the woman's breastbone was punctured by a small, round aperture like that one I'd made with the insect pin. Only a little bigger.

I'd shed tears when I'd been forced to kill the beautiful butterfly to satisfy the demands of a bloodthirsty biology teacher but at least the mission had been clear. It was different this time. I could think of no possible reason for anyone to have rung in the New Year by turning Cricket Koski into a shish kebab.

Well, that's not strictly true. I could think of one reason but I was hoping, in fact, praying, I was wrong.

In the main, we don't approve of murder here in my hometown of Red Jacket on Michigan's Keweenaw Peninsula, a witch's finger of land that crooks into frigid Lake Superior. I mean, we swat the heck out of the black flies that arrive like a tsunami every spring, we

ANN YOST

hunt and we fish and we have more than our share of roadkill, but we don't slaughter each other.

For one thing, there aren't enough of us to spare. For another, we are a close-knit, Finnish American community and our "Bible" is the actual Bible. We are taught to honor our parents, make no graven images and not to kill. Our county jail has only one cell. There is no detective on the sheriff's staff. In fact, there is no staff. Just a part-time deputy. There is no coroner's van. There is, in fact, no single coroner.

Unfortunately, though, things started to change last summer when our midsummer celebration (*Juhannus*) was interrupted by a swan dive off the Painted Rock Lighthouse fourteen miles away on the shores of Lake Superior. And last month, the lifeless body of our reigning St. Lucy turned up in the sauna at the Maki Funeral Home. The death of Cricket Koski last night seemed to confirm what I was beginning to suspect: we were becoming a destination location for murder.

My involvement with the investigation of the previous crimes was purely accidental. I had some credentials. I'd gotten through a year of law school (I dropped out to get married, but more on that later) and I've read plenty of mystery novels but, quite frankly, my deductive powers are closer to those of Agatha Raisin than Agatha Christie. My main qualification though was like that of Chauncey Gardner, who stumbled into the role of president: I was there.

So this was to be my third murder investigation and, arguably, the most important. This time the crime was close to home. Very close. In fact, Cricket Koski was a relation.

If you consider adultery one of the ties that bind.

A one-night stand three years earlier between the pretty barmaid and Lars Teljo, my sister Sofi's husband, had turned my brother-in-law into an ex. Recently, Sofi and Lars had been inching toward a reconciliation based on, in part, Lars's assurances that he'd had nothing to do with the woman during the intervening time. Unfortunately, Cricket's body had been discovered, last night, in Lars's bed and I was pretty sure that the fact that she was dead

2

would cut no ice with my sister. She would be furious with her ex-husband.

I just hoped the news would come as a surprise.

LET ME INTRODUCE MYSELF.

My legal name is Hatti Lehtinen Night Wind but for simplicity's sake and since I have been separated longer than I was married, I don't use my husband's name. Well, not at the moment. Everything about my marriage is up in the air and by that, I'm not talking about castles or rainbows. I guess you could call the outcome pending. Like a patent.

Our relationship started with a bang–love at first sight (at least for me) and it ended with a whimper (mine) thirteen months ago. After a year's separation, we're back on terms (speaking and otherwise) but last night was New Year's Eve and I celebrated it with my friends. Jace Night Wind was, once again, AWOL.

Anywho, as my stepdad, Pops would say, I've returned to the scene of my childhood. Red Jacket, Michigan is a time capsule of a town left over from the days of copper mining and populated by descendants of Finnish miners. And let me just say that, while I don't know what Thomas Wolfe's deal was, I do know that if he'd tried to go home again to a close-knit Finnish-American community in Upper Michigan, he'd have had no problem. It was as if time had stood still during the years I was away.

It was as if it had waited for me.

These days I spend my time managing Pops' bait shop which I've turned into a hybrid enterprise that sells both fishing and knitting supplies. I call it Bait and Stitch, but haven't had a sign made yet. Hybrids, by the way, are very popular up here where people are so scarce we all have to wear multiple hats. My sister owns Main Street Floral and Fudge and our post office branch is located inside the Hakala Pharmacy.

Back to me. I'm nearly twenty-eight years old, about five foot seven with thick, wheat colored hair that gets blond streaks in it during the summer and I have blue eyes. This coloring is not

3

remarkable. You can't swing a dead cat on the Keweenaw Peninsula without hitting a blue-eyed blond.

When I'm with Sofi, who is six years my senior, five inches shorter and more curvaceous and Elli Risto, the cousin who is just my age, my best friend and an elf, we look like a set of Finnish-American nesting dolls. Or at least we did when we all wore our waist-length hair in a thick braid. Nowadays, thanks to a moment of grief-stricken madness, my hair is short and ragged and it flops on my head in a pile of uneven petals. Think of a fading chrysanthemum.

At the moment, I'm back in my parent's butter-colored Queen Anne Victorian house on Calumet Street, sleeping under the glow-in-the-dark stars Pops stuck on the wall twenty years ago. I know that sounds lame but, in my defense, I'd started to move to a little bungalow on Toivo Street when Pops was struck with a snowmobile in the line of duty—he was Red Jacket's police chief. Since then he's recovered but he and my mom decided to spend the winter in Lake Worth, Florida, which is the third point of the Finnish Golden Triangle, along with the Upper Peninsula and Helsinki. I'm keeping the pipes from freezing by flushing the toilets. And I'm keeping Larry, Pops's beloved basset hound, company. Or, maybe it's the other way around.

I stared at the body and tried to focus. The death blow appeared to be a small, perfectly round hole just under the left breast of the woman my sister had nicknamed "the Insect."

"Weird lookin' wound, eh?"

I jumped at the sound of the familiar tenor. I'd forgotten I wasn't alone.

Waino Aho, Sheriff Horace A. Clump's latest in the revolving door of deputies, was hard to overlook, or he would have been if I hadn't known him my entire life. Waino possessed the physique of Paul Bunyan, the stunning baby blues of Paul Newman and the like-able grin of Paul Rudd. He'd broken the rules to let me into the morgue this morning and, anyone in town (at least anyone of a certain age) would have said it was because he was secretly in love with me, a myth that dates back to sixth-grade Vacation Bible

School when we'd been caught playing spin-the-bottle in the cloak closet at church. In fact, Waino was doing me a huge favor. He knew, as well as I, that I was at the top of Clump's people-I'd-like-to-run-out-of-town list. The sheriff and Pops had never gotten along and Clump still resented my involvement with the last two murder cases.

"Weird," I agreed.

"Looks like a wormhole."

I knew he wasn't referring to the hypothetical, topological feature that would be (if it exists) a shortcut through time and space. When Waino said "wormhole" he was referring to the orifice in a piece of fruit created by a burrowing maggot. I shook my head to dislodge some of the cobwebs. It had been a mistake to drive the five miles from Red Jacket to Frog Creek without any coffee but it was too late to worry about that now. I needed to learn what I could here.

"So what do you think made the wormhole?"

Waino shrugged his massive shoulders, a vacant expression on his handsome Nordic features.

"Not a bullet."

I'd already figured that out. There was no torn flesh, no wounding around the pinhole puncture.

"Doc'll know," Waino added.

"Doc" could have referred to any of the four men who share the medical examiner duties but I knew he meant Doc Laitimaki, the general practitioner who had delivered Sofi and Elli and me and, most likely, Waino, too.

"He's still in Lake Worth," I murmured.

Waino shrugged. There was nothing to say to that.

"Could the weapon have been a rapier?"

The baby blue eyes widened.

"A what?"

"One of those long, thin blades people used for sword fights during the Regency."

"The what?"

I sighed and decided not to explain. There probably wasn't a rapier on the entire Keweenaw. Our antique weapons run to Finnish hunting knives.

"What about a skewer," I suggested. He looked uncomprehending. "You know, that long, thin metal thing that people use to roast hotdogs and marshmallows."

"I use a whittled birch stick," he said. I nodded. We have plenty of birch trees. We use their branches for everything from building fires to making a *vihta*, or whisk that we use to slap ourselves on the back during a sauna. I refocused on the wound. I was mesmerized by it. There was something so familiar but I couldn't put my finger on it. A hazy image danced in my mind, as if I were looking at one of those stereograms and trying to relax enough to find the hidden 3-D image.

Waino released a puff of air, an indication that he, too, was seriously concentrating on the matter.

"Ya know, Hatti, a nail gun coulda' did it."

A nail gun? I stared at his blue eyes but they blurred as the answer came into focus.

"Waino," I breathed, touching his arm. It felt like a steel cable. "You're a genius. You figured it out."

"So it's a nail gun?" He sounded pleased. I shook my head.

"No, but the nail gun image got me thinking in the right direction." I paused. "Dollars to doughnuts this wound was made with a long, thin instrument made out of a carbon fiber composite, like the stuff they use in stealth fighter jets and Formula One racing cars."

Waino tilted his head to the side.

"What in the heck are you talkin' about, Hatti?"

"An instrument with tapered tips. The beauty of it is there's one in every household in Red Jacket. It's a weapon in plain sight." He still didn't get it, so I helped him out.

"A knitting needle, Waino. Probably a double-pointed one because it would be the right length and heft for a weapon. I'm guessing a size six. Or eight."

He shook his head. "That's crazy. Why would the killer use a knittin' needle when it would be a whole lot easier to use a huntin' knife?"

"Because," I said, thinking aloud, "it would be harder to trace. And the victim wouldn't see it coming. Because it was handy." I paused and Waino made one of those leaps of logic that was as terrifying as it was unexpected.

"In that case, Sofi musta kilt her, eh?"

CHAPTER 2

Geez Louise. It's what everyone would think. There was no one on the Keweenaw who didn't know that Sofi blamed Cricket Koski for the breakup of her marriage. There was no one who didn't know that Sofi and Lars had finally begun to talk about reconciling. Considering the efficiency of our grapevine, and believe me, it rivals the Internet for speed, folks were, no doubt, already speculating about Cricket's death and the fact that she'd been found in Lars's bed. Wait until they found out the murder weapon may have been a knitting needle.

The anxiety I'd felt when I'd gotten the late-night, jail-cell call from Lars, rocketed. Sofi and her ex were likely already at the top of the public opinion suspect list.

Double geez Louise.

"It wasn't Sofi." I'd waited too long to reply and Waino knew it. "She was with Elli and Sonya and me at the Leaping Deer last night." The Leaping Deer is Elli's Bed and Breakfast and it is on the corner next to my folks' house on Calumet Street. "Anyway, she had no reason to kill Cricket."

"Then it musta been Lars."

I felt a cold sensation in my forehead, as if I'd eaten ice cream too fast.

"Lars had no motive," I heard myself say. "He hadn't even seen Cricket Koski in three years."

"'Cept for last night." I glared at him. "Listen, Hatti, for what it's worth I don't think Lars killed the girl. He seemed floored when I went out there last night. My money's on your sis. You know what it says in the Bible; A woman scorned is mad as a hornet."

I didn't want to contemplate his point so I argued with his reference.

"That's not in the Bible. It's Congreve. *Hell hath no fury like a woman scorned.* The thing is, though, Sofi wasn't scorned. The whole thing happened three years ago and she's not scorned now." He shrugged his massive shoulders.

"Unless Lars started up with the waitress again."

Impossible. At least I hoped it was impossible. In any case, there was no point in arguing with Waino. He was just verbalizing what everyone else would say.

"I need to talk to Lars," I said. He opened the door that connects the morgue to the very short hall and the jail's single cell.

"Make it quick, Hatti. Sheriff's gonna be in early."

"To work on the case?" Waino shook his head.

"Vesta down to the diner's making fresh *pannukakku*. It's New Year's Day."

I took the seven steps necessary to get to the door of the jail cell. The small, square room, located, as I said, between the morgue and the sheriff's office, is made of cinderblock and contains a metal bed with a thin, stained mattress, a wash stand and an extra chair. It is sometimes used during the week as a drunk tank and, regularly on Friday nights for the sheriff's weekly pinochle game.

Lars Teljo was sitting on the mattress, his elbows on his knees. His lean body slumped, as if he'd stayed up all night. He'd clearly been running his fingers through his thick dark hair. I noticed he was beginning to go gray around the temples. He wore an ancient McKenzie plaid flannel shirt my mom had given him for Christmas about ten years earlier, close-fitting jeans and the buff-colored work boots with the sure-grip rubber soles that are standard issue for a Keweenaw winter.

"Go on in," Waino said. "There's no lock. We use the honor system."

Lars looked up at the sound of the deputy's voice. The green eyes looked remote and I got the feeling he'd been a million miles away. I entered the cell, sat down in the chair and cast a glance at a wastebasket full of dead soldiers. Bud Light.

"Not mine," he said. His voice was rusty as if he hadn't used it in awhile. "Waino's. I stuck to pop."

I said nothing but I felt a wave of relief. Alcohol had contributed to the whole Cricket debacle three years earlier and I knew Lars had vowed to stop drinking.

"What about your breakfast," I asked, glancing at the plastic tray propped next to him on the mattress. It was loaded with food, including scrambled eggs, crisp bacon and Trenary toast, a cinnamon-sugar, twice-baked rusk that is one of our UP specialties. There was a carafe of coffee, too, and an empty cup. I knew the food had been prepared by Sheriff Clump's mother-in-law, Vesta Raatikainen, owner of the *Lunch Box*. Vesta had been fond of Lars when he'd served as sheriff's deputy several years earlier and I guessed, from the lavish breakfast, she was still fond of him. Lars had always raved about her food.

"Help yourself," he said. "I'm not hungry."

"You should eat," I said, pouring myself a cup of coffee. "You've got to keep up your strength."

He flashed a lame facsimile of his old familiar grin.

"You're starting to sound like your mother."

After their shotgun wedding during senior year in high school, Lars and Sofi lived with us on Calumet Street for nearly ten years. He had always treated me like an older brother, except nicer. I, like the rest of the family, wanted to see him back with his wife and their daughter.

Coffee in hand, I settled back on my chair.

"Have you been charged?"

"Not yet but it's just a matter of time. I'm the obvious choice. Means, motive and opportunity. It's a slam dunk for the sheriff."

I wondered if it had occurred to Lars that Sofi might be implicated. Normally, my brother-in-law is a smart dude but this morning he was acting like a former NFL lineman who'd been hit in the head too many times. I figured I'd better keep things simple. "Tell me what happened."

He leaned against the wall, his eyes closed, long, black lashes resting on high cheekbones. He spoke slowly, as if by reconstructing the experience, he could hope to understand it. I knew he'd already spent hours going over the same information.

"I spent the day in Houghton with Charlie. We went to a Star Wars marathon at the Frostbite Mall. Afterwards, I put her on a commuter plane to Detroit Metro." Charlotte, or 'Charlie', is Lars' and Sofi's fifteen-year-old daughter. My folks had invited her to come down for a few days to enjoy the pool at the condo. Lars continued. "I got back to town around ten-thirty." He paused and I nodded to assure him I was listening. "I stopped by the duplex."

The duplex, located across Calumet Street from my parents's home, belongs to Aunt Ianthe and her lifelong bosom buddy, Miss Irene Suutula. They live in one half of it while Sofi and Charlie live in the other half.

"Sofi and I had planned to meet and talk," he said, rubbing his eyes with the thumb and forefinger of his right hand, "but she wasn't there."

"You must have forgotten about the New Year's Eve celebration at the Leaping Deer. Sofi, Sonya, Elli and I."

Lars dropped his head back against the cinderblock wall and rolled it from side to side.

"I didn't forget. She was supposed to leave the party early."

And then I remembered.

"Sofi did leave the party early, before we made caramel popcorn balls and just after we'd cast tin." Casting tin, a form of fortune telling, is a new year's tradition. "She told us she was getting sick and left a little after eleven."

"I must have just missed her," he said, his brow furrowed. "I kept falling asleep in the truck and I figured I wouldn't be much good to her until I got some shut-eye, so I went on home."

Home, these days, was a small, rented cabin on Dollar Lake, about a fifteen-minute drive from Red Jacket.

"So you got home around eleven fifteen or a little later," I said, speaking more to myself than to him. And then my curiosity, one of my besetting sins, got the better of me. "What were you planning to talk about?"

The flash of pain on his lean face made me wish I'd kept my mouth shut. He confirmed what I'd been thinking back in the morgue.

"Reconciliation. That's out the window now." He sighed, heavily. "Sofi will never believe I wasn't having a tryst with Cricket at the cabin."

"Were you?"

"No." There was no heat behind his denial. "I hadn't seen her in three years. I told you that on the phone last night. I'd had no desire to see her. That business was a blip on the radar screen during my drinking days. It meant no more to her than it did to me, Hatti. But, at least, she was single. I was the one at fault."

"Was she dead when you got back to the cabin?"

He shrugged. "Like I said, I was exhausted. I thought I was alone in the cabin and I didn't bother to turn on the lights. I grabbed a bottle of water from the fridge, shucked off my clothes and was asleep before my head hit the pillow. I woke up when I heard a knock on the door. I dragged myself out of bed to answer and there was Waino telling me he'd gotten an anonymous phone call about murder at my cabin. I told him he was nuts. He flicked on the light and pointed to my bed or, more precisely to the late Cricket Koski."

"Lars, why was she there?"

"Search me. Like I said, I hadn't seen her in years."

I stared at his defeated expression. I'd never known him to lie. It must be true. And, if it was true, then there was only one explanation.

"It must have been a set up."

He flashed me a weary grin.

"Thanks, Squirt, for believing in me." His smile disappeared. "But that doesn't even make sense. Why would anyone want her dead? She was just a barmaid. Not a threat to anyone."

I tried to look at it from another angle.

"Maybe it wasn't about her. Maybe it was about you. Have you got an enemy? Someone who wants you out of the way?"

"Just Sofi."

It was a bad joke and he knew it.

"Did Waino tell you what the caller said? I mean, exactly?"

Lars shrugged. "Said someone's been killed out at Teljo's cabin on Dollar Lake. Pretty straightforward."

"Pretty eerie," I said. "Your cabin's on a deserted dirt road a quarter of a mile from the interstate. No one happens by. The only way the caller could have known about Cricket is if he killed her."

Lars shrugged.

"There's no way to trace the call. Must've used a burner phone. Anyway, Waino got there, found Cricket and, what with one thing and another, I agreed to come down to the station with him."

"Under arrest?"

"Nah. Waino had Clump's damn Corvette. There was no way to get the body into it. We laid her out in the back of my SUV and caravanned back to Frog Creek." A year earlier, when it had been time to replace the sheriff's department old, woody station wagon, Sheriff Clump had decided to go with a fire-engine red Corvette. There were those who thought it was a questionable choice for a law man whose main job is to rescue motorists stranded in the snow but Clump claimed the sports car would improve the county's image with potential tourists.

"Only on the Keweenaw," I said. He smiled, briefly.

"Lars, shouldn't somebody have come in to look at the crime scene?"

"Waino's new at the job. I took pictures on my phone and jotted down some observations which I'll share with the sheriff if he's interested."

"He's got to be interested," I said, fiercely. "You certainly didn't kill her."

"Nobody'll believe that. I'm the only possible suspect."

"What about Sofi?"

"What?" He jerked into an erect position, his face flushed and contorted. "Don't be ridiculous," he snapped.

I didn't take offense.

"Everybody knows she hated Cricket Koski. And that wound on her chest? The perfect circle? I'm almost positive it was made with a double-pointed knitting needle. People will say it was a woman's weapon. And then there's the alibi. She left the party earlier last night."

"To go home and sleep," he growled. "She told you she was sick, right?"

"Nobody saw her. She could have met Cricket somewhere, killed her and dropped her off at your cabin. She's got a key, right?"

"She wouldn't kill Cricket. She wouldn't kill anybody. Hatti, you know that. For cripe's sake, don't mention this cockamamie idea to anybody else, okay?"

We heard the sound of the front door opening and, an instant later, Waino appeared outside the cell.

"Sheriff's here," he hissed. "You've got to vamoose!"

I looked at Lars. He'd come alive. All his circuits were humming now. "What can I do for you?"

"Besides keeping mum about Sofi? Find out what you can about Cricket. Where did she live? Who were her friends and enemies? Any family? She worked down at the Black Fly in Chassell."

I knew all about the Black Fly. Sofi and I had driven down there a month or two after the incident three years earlier. She'd wanted to get a look at the homewrecker. We only stayed for a few minutes and, afterwards, Sofi threw up in the parking lot.

We could hear Clump's slow, heavy footsteps in the outer office. He is short and built exactly like an egg with his greatest circumference around the middle so that when he walks, he waddles. Still, it was time for me to get out of there.

I opened the cell door, slipped into the morgue and exited out the back without glancing again at the dead girl.

CHAPTER 3

Chassell is thirty-miles south of Red Jacket, pretty much a straight shot down U.S. Route 41, the highway that starts in Miami, Florida and ends at Copper Harbor, (or starts in Copper Harbor and ends in Miami, depending upon your perspective). If I left now, I'd get there by seven-thirty a.m. on Sunday morning, New Year's Day, not an auspicious time to visit a bar. The Fly would open this afternoon so folks could come together to watch the Winter Classic, a hockey game between the Detroit Red Wings and the Toronto Maple Leafs played on the flooded turf of the University of Michigan football stadium.

The whole thing sounded kind of gimmicky to me but there were scores of Yoopers who wouldn't dream of missing it.

I figured I'd spend the next few hours comforting my sister.

The heavy sky broke open as I made my way along the two-lane road from Frog Creek to Red Jacket. Large, heavy flakes hit the windshield first but were quickly followed by snow showers. The wipers on my new-to-me Jeep Explorer worked double time, grinding away, like a metronome measuring my anxiety. It was a weird sensation. I used to be fairly happy go-lucky, a sunny person who saw life as full of possibilities. Jace's defection changed all that. My mind leapt back to that fateful day thirteen months earlier. I'd been in the kitchen of our tiny Capitol Hill apartment mixing a batch of *Joulutorttu*, which is a prune tart traditionally made at Christmas time.

Jace, arrived home from a week-long trip that included a stop to his grandfather's home at the Copper Eagle Reservation a few miles from Red Jacket, came through the door, put down his briefcase in time to catch me as I flew at him. He ignored my squeals of excitement and set me firmly on my feet. He just looked at me until I paused and then he said, "It's over, Hatti."

Oddly enough, I knew just what he meant but, of course, I didn't take it with a stiff upper lip or the stoicism that would have left me with a shred of dignity. I wept and yelled and demanded explanations that I never got. That was Friday. By Sunday, I was making the long, tedious drive back to the Upper Peninsula on autopilot. Somewhere around Cleveland I remembered I'd left the dough for the tarts in the mixing bowl on the counter. It reminded me of an upside down version of the Hebrews fleeing Egypt with unleavened bread and it seemed like a perfect metaphor for my failed attempt at matrimony.

Anyway, since then, I've turned into an all-purpose worrier. Waking or sleeping, I feel an undercurrent of anxiety about everything from war and death to red wigglers and mealworms. Mostly, though, I haven't worried about Sofi. She, like Elli, is true descendant of our strong, practical female forebears who braved the hardships of the isolated new land. If she has an Achilles Heel, (and who doesn't) it is her ex. I know in my soul that Sofi, my sister, would never kill another human being. I also know that Sofi, the bitter ex-wife, would like nothing better than to skewer Cricket Koski with a double-pointed needle.

So I was a little worried. Make that, more than a little. In fact, my stomach was tied up in knots.

The road from Frog Creek turns into Main Street. I followed it up to Third, then turned into the alley that ran behind the houses on Calumet including the Leaping Deer, my family's Queen Anne and the Maki Funeral Home.

I parked next to a three-foot snowbank then waded through a foot of fresh powder to reach the back door of the B and B.

Elli's family has owned the inn as long as I can remember. It has gone through several incarnations from boarding house to cheap motor hotel called the Dew Drop Inn. When my aunt and uncle retired to Florida, they left the ramshackle structure to Elli who rolled up her shirtsleeves and turned the white elephant into a state-of-the-art Victorian hostelry. Elli had not just restored the hotel, she'd made it better than ever, as my Great Aunt Ianthe was fond of saying.

Larry, who had the run of the place, was curled up on a rug on the kitchen floor watching with interest as Elli added flour to the industrial-strength mixer that's nearly as big as she is. He glanced at me, and the white tip of his tail jerked a couple of times in greeting. I knelt to rub his soft ears.

"Thanks for picking up Larry," I said, when the whirring had stopped. "What're you making?"

"Cranberry-orange-walnut muffins."

"Yum."

"They're for tomorrow. Have some *pannukakku*."

I helped myself to the pancake and coffee. I could hear the buzz of conversation and the clink of dishes and glasses on the other side of the swinging door that separates the kitchen from the dining room. I knew that half the town would have shown up for Elli's New Year's morning breakfast feast.

When I'd taken a few bites she started in with the questions.

"How did it go with Lars?"

"He says he didn't do it."

"Uh-huh. Why was she in his bed?"

"He says he doesn't know."

"Weak. He's going to have to come up with something better than that."

"I know."

"Sofi's not here, by the way. The aunts say she's got the flu."

"That means she knows about the Insect."

"Everybody knows, Hatti. You know the grapevine. But she really is sick. Remember, she mentioned it last night."

"That was a dodge. She was supposed to meet Lars but they got their signals crossed."

"Huh. They were going to reconcile, weren't they?"

"How the heck did you know?"

"Everybody knew, Hatti. That time you spent away from home must have dulled your instincts."

I felt foolish but persisted. "So what's everybody saying?"

"The usual. Aunt Ianthe said Lars is a good boy and wouldn't have hurt a fly much less a cricket. "Mrs. Paikkonen claims there's no smoke without fire and Miss Irene backed that up with a quote from Acts: *And there appeared cloven tongues unto them, like as fire.*"

"Pentecost," I interpreted. Miss Irene could be counted on the come up with a Bible reference, relevant or not, for every occasion.

"And then early this morning Mrs. Moilanen stopped in at the IGA to get the ingredients for her vinegar cabbage. She ran into Vesta Raatikainen from whom she got the story. Edna went home and called Aunt Ianthe and Betty Ann Pritula, in that order."

Betty Ann is the host of the radio program, *The Finnish Line*, or as Pops likes to call it, the Finnish-Me-Off Line. It comes on promptly at six a.m. every day of the week so that Betty Ann can inform us of events, teach us crafts and bully us into spending the day doing whatever she considers important.

"You weren't kidding when you said everybody knows about the body in Lars's bed."

I sectioned part of my pancake and dumped it into Larry's bowl. He favored me with another wag while he ate it.

"Hatti," Elli said, sounding hesitant, "you don't think Cricket Koski was trying to blackmail Lars, do you? I mean, if he and Sofi were talking about reconciling, Cricket could have seriously inter-fered by telling Sofi a pack of lies."

I shook my head. "Even if Cricket had tried to blackmail him, Lars wouldn't have killed her."

"Right."

"Anyway, he hasn't seen Cricket in three years. How would she even know he was trying to make it up with Sofi?"

Elli raised one eyebrow. "I think we've just established how impossible it is to keep a secret around here."

I put down my fork. Suddenly, I'd lost my appetite.

"There's some other news, too. Sonya's gone back to New Mexico for the first time since she moved here. She got a call after midnight. Some sort of family crisis."

Sonya Stillwater, a Navajo midwife who showed up on the Keweenaw a couple of years ago, is a close friend and the fourth member, along with Sofi, Elli and me, of our knitting circle.

"She caught an early morning jet."

"A jet? From the Hancock Airfield?"

Elli hesitated, as if she didn't want to explain.

"She flew out of O'Hare," she said, then blurted out the rest before I could ask. "Max drove her down to Chicago."

"Max? Max Guthrie? My Max? I thought those two were sworn enemies. Anyway, why would he go to Chicago without telling me?" Max, a forty-year-old outdoorsman with way more than his fair share of sex appeal, had bought Namagok, an old fishing camp. We'd bonded over bait, a shared sense of humor and (what I'd thought was) a mutual attraction.

This time both Elli's delicate eyebrows lifted.

"That's over, remember? You're back with Jace now."

I hadn't remembered. I wondered now why the recollection brought with it no warmth.

"Anyway, it was just a ride."

"Huh. Anything else I should know about?"

As she was shaking her head I heard my name shouted at maximum decibel level. My real name. Henrikki. I tensed and grimaced at my cousin. I called out, reluctantly.

"In here, Mrs. Paikkonen."

The door from the corridor swung open and a black-clad wraith-like figure exploded into the room. The Wicked Witch of the West incarnate. All she needed was the pointed hat. She shook a long, bony finger in my face.

"You, missy," she hissed, "have a problem."

I was vaguely aware of Elli kneeling by the quivering basset hound and of my great Aunt Ianthe, tall, large-boned and majestic, with her head full of snow-white curls and her magnificent bosom like the prow of a ship as she surged into the room behind Mrs. Pike. Miss Irene, following in her wake, like a small, neat, tugboat, wore her snowy tresses in a coronet on top of her head.

Elli and I had spent many hours of our childhood in the aunts's old-fashioned parlor. They'd taught us to knit and play canasta. They'd provided a haven from the cruel world of grammar school. They'd always been around to protect and defend us and they were doing it again now. Whatever I'd done, whatever I was guilty of, they were the cavalry, here to help.

"My land, Eudora," Aunt Ianthe said, trying to force the witch's attention away from me. "What on Earth is the matter?"

MRS. PIKE REFUSED to be distracted. She bore down on me, her long, spindly arms cartwheeling, her steely gaze so close to my face that my eyes crossed. I expected her to utter something unforgivable, like an accusation against my sister and I found I was holding my breath.

And then she surprised me.

With a black scowl on her long, thin face, Mrs. Paikkonen gripped my upper arm with a surprising strength for a woman in her seventies. She hauled me through the kitchen and dining room and into the corridor that led to the foyer where Elli's handsome, stained-glass, double front door stood open. I glimpsed the airport van parked at the curb. It was disgorging passengers. Very fish-out-of-water passengers. They looked as if they'd come from Oz and gotten dumped in Kansas.

Or Upper Michigan.

I heard Elli's soft Finnish curse.

"*Voi kahua.* Guests? Didn't they get the memo? I'm closed for the month. The plumbers have already started renovations on the bathrooms."

"Maybe it's an alien invasion," I said, making a weak joke.

"Nonsense, Henrikki. These are the television people," Mrs. Pike said in the same tone she'd have used to say, "these are the heathens."

"Television people?" Aunt Ianthe repeated. She and Miss Irene had followed us to the door. "Didn't anyone tell them we don't have a television station on the Keweenaw?"

"They are here," Eudora Paikkonen said, "to film a television show." At that, a small bell dinged in my memory.

"Arvo," I breathed. "This is one of his schemes, isn't it? Something he told us would put Red Jacket on the map?"

Arvo Maki is our funeral director. He holds a string of leadership positions in the community from Head selectman to president of the Library Board and the Historical Society. He is chairman of the Chamber of Commerce. In short, he is the face of Red Jacket, our Grand Pooh-Bah. He had undoubtedly arranged for whatever this was and normally, he'd be in the thick of it. But he was uncharacteristically missing in action because of our last murder.

"They're here now and somebody besides Arvo is going to have to deal with it," I said.

"Not somebody," Mrs. Paikkonen said. "The acting vice chair of the chamber of commerce. You."

"Me?" I stared at her.

"We held an emergency executive meeting before Arvo left town," Mrs. Pike continued. "You were unanimously elected to the post."

I wanted to protest. I didn't have time to deal with one of Arvo's crazy schemes for putting us on the map. I had to find out who'd murdered Cricket Koski. I had to help Lars. I had no time to deal with show biz people. But said people were now mincing their way up the shoveled path to Elli's front door and, really, there was no one else to handle this.

Did I mention that, here on the Keweenaw, we all have to wear multiple hats?

CHAPTER 4

The couple that reached the front door first looked like figures off the top of a Northern-Exposure Barbie-and-Ken wedding cake. They were both tall and slim. His expensively cut, black wool overcoat, white silk cravat and helmet of dark hair, styled with product and sealed with hairspray were complemented by the expressionless countenance of his neat, symmetrical features. Barbie, clinging to his arm, was a vision in winter white, a snow princess clad in an ankle-length coat with a gigantic fur hat with twists and curls of fur as white as the midnight sun. Her features were lovely, small and well-cut and, if not for the sullen scowl on her face, she'd have been beautiful. She batted, ineffectively, at the falling snow.

Oh dear.

The gentleman flashed a mouthful of brilliant white teeth at me when he got close enough to speak.

"I," he said, miraculously holding onto his smile as he spoke, "am Vincent Tallmaster."

The following pause indicated that I should recognize the name. I replied with my name only and he redoubled his efforts to impress.

"You will have seen some of my documentaries, two of which, I have it on good authority, were on the long list for the Academy

Awards." He quirked a perfectly shaped eyebrow. "*Skin: The Secret of Reducing Arm Flab,* and, even more recently, *The True Story of Bryan Mole.*"

"Who is Bryan Mole," Elli asked, after stepping to the door and introducing herself.

"Bryan Mole," Tallmaster said, with just a touch of impatience, "invented the light bulb."

"I thought that was Thomas Edison," Elli said.

"That's a common misconception," Tallmaster sniffed. "Perpetrated by, among others, the U.S. Patent Office."

"Oh," she said. "What is the secret, by the way? About reducing arm flab, I mean."

He shrugged. "Stop eating. Exercise. There's no magic bullet."

"I'm Helena Tallmaster," the woman said, clearly annoyed, whether by the conversation or the weather, I couldn't tell. I soon found out.

"What's with all the snow?"

I didn't bother to explain that we were in the forty-seventh parallel and bounded by great lakes which meant we frequently experienced two hundred feet of snow during the season.

"We get a lot of it," I murmured.

Elli decided we'd done enough fencing and invited the Tallmasters to come in. A moment later three more newcomers approached the porch. The phrase motley crew came into my head. I forced a smile and an apology.

"I'm afraid you've caught us at a loss but please come in and get warm."

Elli, turning away from the Tallmasters, seconded the invitation and added the offer of coffee and pancakes.

"*Pannukakku?*" The familiar word helped me untangle the trio as it was spoken by a slim, blond man of about my age. He noted my surprise and laughed.

"I'm Seth Virtunan. I have an antiques shop in Royal Oak, down by Detroit, but I spent summers in the UP."

"Do you always get this much snow?" The question came from the most colorful woman I'd ever seen. She wore a voluminous cape of many colors. Bright red hair curled up and away from her round face. She looked like a cross between Medusa and the bird lady from Mary Poppins. She was short and plump and introduced herself as Serena Waterfall, a textile artist from New York City. Her question was inquisitive without being critical and I grinned at her.

"You wouldn't ask if you could see the municipal budget. Most of it is used for moving snow from one side of Main Street to the other."

The final newcomer was Harry Dent, a middle-aged man of average height with a decent, compact build, copper-colored hair and penetrating amber eyes. His easy smile seemed to break down all barriers. It was as if he knew my faults and accepted them, as if we were already friends. The seductive twinkle in his eyes sent a not unpleasant shiver up my spine and I wondered what on earth Arvo had let us in for.

"We apologize for what must seem like an invasion on New Year's Day," Harry said, when everyone had eaten and we were settled in the parlor. The local ladies, including Miss Irene, Aunt Ianthe, Mrs. Paikkonen, Mrs. Moilanen and Mrs. Sorensen, had taken up their knitting projects. I winced when I noticed they were all working on socks which meant double-pointed needles. Harry continued.

"Our arrangements were made some time ago with Arvo Maki, your mayor?" He looked at me for corroboration.

"Something like that," I murmured. I couldn't help returning his smile. Mrs. Paikkonen was less charmed.

"Mr. Maki is away on unavoidable business," she said, overhearing us. "In his absence, Ms. Lehtinen will serve as your local liaison."

I swallowed a groan.

"Perhaps," I said, "you would like to give us some idea of why you are here." Harry Dent winked at me and read my mind.

"And what in the heck we want from you, right? That only seems fair. Here it is. Vincent and Helena are producing a new regional television series. The idea is to visit towns off the beaten path and encourage the locals to bring their treasures to be evaluated by experts. We," he said, indicating Seth, Serena and himself, "are knowledgeable about everything from military history to dishes to jewelry to textiles to art. Arvo agreed to let us videotape the pilot here in Red Jacket."

"Excuse me," Vincent Tallmaster said, getting to his feet. He deliberately peered at each of the dozen or so people in Elli's parlor, waiting until the knitting ladies looked up from their work before he spoke. He held his hands in a dramatic pose and intoned a question.

"What is in your attic?"

As his gaze had landed on Aunt Ianthe, it was she who spoke.

"Bats. Probably some mice."

"And the stork, the heron after her kind, and the lapwing and the bat," Miss Irene said, adding, "Leviticus."

Harry Dent seemed to be choking back a laugh.

"What Vincent means," Serena said, in a kindly voice, "is what kinds of treasures are stored in your attics? That's the name of our show, *What's in Your Attic?*"

For a moment I wondered how anyone in his right mind would choose a place to search for treasures where the twenty-two percent unemployment rate had held steady for years and then I remembered the persuasive powers of Arvo Maki. No doubt he'd emphasized the uniqueness of our town and not its poverty.

"Harrumph," Mrs. Paikkonen said. "Sounds like an Antiques Roadshow knock off." Vincent frowned at her.

"That's the idea," Seth said. "The twist is that our show will focus on rural areas, rather than cities. We want to showcase the real America."

"We will be counting on all of you to help us come up with the theme in the next day or two while we get the message out to the community and get our cameras set up," Vincent said.

"Cameras set up where, dearie?" Aunt Ianthe asked.

"Perhaps the church's social hall," Mrs. Moilanen said.

"Or the high school auditorium," suggested Diane Hakala, the wife of our pharmacist.

"The theater!" Aunt Ianthe clapped her hands, pleased at the brainstorm. "We have the oldest opera house in the state."

"I don't know," Miss Irene said. "Someone would have to call Ollie to turn on the heat and the lights. The building hasn't been used since the Salute to Sibelius at last year's Heikkinpaiva Festival."

"Heikkin-what?" The question came from Helena Tallmaster.

"It's a mid-winter festival," the Reverend Sorensen said. "It is to celebrate the bear rolling over onto his other side. In other words, it commemorates the beginning of the end of winter. We have a parade, smorgasbord, a polar dip and a wife-carrying race."

Harry Dent broke into the moment of awed silence.

"The opera house sounds like the perfect venue. I'd like to thank you for your cooperation and your hospitality. We hit the jackpot when we decided to set the pilot on the Keweenaw."

I wondered if he would still believe that when he found out we'd become the murder capital of the UP.

"It shouldn't be hard to come up with a theme," Seth said, smiling at Aunt Ianthe. "This is the land of sauna and smorgasbord and pasties."

Vincent favored him with a cold look.

"It's pronounced pasty," he said, making the vowel long, "and my show will not include a reference to anything as off-color as a strip tease."

"Pasties," Elli said, coming to Seth's rescue and pronouncing the word correctly, "are pocket pies. Vegetables and meat are baked into a crust. They were invented, originally, for miners who wanted a hot meal in the middle of the day when they were underground."

"I doubt whether you will find any treasures in the Keweenaw attics," Mrs. Moilanen said. "More like to find antlers and paintings of dogs playing poker than a Monet or a Picasso."

Harry chuckled. "I'm very fond of dogs playing poker."

"And that's saying something," Serena chimed in. "Harry was on the FBI's art theft investigation squad. He is a bona fide art expert."

"You know, there could be forgotten treasures in our attics. There's almost no new housing stock and families hang onto their homes for multiple generations," I said, thinking about it. "The attics are seldom emptied out."

"Excellent," Vincent said, looking a little calmer. "But I don't want to just do some ethnic theme. We need a better hook."

No one had anything to suggest. Eventually Helena Tallmaster spoke.

"If we are going to stay in this godforsaken icebox, I'd like to get settled in my room."

Elli's eyes met mine. She began to explain the renovations but Helena cut her off.

"Bottom line. Where am I supposed to sleep tonight?"

After a short discussion we decided to put the crew members, who were scheduled to arrive in the afternoon, at the Leaping Deer and to feed everyone there. The cast members were divided between my house (Harry and Serena), Aunt Ianthe's house (Seth) and the funeral home (the Tallmasters.) Mrs. Paikkonen agreed to serve as hostess at the latter although she did so with pursed lips and narrowed eyes.

As we finalized the arrangements I wondered how I'd ever find the time to investigate Cricket Koski's murder. I also thought about the possible ways to punish Arvo if he ever came home. Boiling oil, bamboo shoots under his fingernails and the hoisting of the Swedish flag on the flagpole at the park came to mind.

CHAPTER 5

It was early afternoon when I drove the visitors down to Main Street. The snow had started to fall harder and, for once, I was glad. The fresh fall hid a multitude of sins including discolored brick and faded paint and even buckling rooflines. Our downtown, drab and uninspired in June, looked like a Dickensian village.

Since I've made such a point of our economic problems I should probably explain that it wasn't always this way on the Keweenaw.

Back at the turn of the twentieth century, when the Finns and others arrived to work in the mines, the Keweenaw supplied something like ninety-five percent of the world's pure copper. The community coffers had overflowed and the town fathers used the profits to build, among other things, a medieval cathedral that would have attracted Quasimodo, two downtown blocks adorned with Victorian bric-a-brac and a spectacular library. They'd also built the opera house at the end of the second downtown block on the west side of the street next to the high school and across from the fire station.

Much has been written about our theater, the first one in the state. It is from the Renaissance Revival School, constructed of yellow-brown brick on a foundation of red sandstone from the nearby Jacobsville quarry. There's a copper dome and cornices and a porte-cochere in front where I parked the van. Both the exterior and the inside have been renovated in recent years and the town's historical committee (Arvo) had been careful to ensure that the original color scheme of scarlet and cream was maintained. Plush seats face the stage and proscenium arch and a magnificent chandelier hangs over the audience. Off to the right of the stage, behind the wings, is a green room.

"It's beautiful, Hatti," Serena said. "A little jewel box."

"Stinks of dust," Helena sniffed.

"Limited seating," Vincent said, a note of disapproval in his voice. I stared at him.

"It seats 700. For a town with a year-round population of 800 some of whom are infants."

"The theater will be perfect for us," Seth said.

"It'll be perfect," Harry said, "if it's haunted."

"Some people believe there's a ghost living in the cheval mirror in the green room," I admitted. "An actress named Maud who played here around 1900. She comes back to prompt actors who have forgotten their lines."

Serena clapped her hands.

"Oh, lovely! Mirrors, you know, are portals between this world and the one beyond. They are the natural habitat of spirits. The ghost will add so much to our show."

Serena grabbed Harry's hand and went off to investigate the ghost. Vincent and Helena wandered around while Seth spoke to me about practicalities, like how to publicize the event and where to order flowers to decorate the set. The last question jolted me back to my real life. I told him my sister could handle the flowers then I excused myself leaving him with the keys to the van while I hoofed the three blocks to the duplex.

The entrance to the half that belongs to Aunt Ianthe and Miss Irene faces Calumet Street, while Sofi's entrance is on the side. I climbed the three steps that lead to her stoop. Someone had taped a handwritten note to the door's window.

Sick Bay. Keep out. This means you, Hatti.

It was like Sofi to leave me a blunt message. It was unlike her to hide. What was this about? Didn't she trust me to take care of her and Lars? Or did she think Lars was guilty and she was afraid that, with my intuitive brilliance, I might realize that. In any case I decided to ignore the directive which was easy to do. We on the Keweenaw are more worried about being locked out in the cold than we are about intruders and we have adopted the habit of hiding our house keys in the milk chutes that have been idle for half a century.

I retrieved Sofi's key and let myself in.

All the lights were off in the kitchen and the living room and there was no line of light under the bedroom door. I felt a sudden rush of worry. Had she fainted? Gone to the hospital? Was she dead? I knocked, sharply.

"Go away, Hatti," she said, irritably. "Didn't you read the sign?"

"We have to talk."

"Tomorrow."

"This can't wait. It's a matter of life and death."

"Fine," she capitulated. "Come in then." Even in ill health she was indulgent about my habitual hyperbole and I felt a wave of affection. Together we'd get at the truth.

"Are you really sick?" Even as I asked the question she shot out of the bed and raced into the adjoining bathroom. Retching sounds filled the air and a moment later I was holding her long, thick, sweat-soaked hair above her head so she wouldn't get puke on it. I felt guilty for doubting her as I helped her back to bed. She fell against the pillow, her face white, her eyes closed.

"Is there anything I can get you?"

"Crackers," she whispered. "And Vernors," she added, citing the state's golden ginger ale. We believe there's almost nothing that Vernors and/or VicksVapoRub can't cure. "Then go. I want to die in peace."

"No dying, but I need the answer to one question. What time did you get home last night?"

One blue eye opened.

"You forget you're not the police chief anymore, Hatti."

She was referring to last month when I'd served as acting police chief for Pops after he was injured. A young girl was found dead in the sauna of the Maki Funeral Home and, while I'd caught the murderer (with help) the whole experience had been traumatic enough for the state and county to transfer all criminal justice issues to the Copper County Sheriff. In other words, I'd almost single-handedly stripped Red Jacket of its police department.

"Look, you're gonna need an alibi for Cricket Koski's death. If not for me, for Sheriff Clump. I suggest you start thinking of one."

I wouldn't have thought it was possible for her to look any paler but she looked, as we used to say, like death warmed over.

"You've been to see Lars."

"Of course. And I'm going to clear him, too."

"Think so?" She shoved herself up against the pillows. "What if he did it, Hatti? Have you thought of that?"

I sat down on the bed.

"Don't be ridiculous. Lars isn't a killer."

"Just a cheat."

"Sofi, that was three years ago. I thought you two were on the brink of reconciling."

She said nothing. I tried again.

"I'm trying to construct a timeline, okay? Lars says he was supposed to meet you at eleven but you didn't show so he left."

"When, at eleven-o-one?"

"He said he was wiped out and needed sleep, that he figured he'd try you in the morning. Anyway, it must have taken him fifteen or twenty minutes to get out to the lake where he parked his SUV and fell into bed. He didn't know about Cricket until Waino knocked on the door and woke him up."

She'd turned back toward me by this time.

"Waino went out to see him at one a.m.?"

"Not to see Lars. To check if there was a body. He got an anonymous tip."

"Huh."

"So tell me your story."

"Nothing to it. I came home from the party around eleven. Saw no sign that Lars Teljo had been anywhere near the place, neither did I get any sort of message from him. I felt like crap so I went to bed and I've spent the last few hours throwing up. Scintillating story, huh? At any rate, I can't give him an alibi."

I held her gaze for a moment.

"You can't give yourself one, either."

"What are you talking about?"

"Don't you see? You have as much motive as Lars for killing Cricket. More, probably. Hell hath no fury and all that." I couldn't believe I was using Waino's allusion.

"Well, I didn't kill her. How could I? I was sick. And, anyway, whoever killed her must have carried her into the cabin."

"What makes you say that?"

She hesitated just a little too long.

"I just assumed she was killed somewhere else and planted in his bed."

"You knew he found her in his bed?" She shrugged.

"Grapevine. Anyway, I suggest you let this go." I stared at her.

"You really think it was Lars, don't you? Are you crazy?"

My sister, her face pale and puffy, looked ten years older than her age.

"He lied to me, Hatti. He swore up and down he hadn't seen the Insect in three years but it wasn't true. If he could cheat and he could lie, what's stopping him from murder?"

I found myself thinking about the Ten Commandments, part of Luther's Small Catechism that we were all expected to memorize before confirmation. Thou shalt not covet thy neighbor's wife, bear false witness or murder. If Lars had done any but the first he really had fallen from grace. I didn't believe it.

I opened my mouth to ask for evidence, but I shut it again when Sofi flew off the bed and into the bathroom.

The questions would keep until tomorrow. I held her hair, handed her a moist washcloth and fetched the crackers and ginger ale.

CHAPTER 6

By the time I got on the interstate headed to Chassell it was four o'clock and nearly dark and the snowfall, which had taken a break in mid-afternoon, had resumed. Under any other circumstances I'd have postponed my visit for a day but my conversation with Sofi had lit a fire under me. If Lars had lied to Sofi, if he'd seen Cricket Koski recently, we had a whole new set of problems. I needed to clear him and my sister on the double and it didn't take a genius to realize that all this show biz stuff was seriously going to get in my way.

The parking lot of the roadhouse was packed, which didn't surprise me. We take our hockey very seriously in Copper Country. I parked my Jeep behind a monster truck and prayed the vehicle's owner wouldn't try to leave before I did. My little red car would be squashed like a bug. And speaking of bugs, I glanced up to see the staring eyes of a super-sized, fiberglass replica of a black fly which hung over the roadhouse's front door like a predator drone and I shook my head. Why would anyone would choose to immortalize the ubiquitous creatures that descend on the UP every spring like a Biblical plague of locusts? It boggled the mind.

. . .

INSIDE, some forty spectators, all of them men, all of them dressed in jeans, flannel shirts and work boots like those I'd seen Lars wearing this morning, were focused on the big screen television over the bar. Even the short, thickset bartender with the grizzled beard and his skinny young assistant were focused on the puck. No one looked at me as I made my way through the crowd, except when I blocked their view. Then they'd yell, "down in front!" And "yah, hey!" And "move yer butt!"

I made it to the bar.

"Red Wings winning?"

The older bartender nodded.

"Great," I said. "I'd like a Busch Lite. My name's Hatti."

"Dutch," he replied, filling a glass and setting it on the bar without taking his eyes off the television screen.

"Dutch? Your family is from the Netherlands?"

"Nope."

"Huh." I considered further inquiry into how he'd gotten the nickname but figured that, considering the communication obstacles, it probably wasn't worth it. I got on with the business at hand.

"I want to know about Cricket Koski."

Dutch picked up a glass and started to dry it. I considered it a good sign that he didn't immediately show me the door.

"Does she still work here?"

"Nope."

Well, duh. I knew that. "But she did work here, right?"

"Been gone awhile. Dead now."

News traveled fast even among the hockey-obsessed.

"That's why I'm asking," I said, deciding to lay my cards on the table. "What can you tell me? Did she have a boyfriend?"

He finally gave me an answer but it wasn't what I wanted to hear.

"Just the one. Dat brudder-in-law of yours."

A cold shiver ran up my spine.

"But that was a long time ago," I pointed out, hoping I was right. "Three years."

Dutch shrugged. "Don't know about that. He kilt her last night. In his cabin."

"That's not true!" My voice was high and hysterical. A dozen TV watchers shushed me. "She was found in his cabin. Somebody set him up."

He continued to dry the glass without looking at me. Eventually he continued the dialogue.

"Who?"

"That's what I'm trying to find out. When did she leave the roadhouse?"

"Coupla weeks."

"You know why? She get a new job?" He shrugged, his eyes back on the TV screen. An instant later a commercial for beer brought a clutch of spectators to the bar demanding Dutch's attention and I knew my window of opportunity was closing.

"Just one more question, Dutch. Where did she go?"

He leaned over the bar and accepted a couple of empty pitchers while his assistant filled new ones.

"Heard she went Copper Harbor."

I nodded and dropped some bills on the counter, including a hefty tip. It was a great lead even if I had to balance that against the fact that everyone (if Dutch was to be believed) thought Lars had killed her.

The question I kept asking myself, though, as I maneuvered my Jeep through the steadily falling snow on the interstate was why? What had driven Cricket Koski to leave the (relatively speaking) thriving township of Chassell with its population of nearly 2,000 to relocate to the tiny village at the northernmost point of the Keweenaw? Copper Harbor has a year-round population of fewer than one hundred and, during our eight months of winter, there would be no job possibilities. What then? Was it because of Lars? Was she in love with him? He was technically single now. Had Cricket wanted to build a relationship with him?

Or had she decided to build a stake by blackmailing him? My blood ran cold. How easy would it be to threaten to make up stories to tell Sofi? Cricket Koski could have been a major stumbling block to a reconciliation for my sister and her ex.

I kept coming back to that. It was like the answer that kept turning up on a Magic 8-ball. And I knew why. I believed in Lars, all right, but the fact is, the women in our family are very bad pickers.

My great grandmother left her husband of one year because he pulled a shotgun on her and her baby, my grandmother, *mummi*.

My father, allegedly a charming rolling stone, disappeared when Sofi was six and I just a few months old.

Sofi's teen-age shotgun marriage ended in divorce over Lars's one-night stand with Cricket Koski.

I myself had been married for eighteen months and I'd spent most of that time alone. That situation, never far from my mind, loomed up like headlights in the snowstorm.

Unlike every other girl I knew, I had not fallen madly in love during my youth. I saved that experience until I was in my mid-twenties. It happened like a lightning strike. He'd been a guest lecturer in a law school seminar on Native American rights. Tall, dark and chiseled with flinty gray eyes that had not singled me out in the room.

Later, though, as I was carrying a soggy cardboard box of abandoned puppies through a rainstorm, the guest lecturer had stopped his car and offered me a ride. It had seemed like a fairytale, like my destiny. Right up to that fateful afternoon of the *Joulutorttu*.

I hadn't seen him for an entire year, not until his younger half-brother, Reid, was accused of murdering his girlfriend, Liisa Pelonen, the reigning St. Lucy.

Granted, he'd finally told me what was behind his defection and we'd reached a kind of détente. But I couldn't help asking myself whether marriage was supposed to be this difficult.

The snow plopped on my windshield faster than my wipers could remove it. Sloppy slush covered the roadway making it slippery and I was thankful there was no traffic. It felt like the middle of the night and the clock on my dashboard indicated it was nearly ten o'clock when I pulled off the interstate onto Tamarack and headed for the alley behind Calumet Street. The Jeep's clock was exactly three hours and forty-seven minutes fast, though, so I knew it wasn't even seven p.m. I wanted nothing more than to slip into the Queen Anne, feed Larry and dive into bed but I knew my duty. I climbed the back steps of the B and B.

Elli must have heard the Jeep because she met me at the back door with a picnic basket covered with a red-and-white checked napkin. I blinked at her.

"Little Red Riding Hood, I presume?"

"I was going to take some supper to Sofi but I think you should do it."

"Why?"

"Well, for one thing, you look hungry and there's plenty in the basket. For another, you look tired and Vincent Tallmaster is on a rampage. He needs a theme for the *What's in Your Attic?* pilot and he expects you to come up with it."

"Geez Louise."

"Go. Eat. Check on your sister. Maybe by the time you get back we'll have a theme."

"Finnish-Americans on the Keweenaw," I said. "That's the only possible theme. The story of sauna and *Sisu* and St. Lucy." She shook her head.

"Give Sofi my love."

The duplex was still dark, the door, still locked. As I collected the key from the milk chute, let myself in and knocked on Sofi's bedroom door, I hoped she wasn't still sick. The prayer must have worked because she called out for me to come in and, while she was still in bed, her color was better, her hair had been washed and she'd pulled on her favorite sweatshirt, a dark green number emblazoned with the outline of the Upper Peninsula above the word "yours."

"You look better," I said, "except for the purple crescents under your eyes."

"Thanks for that," she said, eyeing the basket. "What have you got? I'm starved." Then, as if recollecting my cooking skills, she added, warily, "this is from Elli, right?"

I decided not to take offense. We both feasted on *kaljakeitto*, a hearty beer and cheese soup and two large hunks of *pulla*, a cardamom-flavored bread.

"I guess you're over the flu."

"Don't tell anyone." She wiped her mouth, daintily, with the napkin Elli had thoughtfully provided. "I figure Clump will leave me alone as long as there's a chance I'll blow chunks on him."

I regarded her for a minute.

"Why are you afraid to talk to the sheriff?"

She shrugged. "I just don't want to get involved."

"You're a really bad liar."

"Takes one to know one."

I stared at her again. "Did you kill that girl?"

"Of course not."

"Then I don't see what you're worried about. Unless you think Lars did it."

She took another bite of food so she wouldn't have to answer.

Weariness swept over me and I lost what little patience I possess.

"Come on, Sofi. You can't stay holed up here forever. I've got to figure this out and you've got to help me. You've been my sister for twenty-eight years and I can tell when you're keeping a secret. What is it? Tell me?"

"I'm not lying about anything."

"You just said for me to let people think you're still sick."

"I am sick. I mean, I will be sick again tomorrow."

"The way you were sick last night and had to go home right after casting tin?"

"Sarcasm doesn't become you, Hatti. I did have a headache last night but mainly I left early to talk to Lars. I must have missed him be a few minutes."

My eyes narrowed suspiciously.

"You went out there, didn't you? You followed him home."

"You make me sound like a lost puppy. No, of course, I didn't."

"Then why don't you want to talk to the sheriff?" She shrugged.

"I want to stay out of the whole thing."

"But you can help Lars. You can assure Clump that it didn't matter to you whether or not Lars had been in touch with Cricket, that she had nothing to blackmail him about and he had no motive to kill her."

"I can't do that, Hatti."

"Why not?"

She swallowed hard.

"I told you. He lied to me. Look, I found her phone number on a piece of notepaper in the pocket of his jeans."

I stared at her. "What was your hand doing in the pocket of his jeans?"

"You know we've been talking about reconciliation."

"I assumed the rules of engagement included being fully clothed."

"We're not kids, Hatti. We were married for thirteen years." She spoke calmly but her face had turned pink. "It wasn't a one-off."

"Holy moly!" I forgot all about the incriminating phone number as a lightbulb exploded over my head. "You don't have the flu. You're pregnant."

Sofi and Lars had tried for years to have another baby after Charlie.

"Ironic, isn't it? I mean everybody knows how much we wanted another child," she said, wearily. "And everybody knows Lars would do anything in the world to protect our reconciliation, especially if he knew about the baby."

"He doesn't know?"

She shook her head. "But Sheriff Clump isn't going to believe that. That's why I want to stay out of this, Hatti. There's no way I can help Lars and I can hurt him a lot." She sighed. "I'm heart-broken about Cricket's phone number but I don't want to hurt him. Charlie doesn't need to have a father serving a life sentence down at the federal prison in Milan."

"You can't stay in hiding forever."

"I know, I know. That's why you've got to pin this on somebody else and fast. And, for pity's sake, Hatti, don't breathe a word to anyone about the phone number."

"Wait a minute. How did you know it was Cricket's phone number?"

Sofi lips twisted.

"For one thing, her name was next to it. For another, there was a printed message on the notepaper. It said, anything your heart desires will come to you."

"A line from *When You Wish Upon a Star,* Jiminy Cricket's song in *Pinocchio*," I said. "Sounds like she was a romantic."

"Or, at least, she knew her cartoons."

CHAPTER 7

My head and heart were so full of the news about the baby, both the joy of it and the potential danger to Lars, that I was surprised to find half the town of Red Jacket at the B and B, assembled for the purpose of coming up with a theme for *What's in Your Attic?*

Miss Irene was seated at the upright piano softly playing Victorian parlor tunes like *Love's Old Sweet Song*, and *The Lost Chord*, and a medley from Stephen Foster.

Music was something my great aunt and her best friend had in common. It was also the one thing that had threatened their eighty-year friendship.

The near-disaster was precipitated by the departure, some twenty years earlier, of the organist at St. Heikki's Finnish Lutheran Church. Miss Irene, who had taught piano to the children of Red Jacket all her professional life, was considered the natural successor but it turned out that Aunt Ianthe, a primary school teacher who is also musical, wanted the job. Needless to say, the conflicting wishes set up an awkward situation and (according to my mother) the town was on tenterhooks until the then pastor, the Reverend Virjo came up with a Solomon-esque solution.

Aunt Ianthe, he'd decreed, because of her aversion to sharps and flats, would perform the hymns written in the key of "C" and Miss Irene would get all the rest, including the coveted, jewel-in-the-crown, *Be Still My Soul*, by our musical uberhero, Jean Sebelius.

"And so," Pops said, out of earshot of the ladies, "thanks to the wisdom of Pastor Virjo, peace was restored in the valley. And without cutting a baby in half."

BUT, back to the present.

Aunt Ianthe, Mrs. Moilanen and Diane Hakala were knitting socks out of the new, self-striping yarn that I'd ordered for my shop. Mrs. Paikkonen, sitting on a straight-backed dining room chair, was working on a pair of plain gray socks and Mrs. Sorensen, perched on a settee, was creating a Fair Isle sock with a ring of tiny reindeer around the cuff. All the finished socks were intended for Fibber McGee's Closet, our local charity outlet.

Seth sat next to Helena Tallmaster on the mahogany-framed love seat Elli had reupholstered in a lush green-and-pink striped fabric and Harry Dent, who favored me with an amused glance, leaned against the wall next to the fireplace, his arms crossed over his chest. Serena Waterfall dressed in a fuchsia-colored sweater and an immense pair of puce-colored bib overalls that did nothing to minimize her bulk, was plopped on a chintz-covered hassock. She appeared to be eating yogurt out of cup and the comparison with Little Miss Muffet was inescapable.

I joined Elli on the shallow step that separates the front hallway from the parlor.

Everyone, including Miss Irene who remained at the piano but stopped playing, was watching Vincent Tallmaster who stood in the center of Elli's thick, maroon-colored Persian carpet, a scowl on his handsome features, his hands clasped in front of him as if he were about to perform an oration. Or an aria.

"We've been spitballing," Harry said to me, out of the corner of his mouth, "in the time-honored manner. Each of us has written down an idea and the good padre here has volunteered to read them aloud for consideration without giving away the author."

I managed to look at the Reverend Sorensen who was shuffling a handful of post-it notes but my main attention was on the lifted eyebrows of Aunt Ianthe and the pinched expression on Mrs. Paikkonen's face. Dent's use of the word "padre" smacked of Catholicism, and therefore, blasphemy.

Harry, unaware of his faux pas, smiled at the minister.

"Go ahead, Dick."

Dick! I'd forgotten that the pastor's given name was Richard. Folks in Red Jacket always called him by his title but the reverend didn't flinch. He withdrew his reading glasses from the pocket of his cardigan, put them on and cleared his throat.

"Our first suggestion is the Finnish-American tradition including a brief history of the farmers who immigrated to copper country in the late 1800s." He looked up, over his glasses, apparently unable to resist an opportunity to educate. "It was to be a temporary move. The Finns were farmers, not miners, and in nearly every case they intended to earn enough money to buy land when they returned to the homeland. What happened, and this is the exciting part, is that they stayed to embrace and enrich America. They started unions and newspapers and churches. They put down roots and lived by example. They revered education and founded a fine liberal arts college here on the Keweenaw."

"Oh, yes," Mrs. Sorensen said, jumping in. "With a theme like that we could educate viewers about the historical highlights of the region, like the Italian Hall Disaster of 1913 when seventy-three persons, most of them striking mine workers and their children, lost their lives during a Christmas party when someone falsely yelled Fire!"

"That seems a little downbeat," Mrs. Moilanen said, looking up from her knitting. "We should highlight something more positive, like *Sisu*."

"See-soo?" Vincent frowned. "Is that the way you pronounce see-saw?"

"No, dearie," Aunt Ianthe said. "*Sisu* is a quality of perseverance in the face of adversity." She smiled as her needles clicked. "It refers to tenacity and stoicism and bravery in the Finnish culture."

"Too earnest," Vincent pronounced. "Not what I'm going for. And, anyway, that theme must have been done to death. What else have you got?"

The Reverend Sorensen peered at the notes in his hand.

"Ghosts and ghost towns." He looked up over his reading glasses. "There are quite a few small mining settlements that have been completely abandoned on the Keweenaw," he explained. "Some buildings remain but they are empty."

"The ghost town idea is interesting," Seth said, diplomatically, "but I can't quite see how empty houses would play into our goal of finding forgotten treasures in local attics." I had to agree with him.

"In any case," Serena Waterfall said, "the ghost towns may be the homes of the departed. We would not want to disturb them any more than we want to disturb the ghost in the mirror down at the theater."

"Our departed are located on Church Street," Mrs. Paikkonen said, stiffly. In the Old Finnish Cemetery or, as Pops calls it, the marble orchard. "And, of course," Mrs. Moilanen added, "in heaven."

"Or *Tuonela*," Aunt Ianthe said, with a twinkle. "That's the land of the dead in Finnish mythology." She paused and nodded at Miss Irene who quoted First Corinthians.

"O death, where is thy victory? O death, where is thy sting?"

"If we're going to have a theme about death, maybe we should focus on the rash of killings we've had up here this year," Mrs. Moilanen said, practically. She measured the red, blue and yellow striped stocking with her hand. "Murder is always popular."

During the sudden silence that descended on the room, Elli whispered in my ear.

"Somehow I don't think Arvo will see that as the best way to lure tourists up here."

Vincent seemed to be considering the suggestion but, after a moment, he shook his head.

"Too specific. We don't want to turn this into a true crime show."

"In other words," Harry drawled, "we don't want the murders to eclipse the attic treasures." Vincent frowned.

"We need something dramatic but not life-and-death. Something more than long-dead copper mining and Finnish kitsch."

"I know," Aunt Ianthe said, with a smile. "What about Hatti's new yarn shop? She could use the publicity and everybody in the UP loves knitting you know."

"You have a yarn shop?" Serena's pale blue eyes focused on me.

"A hybrid. Knitting and fishing supplies," I said. "It's called Bait and Stitch."

"That sounds unique," Serena said, thoughtfully. She turned to Vincent. "You know, it wouldn't be a bad idea to shoot some scenes in local shops. And a yarn shop would make a colorful backdrop."

"But that's just a venue, it isn't a theme!" Vincent wailed.

I wanted to offer something and suddenly, I knew what it was.

"There is something at my shop that might be suited for the show," I said. "I've got a Rya Rug hanging on my wall. It was originally woven as a wedding gift for a bride in Finland. Somehow it wound up in our attic and Pops gave me permission to hang it in the shop."

"What is a Rya Rug?," Harry Dent asked. Serena answered him before I could.

"It's got long, dense pile double-knotted for extra warmth," she explained. Her cheeks were flushed and her eyes sparkling. The animation made her almost pretty. "A Scandinavian handicraft created originally for sailors heading out to sea. I can't believe you have one," she added, looking at me. "They're not easy to find, at least not in good condition."

"Since this one was a wedding present and was never used at sea, it still looks good if a little yellowed. It's got a white wool background with a tree of life woven in red."

Vincent's quick frown revealed his lack of patience with the subject.

"We need more than a rug. We need a theme," he said, injecting a note of impatience in his voice.

The Reverend Sorensen adjusted his glasses and read,

"Romanovs."

It didn't take much imagination to know who had suggested the idea of featuring Russian artifacts and, after a short pause, Helena said, "we could use this annoying snow as a background for keying in on the Russian Revolution and featuring such things as jewels, crowns, goblets, Faberge eggs. Russia is the quintessential metaphor for winter."

"Good gracious," Aunt Ianthe said. "I don't believe there is even one jeweled egg in Red Jacket, then." Her comment prompted another quote from Miss Irene.

"Or if he shall ask an egg, will he offer him a scorpion?"

"A scorpion?" Helena Tallmaster shuddered.

"I'm certain Luke meant it figuratively, dear," Aunt Ianthe said, comfortingly.

"I'm afraid there is another problem with a Russian theme," the Reverend Sorensen said, apologetically. "Russia is Finland's neighbor to the east and the Finns's greatest nemesis. In fact, there was a series of wars in that region during the 1930s and 40s."

"You mean World War II, of course," Vincent said, condescendingly. "That's been done to death."

I darted a look at Elli and I could tell, by the stricken expression on her face that she foresaw the same disaster that I did. A hush came over the others, too. Aunt Ianthe and Mrs. Moilanen stopped knitting and Miss Irene, who had resumed playing with the soft pedal, froze in the middle of *Lumi, Lumi, Lumi,* (Snow, Snow, Snow). I held my breath, hoping no one would correct him. And then I heard Harry Dent's pleasant voice unwittingly pounding the final nail in the coffin.

"I believe the good reverend refers to the Winter War between Finland and Russia. It was that conflict that prevented the Finns from joining Great Britain and the Allies in the war against Hitler."

"Oh, yes," Serena said, trying to be helpful. "Finland was neutral during World War II. Like Sweden."

I squeezed my eyes shut, hoping against hope that the Reverend Sorensen, a man of the purest ethics, would not feel that he had to clarify the situation. Once again, though, Harry stepped in.

"Finland," he said, "was greatly outnumbered by the Russians and needed an ally. Neither the United States, the United Kingdom nor France could help out because of the non-aggression pact they had signed with Stalin. Hitler offered troops in exchange for access to the nickel mines in Karelia. Finland really had no choice."

Helena Tallmaster was quick to grasp the relevant point.

"So the Finns became Nazis?"

That wasn't strictly true but it wasn't strictly untrue, either. If only, I thought, Vincent would dismiss this tidbit the way he'd rejected the others. Unfortunately, he was enchanted.

"The Finns fought on the side of Germany? That's amazing! That's stunning! Why doesn't anyone know about this? We can break the news! Think of the marketing possibilities! Finnish-American boys fought native Finns. Just like the Civil War! Brother against brother!"

"More like second cousin against second cousin," the Reverend Sorensen said, uncomfortably, "and, in fact, no Finnish soldiers ever fought American soldiers. All the conflict was on the Eastern border against the Russians."

"No one has to know that." Vincent's color was high and he raked his long fingers through his spray-stiffened hair. "That's the theme. This is the theme! The Finnish role in World War II as depicted through attic treasures from Northern Michigan. It's a winner! A sure winner!"

I exchanged another glance with Elli. Arvo was going to be distinctly unhappy about this. It's not that we Finnish Americans are ashamed of any of our history but the World War II connection with the Nazis, which we are taught was forced upon Finland, is not a period we like to emphasize.

The summit meeting broke up soon after that and while I was standing in the kitchen loading coffee cups into the dishwasher, I heard Harry Dent's voice in my ear.

"Surveys show that ninety-five percent of viewers will watch anything on TV with Nazi in the description. This idea may actually produce an audience for the show and it can't really hurt the Keweenaw."

I turned to find him only about twelve inches away and I inhaled his masculine essence. The man had an undeniable sex appeal.

"Where are we going to find enough objects that relate to World War II, never mind the Nazis, in attics that are full of kerosene smelters, snowshoes, and old bathtubs?"

"I imagine we'll have to expand the perimeters," he said. "But just think about the excitement of revealing the little known secret about the Finns."

I scowled at him. "Just so you know, Finland was the only country to pay back its war debt." He chuckled.

"Most commendable."

"What we need," said Vincent, bursting into the kitchen through the swinging door that connects it with the dining room, "is Nazi memorabilia. Swastikas and that sort of thing. And, anything that connects the two countries. There must be books and letters written about the partnership. Find those. And we'll need a clever tagline, something like, Swastikas and Saunas or Finns against Kin, or The Finns had an axis to grind." He looked at me standing at the sink with my hands in dishwater. "Get on that, will you?" Vincent exited with a flourish.

"Look, Cupcake," Harry said, "we can keep this dignified. There must have been some contact between the Finnish-Americans in Michigan and the Finns facing the Winter War, you know, relief efforts and so on." I searched my memory.

"There was the Finnish Relief Fund established by Herbert Hoover. Americans, many of them Finnish-Americans raised millions of dollars to help the refugees from the Winter War. And, of course, it is well known that even when Finland was a co-antagonist with Hitler, Helsinki refused to indulge in any of the anti-Semitic practices."

Vincent whirled into the room again but only briefly.

"Take a memo," he said, focusing on me. "I want replica Nazi flags for the backdrops and flower arrangements in Nazi colors whatever they are. Handle that." He disappeared before I could speak.

"Why," I said to Harry, "is he behaving as if I'm his private secretary?"

A warm, male hand ruffled my hair and sent shivers of awareness down my spine.

"Must be your Aryan coloring," he said, with a grin.

I wasn't sure whether he snatched his hand back or I moved away first when, an instant later, Serena Waterfall came through the swinging door.

"Did you know that Hitler had no red in his aura?"

Since the war-mongering dictator had been dead for seventy years I wondered how she could know.

"No red?"

Serena shook her head and the twists and corkscrews of orange hair bobbed and weaved. She had her cell phone with her and had clearly consulted Google.

"Blue and yellow. It's surprising, really, since red is the color of aggression. It's also the color of sexuality, though. And the theory is that he was impotent."

I felt the red that was missing from Hitler's aura flood up into my face but neither of the other two was looking at me. Harry's lips had quirked into a half grin and Serena was gazing at him with stars in her eyes. I wondered whether her infatuation with him was new or whether they had a history. She certainly didn't seem to be his type. Not that it was my business, I reminded myself. My job was to get back to investigating Cricket Koski's murder, and, if at all possible, to deflect Vincent from ruining Finland's good name on national TV.

When I returned to the parlor I found Elli sitting cross-legged on the floor. Most of the others were gathered around, watching her remove items from a very old, very stained cardboard box.

"I noticed this up in the attic recently," she said, with an apologetic glance at me. "I don't know what's in here but somebody has written "The War Years," on it."

"Maybe it's Hitler's ashes," Vincent Tallmaster said. "Open it, open it, open it!"

"Geez Louise," I muttered.

CHAPTER 8

S he didn't open it. At least not right away. Instead we all stared at the corrugated cardboard that had gone limp with time as if it held, instead of memorabilia, a terrorist bomb.

"That doesn't look familiar," Aunt Ianthe said, with a slight frown. She and Miss Irene were among the oldest lifelong residents of Red Jacket and, as such, represented our institutional memory. "My brother fought in the Korean War and, I believe, Elli's grandfather did, too. This must be letters from those days."

"No, no," Vincent shook his head decisively. "No one is interested in that war. Evil is what draws an audience. People are fascinated by Hitler. Hitler is the key to the success of *What's in Your Attic?* This refers to World War II. There can be no argument about that."

Eventually Elli tried to untie a knot that had hardened in place some seventy years earlier. After a few seconds though Harry Dent produced a folding knife from his hip pocket then he neatly slit the twine. Elli didn't thank him. She just opened the top of the box and once again we were all staring at it.

"Holy moly," Elli said, echoing my thought, as we stared at a heavy-looking, old-fashioned gun.

"Looks like a Mauser," Seth said, "standard issue for German soldiers during the war. Probably picked up as a souvenir."

"Eureka!" The exclamation came from Vincent Tallmaster.

"Is it loaded?" Aunt Ianthe asked, anxiously.

Harry took it out of Vincent's hands and peered into the chamber. He looked very comfortable with the weapon in his hands. "No bullets," he said, smiling at the elderly lady.

"What else is in the box?" Mrs. Moilanen was so interested that she'd set aside her knitting.

Vincent held up a medal on a ribbon.

"An iron cross," Seth said, in a stunned voice. "It's almost as if this stuff was planted, as though someone knew we were going to use a World War II theme. Look at the swastika on the medal and the pair of oak leaves."

"Another souvenir," Harry Dent said. "These are almost certainly the belongings of a Finnish-American soldier. The pistol and the medal may have been taken from a fallen officer. I have to tell you there's nothing too remarkable about this. I ran into quite a bit of war memorabilia when I was on the art theft squad. In fact, you can buy this kind of stuff on the Internet."

"There are letters, too," Aunt Ianthe said, peering into the box. "Maybe they explain about these German artifacts."

Elli held up a stack of envelopes, all of which had been neatly slit with an opener. The letters were still inside. She handed them to Harry who extracted one and examined it for a moment. Vincent became impatient.

"What does it say?"

"Pure gobbledygook." Harry grinned and handed me the letter.

"It's Finnish," I said, recognizing the umlauts. "It is dated July 22, 1942 and it starts off, *Rakas Tati.* Dear Aunt. And the sign off is *Kunnioittavasti.*"

"Ah, that is very, truly yours," Aunt Ianthe said. "Who wrote the letter, dearie? And who is the aunt?"

"It's signed, Ernst." I examined the back of the envelope. "And the recipient is Mrs. Bengta Hautamaki, Red Jacket, Michigan. No postal code, of course."

"I don't remember anyone named Bengta," Miss Irene said, thoughtfully. That didn't surprise me, as she and Aunt Ianthe had been children at the time the letter was sent. "The sender was Ernst Hautamaki," I said, reading the return address. And then I looked at the postmark and a tremor ran down my spine.

"I don't remember any Hautamakis," said Mrs. Moilanen, who by my calculations must have been little more than a baby in 1942. "There have been Victormakis, Lahtimakis, Vihreämakis."

"Mustamakis, too," Aunt Ianthe said. "Remember Lula?"

"Why so many Makis?" Harry asked.

"Maki means hill," Elli explained. "There are a lot of lakes and fens in Finland. Apparently there are a lot of hills, too." And then my great aunt asked the question I'd been dreading.

"What about the postmark, Henrikki," Aunt Ianthe asked. "Was it sent from Helsinki?"

The postmark was blurred and faded but legible enough to understand. I spoke with some reluctance.

"Not Helsinki. It was posted from Munich."

There was a stunned silence. Mrs. Moilanen recovered first.

"Munich? You mean the Munich in Germany? Was this young man, this Ernst Hautamaki, a Finnish Nazi?" She had pushed herself to her feet.

"No, no, Edna, I am certain that is not correct," the Reverend Sorensen said. "I am certain there will be some other explanation. My Finnish is a bit rusty but I imagine I will be able to translate enough to get an understanding of it."

"I will translate the letter," Mrs. Paikkonen said, twitching it out of my hand. No one argued with her. For one thing, we all knew that she read a Finnish edition of the King James Version every night. For another, well, no one ever argued with Mrs. Paikkonen. She was formidable. When we were younger, Elli and I had believed she was a witch. And not the good kind, like Glinda.

"I will study this carefully tonight and give you an accurate reading tomorrow."

"Absolutely not," Vincent said, glaring at the older woman. "I have to know what is in the letter now." He sounded like a thwarted five-year-old.

"Mrs. Paikkonen is correct," the pastor said. "The position of

Finland during World War II was a delicate matter. It wouldn't do to exploit a letter from a nephew to his aunt. It is important to get the translation right."

As curious as I was about the letter I was also relieved to get a reprieve. I needed time to work on Lars's predicament and I needed time to think. As I walked back to the Queen Anne with Larry and my guests, I couldn't believe that just last night Elli, Sofi, Sonya and I had been celebrating with confetti and molasses popcorn balls and cheap wine. It was less than twenty-four hours into the New Year, Sonya was long gone, Sofi was hiding out (and pregnant) and I was up to my forehead in Nazis and murder.

I GAVE Serena the master bedroom and assigned Harry to the one formerly used by Sofi and Lars. It had crossed my mind that it might feel weird to have the out-of-towners in the house but it turned out I was too tired to care. As soon as I snuggled under the woolen blanket in my childhood bed with Larry serving as a hot water bottle for my feet, I was out like a light. In fact, I was smack in the middle of a very enjoyable scene in which Jace was on his knees apologizing to me for our breakup when a familiar, rasping voice interrupted.

"Rise and shine," Betty Ann Pritula shouted. "In the words of Thomas Jefferson, early to bed, early to rise, makes a man healthy, wealthy and wise. It's the second day of January and there are big, big doings on the Keweenaw!"

CHAPTER 9

I'd instinctively crushed my pillow over my head and missed part of her patter. By the time I sat up, Betty Ann had launched into her public service announcement.

"You, too, can be on television! Come one, come all to the once-in-a-lifetime opportunity that awaits you this morning at the historic Red Jacket Opera House, where world-renowned television producer-slash-host-with-the-most Vincent Tallmaster is taping the pilot episode of the soon-to-be-smash-hit show *What's in Your Attic?*"

The thought flashed through my mind that Arvo had not left us completely high and dry as regards the invasion of the television people. He'd written a press release for Betty Ann, possibly a month ago, before the discovery of a body in his sauna had changed his life forever. I listened as Betty Ann continued.

"Scour that attic for heirlooms and family treasures, everything is worth considering, from that ancient toboggan to your grand-mother's mangle iron to that set of Wedgewood china to those brilliant Marimekko tapestries from the 1970s. Look for paintings, too. You never know when something that you thought was just a doodle by your Uncle Paavo might turn out to be an authentic Picasso. International experts will evaluate your treasures and offers will be made on each and every valuable. Show your community spirit and your acting chops and help put Red Jacket on the map!"

At least, I thought, trying to find a silver lining, the announcement hadn't included the word Nazi.

My sense of relief, though, turned out to be premature. A few minutes later, while I was toweling dry my short hair, Betty Ann returned to the subject.

"Friends," she said, with slightly less enthusiasm in her voice, "I have an update on the television pilot. The powers that be have informed me the show's producer and host, Vincent Tallmaster, has decided to build his show around a specific time in history, that of World War II. He wants to encourage you to bring artifacts that reflect that time, in particular, the role of the Finns who were, as you know, engaged in several wars during that period. Items might include weapons, souvenirs or objet d'art from the, uh, Third Reich or something more domestic, such as a poster of Rosie the Riveter." She paused. "In other announcements, four to six inches of snow is predicted for this afternoon and the Copper County High School Miners will face off against the Watersmeet Nimrods tonight at the ice arena in Hancock. Come down and root for your team!"

I made a face in the bathroom mirror. Surely there couldn't be much in the way of Nazi memorabilia in Red Jacket. After all, Finnish Americans had been solidly on the side of the Allies, the U.S. and Britain. The worst that would happen would be a set of Hummels or some other teutonic bric-a-brac. But I frowned as I thought about the Nazi flowers, flags and colors planned for the television pilot. I had to find a way to derail that.

I dressed hurriedly in a gray sweatshirt bearing the words *I have a crappie attitude* under the emblem of a grinning fish, a pair of clean jeans and some hand-knitted socks, then I ran a brush through my still wet hair, slapped on a little lip gloss and headed for the stairs. I was aware of a slight feeling of excitement at the thought of Harry Dent sleeping across the hall in Sofi's old room. And then I wondered at myself. I'd been devastated by the breakup of my marriage but sometime, during the months apart, I'd begun to be aware of men. Other men, that is. There was Max Guthrie, for example. Gradually, I'd been attracted to what I saw as his masculinity combined with a genuine liking for women. Harry Dent, I thought, seemed to fit into the same category. Off-limits but intriguing.

I couldn't understand this attraction and, I told myself, I didn't have to explain it. My so-called husband wasn't here and I didn't know where he was or what he was up to. I had no one to answer to except myself. I thrust my thoughts into a mental drawer, closed it and threw on my snowboots and pink parka. Then Larry and I waded through the snow between our house and the B and B.

BOTH THE KITCHEN and dining room were buzzing with activity. Residents had stayed up late cooking and baking to help Elli feed the visitors and they'd come over early to set up a smorgasbord that included Mrs. Sorensen's delicious *kalakukko*, a casserole of fish and pork, Diane Hakala's almond buns and Ronja Laplander's three-berry relish (blue, cloud and boysenberry). Elli had made fresh *pulla* and an egg strata and Mrs. Moilanen had contributed her signature dish, vinegar cabbage.

Seth Virtunan had come across the street with Aunt Ianthe and Miss Irene and their sticky buns, and I filled a plate and took a seat next to him.

"You seem like a nice Finnish boy. How did you end up in a place like this?" He laughed.

"I love the UP, especially the Keweenaw," he said. "I spent several summers up here as a kid. But if you're asking how I got involved with Vincent, well, he posted some notices at an antiques show I was attending. I have a little shop inherited from my folks and I spend a lot of time at flea markets and so on. Business is slow because, frankly, the younger generations aren't much into sets of china or collectibles. I'm always trying to figure out how to drum up business so when I saw his notice, I called him. When he told me they were going to videotape in Red Jacket, I was sold. It's Little Finland up here. It feels like my spiritual home." He made a self-deprecating gesture.

"I'm sorry about this World War II theme, though. Vincent clearly doesn't understand how sensitive a subject that is. Not," he added, honestly, "that it would stop him. And, in a way, he's right. People are interested in Nazis."

"What's the story with Helena," I asked, realizing I was being extremely rude. "She seems like she'd rather be anywhere else."

"She's okay. She's just unhappy. She made a mistake in her marriage. Vincent's got a good act and apparently she fell for it. Other than that, she's smart."

"So Helena's the brains behind the operation?"

"Oh, no. That's Harry. Lord knows why he joined our motley crew. I overheard him talking to one of the cameramen and it sounded as if he'd done it as a favor to Serena, although why she'd bother with this, I don't know. She's got her own little gallery in Tribeca in Manhattan. Mostly textile art and some pottery. Maybe they just thought it would be a kick."

"You speak about them as if they were a couple," I said, unable to resist a little more prying.

Seth's blue eyes revealed concern.

"They were married for about two minutes years ago but they've remained friends. At the moment, I think he's interested in you, Hatti. I know it's none of my business but you should watch your step. The guy has broken a lot of hearts from what I hear."

His words gave me a little tingle of warmth which I knew was just plain silly. What possible interest could I have in someone twenty years older than I? And a sophisticated playboy to boot? Anyway, I thought Seth was wrong about one thing. I'd recognized the adoration in Serena's hazel eyes when she looked at her ex. This wasn't about friendship for her.

"You know," he said, "this theme business might just work. The Keweenaw has been trying to lure tourists up here with sauna, smorgasbord and *sisu* for years. If we could find a real historical connection with Nazi Germany, I'll bet that would be a strong lure."

"But there is no connection, Seth. You know that."

We were speaking only to each other but he inched even closer and lowered his voice to a whisper.

"Listen, last night I did some research on my phone. Get this. In 1942, Finland sent a small contingent of quasi-diplomats to Munich. The individuals were chosen because of their facility with languages, specifically because they could speak German. They were housed at Nazi Headquarters, a place called the *Fuhrerbrau*, which was one building in a complex that also housed Nazi-looted artwork."

I stared at him. "Are you saying that our letter writer might have been one of those diplomats?" Seth shrugged.

"The letter's postmark is Munich. What if that letter includes information about what the Nazis were warehousing at the headquarters? What if he was trying to alert the rest of the world to the looting that was taking place?"

"Through his Great Aunt Bengta?"

"Why not? Who would suspect a correspondence like that?"

"But, to what end?"

"Maybe there's a reference in the letter to a specific work of art. Maybe it reveals where a lost masterpiece is hidden."

I thought about that for a minute.

"It would be interesting, if not important. I mean the artwork was probably discovered decades ago. But I don't see how that contributes to *What's in Your Attic?*"

"Sure you do," he said, with a smile. "A letter of historic importance would be fascinating for viewers, especially if it does name a painting that we can locate in a museum somewhere. Or, another possibility. It's well known that the Nazis hated modern artists and that, in some cases, they destroyed works by Matisse, Monet, Picasso and Klimt and the others. Maybe Ernst Hautamaki witnessed a bonfire. Just his account would be historically interesting."

"Okay, okay," I said, laughing, "you've sold me. We'll just have to wait for Mrs. Pike to translate the letter to see if there's anything there."

"You know what would be really cool? If Ernst managed to get a hold of a painting and shipped it to the Keweenaw."

"That would have been hard to do when Germany and the U.S. were at war."

Seth appeared to think about that.

"But Germany and Finland were on the same side. The Axis. What if Ernst salvaged a painting and sent it to relatives in Finland with instructions to ship it to the U.S. for safekeeping?"

I grinned. "I guess he'd be a real Finnish hero. It would be interesting to see what he did after the war, wouldn't it? I wonder if he ever visited the Keweenaw. Maybe he came to collect his Monet?"

I'd spoken teasingly but Seth stared at me.

"Monet? Why did you choose that particular artist?"

"No reason. Why? Is it significant?"

"No. No, it's not significant, exactly. Just coincidental. Harry started collecting art when he was working for the FBI. I believe he has several impressionist masterpieces. At least one is a Monet."

"*Holy wha,*" I said.

CHAPTER 10

I was glad to get in under the wheel of the Jeep and head up U.S.-41 to Copper Harbor. I needed to make some progress on the Cricket Koski murder investigation and I wanted to get away from town and the craziness of the newcomers. Also, I needed time to myself. Time to figure out what I should do about Jace. What I should do about Max. And why, with those two studs in my mirror, I found myself fantasizing about Harry Dent. My nerves were spinning out and forty minutes of gazing at the cloud-filled sky, the empty road, the leafless trees and the mounds of unbroken snow in the fields to the east and west, soothed me. Sort of.

A third of the way into the thirty-mile trip, the sun behind the tree-line rimmed the clouds with a kind of rose gold color that was breathtaking. I glanced at my sidekick posed on the passenger's seat with his nose out the half-opened window.

"See the sun over there? I think it's a sign. We're gonna have a breakthrough on this case."

Instead of turning his head when I spoke, Larry angled his neck a little. His ears fell back and he stared up at the ceiling of the car. The move reminded me of the awkward way Sheriff Clump holds his head. The lawman's resemblance to Humpty Dumpty is partly because of his exceptionally expansive circumference but also because the skin between his ears and shoulders does not constitute a neck in the traditional sense. His head moves forwards and backwards but not left and right. Anyway, Larry reminded me of the sheriff which reminded me that Sofi had found Cricket's phone number in Lars's jeans which reminded me that Lars had lied to Sofi and to me. My quick flare of anger probably had as much to do with my own faltering marriage as with hers but, if I was going to defend the man, I needed to know the truth. The trouble was time. I made a mental note to stop in at the jail in Frog Creek as soon as possible but first I'd see what I could find out about Cricket.

Copper Harbor is built on a grid—well, a mini grid. It consists of the interstate which turns into Gratiot Street for two blocks before morphing back into the tag end of the 2,000-mile highway that starts in Miami and a parallel block north of that and then there's a kind of road that hugs the shoreline of the lake. In between are short cross streets, most of them consist of one establishment on either side of the road. The surrounding area includes a snowmobile trail, campsites and Lake Fanny Hooe, which legend has it was named for the sister-in-law of a young officer, a woman who disappeared while picking berries and was believed to have been eaten by a bear. The town developed around the shipment of copper in the mid-1800s which resources were exhausted well before the turn of the twentieth century. Nowadays it serves as a port for the ferry that carries visitors to Isle Royale, a national park that is also the largest island in Lake Superior.

The small shops in Copper Harbor are located in old houses with few exceptions. Most are gift shops which are closed during the winter. A few businesses stay open all year for the convenience of the hundred full-time residents. One of those is the Gulp 'n Go on the corner of U.S.-Route-41 and Walnut Street. I drove past a small art gallery, Ole's Gift Shop, the Whitefish Bar and Saampi's Ice Cream Parlor then turned down Pine Street where I parallel-parked on the street in front of a worn-looking, gray, wooden house with the standard A-frame roof that allows snow to tumble off. There was no sign to indicate the nature of the business but a card in a lighted window proclaimed it open.

I felt a jolt of déjà vu as Larry and I made our way up the short, shoveled walk. Even though I hadn't been there in several years, it looked and smelled the same as the days when I'd come up here with Pops to visit his friend. For a moment, I felt the warmth of my step-dad's presence as strongly as if he were there and, when I got inside, I found myself glancing at the low freezer by the door, the one that had always been stocked with the much-coveted blueberry popsicles.

An old man stocking the shelves with cans of food turned to greet me and I was shocked to see that he wasn't nearly the physical giant I'd remembered. His abundant white hair still connected with his moustache and beard outlining rosy cheeks and twinkling blue eyes, though. We exchanged wide, delighted smiles.

"Hatti-girl! Such a long time! And, Larry. Come here boy. I have meaty bone for you, yah?"

A moment later Larry was lying on the wooden floor, gnawing on his gift in front of the pot-bellied stove while Nestor Hyppaa and I sat nearby with mugs of coffee.

"You have been out in the world spreading your wings, then? I keep track of you from your *isä*," he said, using the Finnish word for father. "He says you go away to college, eh? And get married? So where is he, this husband?"

"In Washington, D.C.," I said, opting for the simplest response. "Things between us are complicated." Nestor nodded and didn't pry.

"You are glad to be back home?"

"I am glad," I said, meaning it. "It's comforting to know that some things don't change."

"*Voi*, Hatti-girl. Life is change and all of it is good, even the bad parts." We both laughed at the apparent contradiction. "There is change here, you know." It occurred to me, belatedly, that Mrs. Nestor was nowhere to be seen. Since Nestor, his wife and three children had lived in the top floor of the old house, she had always been around when I'd come up here with Pops and I was stricken by the possibility that something had happened to her.

"Where is Hulta?"

He chuckled. "That's the change. We don't live above the shop anymore, Hatti-girl. We got a little place in Eagle Harbor."

That was news. "You drive in every day to work then?"

"Hulta wanted to live near Rini and her children. We live next door to them." He pulled out a cellphone and showed me photos of his grandchildren. Frankly, I was impressed with his mastery of the technology. Pops would have nothing to do with a cellphone or computer and we still handled all transactions at the bait shop with an old-fashioned cash register.

"So tell me," he said, snapping off the phone, "why you come up here today? Snow is going come, you know."

I grinned at him. "That's something that doesn't change. Snow is always going to come. I was hoping you could tell me something about a young woman named Cricket Koski. She used to work at the Black Fly in Chassell but moved to Copper Harbor a few months ago. Have you heard of her?"

The warm grin faded on his kindly face.

"I know she is dead, then. The police came to tell me."

That startled me. "Why you?"

"Because my address was in her purse. She lived here, Hatti. Upstairs in our old home."

I just stared at him, shocked at my good fortune but sobered by the note of sorrow in his voice.

"She came in November when everything is closed. She asked if I had a job for her or lodging cheap. It was cold outside, eh? I felt sorry. She was all alone and not too bright. I don't mean stupid, you understand, just a little simple."

"Naïve?"

"*Joo.* Yes, that's it. She did some chores for me, straightening up, sweeping the floor, that sort of thing. It seemed to me good to have someone in the house at night, you know?"

"It sounds as if you liked her company."

"She reminded me of Rini when she was a child. Everything romantic. Magical. Cricket was waiting for her Prince Charming."

I stared at him. "She told you that?" He nodded.

"Many times. Prince Charming and her ship coming in. These were favorite subjects."

Was Prince Charming Cricket's killer? Had she gone somewhere to meet him thinking he was offering happily ever after?

"Did she tell you his name?"

He shook his head but not before I'd seen something flash in his kindly blue eyes.

"What, Nestor? What is it?"

"Henrikki, it could be Lars."

"No, no. There's no way." I refuse to hear that theory, not even from an old family friend. "There's something else, isn't there? You know something about this guy."

He shook his head again.

"Cricket had no family, no friends. She said she had the big date, though, for New Year's."

"The big date? That must be the guy. This so-called prince. And he must be the killer, too. But who is he?"

Nestor shook his head and a tremor of fear rippled down my spine. I shook it off. Prince Charming wasn't Lars. It couldn't be.

"Why would anyone want to kill Cricket Koski? It's not like she had any money."

"Not yet. Remember the ship coming in."

"You think she was mixed up in something dangerous? Smuggling? Drugs?" He shrugged.

"She was excited for the money but more excited for the man."

After an uncomfortable moment, I got to my feet and asked if I could see Cricket's room. Nestor nodded and pointed to the narrow staircase behind the counter. As soon as I reached the landing, it was obvious which room had belonged to the barmaid. It was full of pink and purple items, feather boas, glittering plastic crowns and necklaces of sparkling beads. Ruffled tops and slinky tops, leather slacks and pairs of tights, half a dozen pairs of four-inch heels were strewn on every surface as if someone had opened a closet and dumped it all out. The scent of hairspray mixed with a strong perfume and the small dresser top was littered with makeup brushes and containers of powder and blush and eye shadow and an array of lipsticks. A bottle of purple opalescent nail polish had been left open and there was a (luckily unplugged) curling iron on a chair. The barmaid must have spent most of her income on her back.

Cricket Koski had been twenty-eight, my age, but her room was that of a teenager preparing for the senior prom. And her date? Had he been her killer? Another shiver rippled up my spine and made the little hairs on the back of my neck stand on end.

I perched on the edge of her bed and tried to think. What was the ship she was waiting for? What had Prince Charming promised her? Was it something illegal? Was that why he'd killed her? But why tell her about it in the first place? Of what possible use had an immature millennial been to a criminal? And why her?

That last was easy enough to explain. Cricket Koski had been alone in the world, with no one to care whether she lived or died except Nestor.

I closed my eyes and tried a technique that a yoga teacher had taught me. I breathed in through my left nostril and out through my right, concentrating on the breath, concentrating on staying in the moment. It was a form of meditation that could be calming. It could also, I'd discovered, allow new ideas to penetrate the general haze of anxiety in my conscious mind. I found my mind jumping back to my pre-teen, princess worshipping years. I'd kept a flashlight in my bedside table and, after lights out, I'd use it under the covers to write in the diary I kept under my pillow. With my eyes still shut, I slid a hand under the pillow, hoping that Cricket, had confided her hopes and dreams (and the names of possible murderers) in written form.

There was no diary there.

But there was an envelope. The slit at the top was neat and precise. It had been opened initially with some care and, judging by the slight fraying near the cut, it had been opened several times. It was important then. Or, it had been to Cricket.

I recognized the Christmas card as one of those from the ninety-nine-cent rack at Shopko. The cover consisted of a picture of Rudolph the Red-nosed reindeer, a wreath around his neck, and a toothy smile on his face. Inside the printed message read: Merry Christmas, deer!

The sender had repeated the greeting in a childish hand, accompanied by a signature.

"Merry Christmas, from Cloud."

For some reason, tears stung the back of my eyes. It was such a simple card to be so cherished. Cricket had not been just a cardboard princess-wannabe. She'd been a person with real emotions and, at least, one connection. A connection so important that she'd kept the card under her pillow where she could look at it every night.

So who was Cloud?

There was no return address on the envelope but, as with the letter from Munich, the postmark provided important information.

The card had been mailed from L'Anse, a settlement near the Keweenaw Bay that was home to an Ojibwe Reservation.

Cloud. Cloud must be an Indian.

As I slipped the card back in the envelope, I noticed something I'd missed before. A phone number! My heart started to pound. I could call Cloud! Or, better yet, I could use the number to get her address. I could be down in L'Anse in an hour.

I pulled my phone out of my pocket and started to copy in the number. A heady feeling swept over me. I might not be Jessica Fletcher but I was getting the knack of this detective business. Suddenly I couldn't wait. I hit the call button prepared to introduce myself and ask Cloud if I could come visit her. The phone rang a few times, six, I think, and then it was answered by a machine.

"This is Lars. Leave a number and I'll call you back."

CHAPTER 11

I was thunderstruck, not to mention sick to my stomach. He'd lied to me. Lars had lied to me. And what was worse, he'd lied to Sofi. He must have been in contact with Cricket Koski, why else would she have his number? And it was a new number. During the past three years we'd changed cellphone services in the UP and this was not the number Lars had been using three years ago.

A jury would believe they'd been in touch either to resume their long-ago, one-night-stand affair or because he intended to kill her. Or maybe both. In any case, it wasn't good.

And he'd had her number, too. I could think of no good reason why Lars should have risked his reconciliation in this way. The phone numbers, it seemed to me, were as damning as the fact that Cricket had been found in Lars's bed.

Poor Sofi! Her happy ending seemed to be drifting farther and farther out of reach.

She needed help. And pronto, as Pops would say.

The morning sun had disappeared behind the clouds and a rising wind caught the snow on top of the drifts and streaked it across the road in front of me. I knew I had to control or, at least, compartmentalize the hysteria so I forced myself to review Lars's story about New Year's Eve.

He'd spent the day with Charlie down at the Frostbite Mall and he'd driven her to the regional airport near Hancock that evening to catch a puddle-jumper down to Detroit Metro. It had been snowing, though, and I made a mental note to check whether there was a flight available. After that, he'd returned to Calumet Street some-time before eleven p.m. with the intention of meeting Sofi.

Lars said he'd been too tired to wait for Sofi to come home, that he'd headed straight for Dollar Lake and his bed where he'd fallen asleep as soon as his head hit the pillow. So he was in bed before eleven-thirty. Had Cricket already been there? Had he been too tired to notice her? Or, equally as improbable, had someone broken into his cabin and planted her body in his bed without waking him?

In any case (according to him), he'd awakened sometime after one a.m. when Waino pounded on his door. At virtually the same time, if he was to be believed, he'd become aware of the corpse next to him. I groaned. None of it seemed possible.

And then there was the bit about Waino getting an anonymous phone tip. Why would Lars have called in if he'd been the murderer? Why would someone else? That part was easy. It was to set him up. Law enforcement on the Keweenaw was neither high tech nor sophisticated and finding a body in someone's bed was pretty much of a slam dunk for that someone getting arrested. By two thirty or three a.m. on New Year's morning, Lars Teljo was locked up in the Keweenaw County Jail. Had that been the killer's goal? Why?

Was the barmaid merely the vehicle? Had she been killed just to frame Lars? I still couldn't come up with a good reason for that. As far as I knew, his only enemy was his ex-wife and she couldn't have killed Cricket Koski.

Could she?

I felt antsy and irritable, a sure prelude to a panic attack. What I needed to do, and ASAP, was to find this Cloud person and learn more about Cricket.

I'D JUST PASSED the exit for Red Jacket when my cellphone chimed.

I dug it out of my pocket, knowing it would be a mistake to answer it. I answered it, anyway.

"Hatti, get back here STAT," Elli said. "World War III has broken out."

I grimaced. "Is this about the Nazi thing?"

"Let's just say that Vincent wants to sew black Swastikas on the antique velvet stage curtains. Helena Tallmaster is making fun of the ghost in the mirror which has reduced Serena Waterfall to tears and Mrs. Paikkonen to curses. Oh yeah, and the safety catch was off the antique blunderbuss Ollie Rahkonen brought for the video-taping and he accidentally blew a big hole in the proscenium arch."

"Geez Louise."

"But wait, there's more. Lydia Saralampi showed up with her collection of chicken-themed cookie jars and she fell off the stage into the orchestra pit and claims to have a concussion."

"Let me guess. She was flirting with Harry Dent."

Lydia, who was in Elli's and my high school class, was constitu-tionally incapable of passing up an attractive man. She was a boundary jumper from way back and both Elli and I had lost boyfriends to her back in the day. Actually, it was a miracle she'd never been physically hurt before.

"So what happened?"

"She was walking too close to the edge," Elli said, tongue-in-cheek. "She claims Serena Waterfall shoved her. Naturally Serena denies it. Lydia's threatening to sue. Hatti, it's Armageddon."

Dang. My instincts had been right about Harry and the textile artist. The petty part of me was glad Lydia had finally paid a price for her behavior. The other part of me realized I had to postpone my visit to Cloud. Elli definitely needed help.

I swerved into a sharp U-turn, bouncing across the grass median.

"On my way."

Minutes later I skidded to a stop in front of the opera house, parked the Jeep and, with Larry beside me, hightailed it up to the porte-cochere where Vincent and Helena Tallmaster stood, in their full length coats with fashionable scarves arranged around their necks. Each of them was holding a long, gold cigarette holder in which was inserted an unlit cigarette.

Helena glanced without interest at Larry then glared at me. "Does it ever stop snowing around here?"

I nodded. "During the months with no 'R' in the spelling." She blinked.

"You mean the summer. What do you do for entertainment then?"

"Black flies," I said. "Snow is better. Trust me. How's Lydia?"

The television host blinked at me. "Who?"

"The woman Serena Waterfall pushed off the stage."

"She wasn't pushed." He took a drag on his cigarette. "She lost her balance and fell. You know how it is with these overweight women," proving he didn't know what he was talking about. Lydia Saralampi is tall and willowy. The only thing fat about her is her thick, wheat-colored hair. And her long, enhanced eyelashes. Helena, naturally, was more clued in.

"She was interacting with Harry. That's why she didn't see the edge of the stage. He has that effect on women. Serena saw her stumble and she tried to catch her."

"Without success, I gather."

Helena shrugged. "Not much you can do about gravity."

"You don't think Serena was jealous?"

Vincent looked at me. "Hell, no. Harry and Serena are just friends."

"I understood they used to be married."

"Is that right?" Vincent sounded uninterested.

"Ancient history," Helena said.

I wondered if I'd be jealous of Jace even if I hadn't been married to him in twenty years and I figured I would.

"I'll just go check on things," I said.

Lydia looked like a soap opera heroine the way she was draped on an antique chaise lounge in the Greenroom. She wore a gauzy chartreuse blouse with the first three buttons undone and her braid had been released so that her long, thick, fair hair billowed around the high cheekbones of her face. Tapered, manicured fingers wrapped themselves possessively around Harry Dent's square, masculine wrist. They reminded me of snakes slithering among the rocks.

Harry looked up at me, an amused expression in his eyes. It was as if he were inviting me into the ridiculous situation. I looked away.

"Hello, Hatti," Lydia said, in a melting voice, her eyelashes fluttering, "it's wonderful to see you. How exciting it is to have these guests in town." As she spoke, she drew Harry's captive hand up to her cheek and caressed it.

"Elli said you hurt your head."

Lydia's laugh trilled. "Dear Elli. Always so tactless. I didn't hurt my head. I was pushed off the stage, bumped my head and got a concussion. I'm starting to recover though. If someone could just take me home," she said, smiling at Harry and squeezing his hand.

"Of course, of course. I think just to be on the safe side though, we should have a doctor check you out. I'll drive you over to Frog Creek to see Doc Laitimaki."

"He's still in Lake Worth," she said, her grip tightening on Harry's fingers. "Anyway, I don't need a doctor. Just a strong shoulder to lean on." She smiled up at Harry.

"Sonya can take a look, then," I said, offering the midwife's services. During her short time in Red Jacket, my friend had gotten used to handling all sorts of medical crises.

Lydia shot me a sly look. "I heard Sonya went on a road trip with your boyfriend."

It was a typical snarky comment from the woman and I pressed my lips together to keep from responding. After a few seconds, I smiled at her.

"Are you referring to Max Guthrie? He's a great guy, isn't he? It was nice of him to drive her to the airport. But, as far as Harry here, he has to stick around for videotaping. I can take you home."

"Wait, what about my cookie jars? They were made in Finland during the war."

I picked up a ceramic rooster and checked the writing underneath which read *made in China*.

Seth Virtunan materialized suddenly to tell me Elli needed me in the Greenroom.

"I will take care of Miss Saralampi," he said, flashing her a warm smile.

"It's Mrs.," She corrected him but I noticed she released Harry's hand. Harry said a hasty goodbye to Lydia and followed me into the Greenroom where I found Elli, Aunt Ianthe, Miss Irene, Mrs. Moilanen and Serena standing in a semi-circle in front of the mirror. I joined them.

"She's gone," Aunt Ianthe said to me. Her face was bereft. "Maud, I mean. She has left the mirror."

I stared at the glass in the antique, free-standing mirror.

"How can you tell?"

"I felt her vibes," Serena explained. "Earlier, I mean. Then there was that unfortunate gunshot and, well, some things were said. Maud took offense. It is really unfortunate. Such a bad omen."

"Most likely Maud took exception to all the activity at the theater," Harry said, "And she's moved, temporarily, to greener pastures.

It was a good opening for Miss Irene and she seized it.

"The Lord is my shepherd," she said. "He maketh me to lie down in green pastures."

"Amen," said Aunt Ianthe.

"Maybe," I suggested, "she went on vacation. She probably needed one after being stuck in the mirror for more than a hundred years."

"I believe you're right then," Aunt Ianthe said. "Everyone needs a fresh start sometimes."

The older ladies began to leave the room and Harry accompanied them. I waited for Serena who put her face in her hands.

"This was my fault," she said, softly. "If I hadn't been distracted by that Chicken person, I'd have kept a closer eye on Helena. She has no respect for spirits."

"I don't think there's any real harm done," I said, feeling an obscure need to comfort her.

"Women always flirt with Harry. That's just the way it is. That

Lydia wasn't a real threat. Not like you." Her eyes were watery as she gazed at me. "He likes you, you know. It's because you're funny. And authentic. And pretty, of course."

"Oh, no, no."

"Are you trying to convince me or yourself? Don't worry. He's fair game. We're no longer married. It's just that," her voice trailed off.

It was just that she still loved him. I didn't think she needed me to make that point.

We were all out on the stage when the front door slammed open and we could see an outline of a man in the back of the house. It was a classic scene out of the old west with the local sheriff making a dramatic entrance. If, that is, the local sheriff had been shaped like an egg. He waddled up the carpeted aisle, his fists attached to the center of his body where his waistline should have been. Behind him, Waino was forced to take baby steps.

Horace A. Clump, demonstrably lazy, penurious and mean-spirited has, nevertheless, been re-elected sheriff in Copper County more than a dozen times which may prove the cantankerousness of Keweenaw voters or it may indicate the lack of interest in the job or it may mean nothing at all.

He doesn't appear to approve of anyone (with the possible exception of his wife and grown daughters) but he is especially acrimonious toward me. He'd had a contentious relationship with Pops and my involvement in the last murder case in Red Jacket had him raging. He climbed the stage steps and made a beeline toward me.

I braced myself for what I knew was coming.

"What in the H-E-double-hockey-sticks makes you think that corpse was killed with a knittin' needle?"

CHAPTER 12

I was paralyzed by a combination of humiliation and fear. Why had I opened my big mouth in front of Waino? What if Clump made the same jump as his deputy and figured that Sofi had killed Cricket Koski? I scrambled to find some kind of answer that would distract the sheriff.

"It was just a guess," I said. "A shot in the dark." I winced. That probably wasn't a good image to use, either. "The weapon could have been anything from an ice pick to, uh, uh, nail-gun to an awl."

"A owl?"

Help came from an unexpected source.

"A nail-gun's my idea," Waino said, coming up next to the sheriff. "Or one of them skewers."

Clump was unmoved. His beady eyes remained on me, his mind on its original track.

"You sold any of those double-points, lately?"

"Sure," I replied. "Actually, quite a few packages." It was a cheering thought. The more people who owned needles, the harder it would be to pin this thing on Sofi. I hoped. "Our expanded knitting circle is working on socks this winter."

Clump's stare turned into an uncomprehending glare.

"You see, sheriff," Aunt Ianthe said, helpfully, "you cannot make a tube shape with straight needles." She smiled, graciously, at both the sheriff and Waino, as if she were welcoming them to an afternoon tea party. "So we use a set of double-pointed needles, that is needles with points on either end so that the stitches can be knit in a circle."

Aunt Ianthe took his silence for confusion. She produced her knitting bag and from it she extracted her work-in-progress.

"See how the stitches are arranged in a circle? Not only can you make a tube, you avoid seaming."

"Avoid seeming what?"

"While we look not at the things which are seen, but at the things which are not seen: for the things which are seen are temporal; but the things which are not seen are eternal." Miss Irene beamed at the sheriff after delivering the words from Corinthians. He stared at her for a long minute. They were about the same height.

"Never mind about that," he yelled, "I wanna know how in the Sam Hill that hole got into that corpse's chest and I wanna know why."

"Not an unreasonable request." Harry Dent's voice was pitched for my ears only but I couldn't summon a smile.

"Well," Aunt Ianthe said, in an instructing voice, "I should tell you that it is also possible to make socks using two identical circular needles. It's rather a new method. You line the shafts up next to each other only pointing in opposite directions."

"Like earthworms," Waino put in. The sheriff craned his non-neck to look up at the deputy who was a head taller.

"What are you talkin' about boy?"

"It's the way they have sex. I can remember cause I took biology twice." He grinned at me. He paused. "And because it's about sex."

"Never mind about the damned worms," Clump stormed. His face flushed the color of eggplant. He looked as if he were about to blow. "I wanna know all the folks that had access to these two-pointed needles."

"Well, Horace," Aunt Ianthe put in, "Hatti told you the entire Ladies Aide and the Martha Circle are working on socks for Fibber

McGee's Closet this winter. Children go through their socks so fast! We're calling it Toasty Toes! Anyway, we wanted to try out the new striped yarn for toe-up and toe-down patterns. They are turning into works of art, if I do say so myself." She paused, noticed his glare, and continued. "All of us have sets of DPNs."

"Mine are bamboo," Mrs. Moilanen said. As the holder of the most powerful position at St. Heikki's Finnish Lutheran, Mrs. Moilanen was well aware of her own importance. When she spoke, people listened and she could see no reason to exclude the sheriff from her followers. "Some folks – I won't name any names – still use aluminum needles but, trust me, the stitches hold much better on the bamboo."

"You know, sheriff," Aunt Ianthe said, "I'm surprised Agatha Christie didn't use DPNs in *Murder on the Orient Express*. They would have done the job and been a lot less messy than a knife."

I closed my eyes and waited for Clump to fly into a million pieces but I had underestimated him. He nodded at my great aunt and asked, in a deceptively mild voice, whether Charlie was a knitter, too.

Aunt Ianthe's smile covered her entire face.

"How kind of you to ask, sheriff. Yes, Irene and I are teaching her the skills. She has her own little knitting bag."

"And her own set of needles?"

"Yes, yes, of course."

I managed to suppress a groan.

"She keep that knittin' stuff out at her father's cabin?"

"I believe she takes it back and forth from Sofi's home to the cabin." My aunt's voice trailed off as she began to understand what he was getting at.

"Funny thing," Clump said, in what clearly a fake chatty tone, "deputy here says he found a knittin' basket at the Dollar Lake cabin and it was full of those little two-pointed needles. Two dozen of 'em."

Waino mouthed *I'm sorry* over Clump's head but the damage was done. I'd suggested the weapon and they'd found one at the apparent scene of the crime. Geez Louise, not one. They'd found two dozen. I knew my cheeks were burning but I tried to keep my face expressionless.

"Tell your sis I wanna see her," Clump said.

"She's sick. She has the flu."

"Most likely got chilled when she was out in the snow Saturday night."

I stared at him.

"She was only outside long enough to cross the street from the Leaping Deer to her house."

The small beady eyes narrowed in satisfaction. I'd been too quick to answer. Too defensive.

"Are you lying to the law?" He kept his voice soft. "Or did I hit on something you don't know? Tell me this, Missy. Did your sis go home before or after you blew the horns and threw the confetti?"

I frowned, unsure what he was getting at.

"We didn't have any horns, or hats or confetti."

"You sure about that?"

All of a sudden, I wasn't. We'd been eating popcorn balls and Elli poured glasses of wine and handed each of us a little baggie filled with the funny papers cut into little squares. Sonya had laughed and said it would make more work for Elli in the morning but we wound up flinging the confetti anyway.

Sonya had been right. It had made a mess.

"Why do you want to know?"

Clump shrugged. "Just tying up loose ends. "Deputy here found some bits of colored paper iced into the snow out to the cabin. Right next to boot prints. Ladies size six."

The words took away my breath. I tried to marshal arguments about why that hadn't been our confetti and how the boot prints couldn't have belonged to my sister but my mind was whirling. Before I could speak, the front door of the theater opened again. This time it was Patty Ojanpaa from Patty's Pasties. It was time for lunch and Elli, always innately polite, invited the sheriff and Waino to partake.

"Hell, yeah," Clump said. But before he waddled over to the

table to join the others in claiming a beef-and-vegetable pasty, he had a private word with me.

"Here's what I think. Teljo and your sis had plans to get back together and this here barmaid got in the way. Now I don't know if he done it by himself or if she was an accomplice but I aim to find out. And, if you know what's good for you, missy, you'll stay out of my way."

My mind was roiling as Clump turned his attention to lunch. Lars and Sofi needed someone in their corner who knew what she was doing. In the earlier murders I'd had help from Sofi, Elli and Sonya, not to mention Max Guthrie and Jace.

This time, there was only me and I felt horribly and woefully inadequate. After a moment I became aware of Harry Dent's presence nearby. His tone was soft and there was no hint of amusement.

"I can help you, you know. I was a detective. Think you can trust me?"

"I don't know." He chuckled.

"Are you always that honest?"

"Probably. It's less virtue than 528 hours of Sunday school instruction."

This time he laughed aloud.

"The offer's there. Think about it."

When lunch was over and the sheriff and Waino (and Patty) had left, Vincent called for a status report. He then read a statement he had prepared.

"Mrs. Paikkonen," he said, butchering the pronunciation of her name, "continues to work on a translation of the Finnish letter. We will get a report from her tonight. In the meantime, we have to up our game, people. I want you to spend the afternoon ransacking the attics of this town. Tonight we will hold a show-and-tell of treasures from the 1940s. Seth has agreed to research the extraordinary relationship between Upper Michigan and the Third Reich. The rest of you need to find relevant *object d'arts!*"

Waino popped his head back into the theater.

"Big storm's coming up. You folks better get back up to the B and B unless you want to sleep in the theater tonight."

I found Harry Dent next to me as we exited the theater.

"I think I'd like to take you up on your offer," I said. "Maybe we could just talk over this case."

"I won't pry," he assured me. "But I'll be happy to give you the benefit of my experience."

It would be a relief to share some of this frightening responsibility. I imagined Miss Irene's light high voice with a line from the New Testament.

"Bear ye one another's burdens, and so fulfill the law of Christ."

CHAPTER 13

Calumet Street, in case I haven't mentioned this before, is the highest vantage point in town. The rest of Red Jacket, a lattice of numbered streets (east-west) and those named for trees (north-south) lies on a slight incline. Main Street, at the base of the hill, sits atop seven abandoned mining chambers which are no-doubt filled with water. Doomsayers have suggested that someday the ground will give way and the downtown blocks will collapse in on themselves like a dying star. Mostly, though, we don't think about that.

Anyway, Elli's Bed and Breakfast, by far the largest and most opulent structure in town, consists of forty-six rooms. My family's Queen Anne Victorian is much smaller but dates back nearly that far. Both dwellings were conceived by the same architect and both boast wrap-around porches, front and back staircases, quirky rooflines and, in our case, a round tower bathroom with a witch's hat roof.

The Maki Funeral Home, to the west of the Queen Anne, looks like something from a different planet. It is generally thought (but seldom expressed) that its creator was either terminally depressed or prescient about the structure's eventual use. It looks like a house of death. Constructed of dark brick that has blackened over the years, with slitted windows that would have been useful for archers during the War of the Roses, a dark, covered entrance and a roof of thick shingles that curls over the eaves like a lazy python, the place always makes me think of a predator lying in wait.

Across the street is Mrs. Moilanen's mid-sized colonial, Mrs. Paikkonen's tall, narrow home and the cheerful duplex that is the home of Aunt Ianthe, Miss Irene, Sofi and Charlie.

We split up the attic-searching duties. Mrs. Paikkonen and the Tallmasters headed for the funeral home while Serena accompanied the elderly ladies to their duplex. Seth stayed at the B and B to help Elli. Somehow I wound up at the Queen Anne with only Harry Dent for company. As soon as we were alone, I felt butterflies in my stomach, a sensation that annoyed me and brought me to my senses. He wouldn't make a move on me while we were searching for treasure, surely, and if he did, I could handle it. I was pretty sure I could handle it.

"Cupcake," he said, when we were standing in my mom's kitchen, both of us wet and chilled from the storm outside, "I am perfectly willing to search your attic but at the moment I feel like the abominable snowman." His grin was friendly but his shiver was real. "I'd like to suggest that first we take a sauna. No shenanigans, I promise."

The butterflies threatened to return but it was a legitimate request and he did look cold. I was cold, too.

"Only if you pronounce it correctly. It's sow-na. We Finns articulate all the vowels."

"Agreed. And while we're sweating it out, maybe you can fill me in on the other arcane elements of Finnish culture."

"And you can tell me about your art collection."

"Done." He started to take off his clothes and I panicked.

"What? What is it?"

"Just that you need to wear a bathing suit."

"To take a bath?"

"It's more than a bath. It's a ritual. Really, almost a religion. When men and women bathe together we always wear a bathing suit."

He quirked an eyebrow at me.

"Even if you're married?"

It was just a casual comment but it slingshotted me back to an afternoon a week ago in which Jace and I had shared a sauna without benefit of beachwear.

A few minutes later, respectably clad, we entered the sauna attached to the kitchen. He sat on the lower bench or *lavat*, while I turned on the electric heating element and filled up a bucket of water to throw on the stones to create the steam.

"Nice threads," he said, eyeing the tank suit I'd worn during my only season of competitive swimming in junior high. It was navy blue with a faded logo that spelled out the team's name *Hancock Hematites.*

"Thanks. I like your boxers." He grinned at me and I had to admit, if only to myself, he looked good. Stripping his clothes had not diminished his sex appeal. Not a bit.

The steam rose to engulf us and I took a seat next to Harry. It felt good and warm and, more than that, it felt familiar. I ladled more water onto the heated stones and watched the steam sizzle up into the air.

"It's called *loyly*," I said, apropos of nothing. "The bursts of steam, I mean."

He pronounced the word.

"I thought sow-na involved slapping silly yourself with birch twigs."

I giggled. "They're called *vihta* and intended to increase circulation. They are also strictly optional."

"I'm glad to hear it. I think I'm suffering enough with this heat."

"You said you were cold."

"I was cold but I could also breathe."

I chuckled again. I knew it wasn't uncommon for newbies to panic in the steam room.

"You get used to it with practice," I assured him.

"Tell me something. Why is the sow-na the exclusive property of the Finns?"

"I guess we're just smarter than everybody else. Actually, American Indians have a similar ritual with their sweat lodges and I believe that, at one time, many European cultures used something similar. I read that a sixteenth century syphilis epidemic gave communal bathing a bad name. Finland may have been exempt from that because of its low population and isolation. It's kind of off by itself."

"Except for its proximity to Russia," Harry pointed out. "Don't forget about the wars."

I decided to let that pass.

"When the Finns came to America the first thing they'd build on their land was a sauna where the family would live until a cottage could be constructed. The sauna was warm and hygienic and it was often used for giving birth. Nowadays, in Finland, anyway, businessmen conduct meetings in the sauna."

"Businessmen and women," Harry said. "Catch up with the times, Cupcake."

"Right." I smiled. "Families use it for bonding. There can be a spiritual aspect to it. It's said that more Finns and Finnish-Americans spend time each week in the sauna than they do in church."

He inched closer to me and our shoulders touched. His voice was low, unthreatening but intimate.

"I'm going to kiss you."

I appreciated the warning but I didn't pull away and the kiss was nice. I mean, it was really expert and I felt an inner tingle but it was very mild. When he'd finished he searched my face.

"Nothing, huh?"

He sounded so abashed I had to smile.

"I wouldn't say that."

He shook his head. "But the earth didn't move for you."

"No," I admitted. "Thank goodness. My life is complicated enough at the moment." He gazed at me for a few more seconds and then he chuckled.

"Mine, too," he said.

"Harry," I said, relieved to have the whole attraction thing put to bed, so to speak, "what's going to happen with this television pilot?"

"The truth? I doubt whether it will ever see the light of day. Vincent's talents don't lie in crossing the finish line. I doubt whether this will go anywhere at all."

"Helena could do it," I pointed out.

"She could but if I'm any judge of character she's not interested in show business. She's just looking for an escape clause that won't leave her destitute. Her marriage is a classic case of marry in haste, repent forever."

I eyed him curiously.

"If you knew that about Vincent, why did you join up with him?"

"I told you, Cupcake. It was Serena's idea. She wanted an adventure, with me. And if you're asking why I'd go along with my ex-wife, all I can say is I was bored."

"Maybe you felt you owed her something."

"Maybe I did," he said, with a sigh. "I just wasn't good husband material and it made her unhappy." He picked up my hand and lightly kissed the fingertips. "Look. Stop worrying about Vincent's folly. I'm offering you my well-honed detection skills to solve the murder of the unfortunately named Cricket. What do you say?"

I couldn't think of a good reason to say no. What possible motive could he have for helping with Cricket's murder other than to be helpful? And, anyway, I needed his help. My investigation had gone nowhere so far. I told him about Cloud and the Christmas card and my plan to head down to L'Anse first thing in the morning.

"May I come with?" I giggled. He sounded like a teenager willing to do anything in the world in place of visiting Aunt Agnes. I nodded.

"And now," he said, "much as I hate to break up this tete-a-tete, I've got to get out of here and cool off."

"Your wish is my command." I grabbed his hand and pulled him off the bench, through the back door and into a snowbank. Harry yelled a curse.

"You Finns are crazy!"

"That's what they say."

CHAPTER 14

T he attic of the Queen Anne held good memories for me as Elli and I had used it as a hideout or clubhouse during our formative years. The scent of sawdust from the bare rafters transported me to the rainy and snowy afternoons when we had raided the kitchen then brought our ill-gotten snacks up to the cozy spot under the eaves. There was a twin-sized bed against the wall under a window and I had sometimes crept up here to sleep, like when baby Charlie cried all night with an earache and later, when Sofi and Lars had begun to argue.

The attic stairs were behind a door on the second floor hallway so the stairwell was narrow. I balanced two full mugs of coffee on a tray with prune tarts left over from Christmas. I hadn't hurried and wasn't surprised to find Harry was there ahead of me. He was standing by the bed, gazing out at the falling snow and he turned as I emerged into view.

"That staircase is like a magician's trick," he said. "You look like you're coming up out of the ground. By the way," he held up a porcelain pot, "this was under the bed. Is it what I think it is?"

"Hey, it's a steep climb down to the bathroom in the dark. Geez, I haven't been up here in years. The junk looks as if it has multiplied. What if we really found a treasure?"

"Unlikely."

"Maybe not. I forgot to tell you. Seth did some online research and discovered that a couple of professors in Finland have made a connection between that country and art that was looted by the Nazis."

"Nazi loot! I hadn't heard about Finland's involvement but it isn't surprising. Ever since the fall of the Soviet Empire there's been a push to locate stolen paintings in museums and private collections all over the world. It's hard to see how the loot could have gotten to Finland."

"But, remember, there were some Finnish diplomats and soldiers in Germany during the war years. Maybe some of them acquired stolen artwork."

He gaped at me.

"Do you think that's what Ernst Hautamaki did?"

"It's possible. When I skimmed that letter I thought I saw the word for package. Later I looked it up and discovered I was right. I think Ernst was telling his aunt he was sending her a package and it seems like it must have been something significant. We'll find out when Mrs. Pike reports tonight."

Harry appeared to think about that as he drank his coffee.

"Is there any chance that Aunt Bengta stayed in this house?"

"Sure. As you've heard, we're mostly all related, although I don't know where the Hautamakis come in. Anyway, a lady visiting for a whole summer would likely have been rotated from house to house to give each family the benefit of her company. But if Bengta did receive a package from Ernst, surely she'd have taken it with her when she returned to Finland."

"Maybe not. It was 1942. The world was still at war. Ernst may have asked her to leave it in Michigan for safekeeping."

"But he'd have come to get it after the war, though."

"True enough. It probably isn't here." His eyes ranged over the stacked boxes, barrels and trunks, and the sleds and skis standing on end. He looked at the pieces of furniture that had been retired, like the crib and dresser my mother had used for Sofi and me and that Sofi had used for Charlie. I wondered if the crib met modern day safety standards and figured it did not. The old dollhouse would be useable, though, and the tricycle. I felt a surge of excitement about the coming child and just hoped he or she would be welcomed by both parents.

Harry pointed to a bookcase filled with children's volumes, board games and puzzles. Next to it was a basket that contained several dozen partial rolls of wrapping paper.

"I see your family comes from the never-get-rid-of-anything-school of thought," Harry said, gazing around.

"We're not much on change. Not even the pets. When my maternal grandfather died and his house on Second Street was sold, my parents brought his cat here but Snoopy kept returning to the Second Street house. Finally, the new owners agreed to keep her. Of course, they were distant relatives, too."

"It takes a village," he said, looking at one wall. "Why are you keeping the antlers and the beer mirror?"

"Are you kidding? Those are classic Yooper items. I know of one house in Red Jacket where the guy turned his antlers into a chandelier."

"You know why people hang onto stuff, Cupcake? Psychologically, I mean. It's because they think it makes them immortal. If you are still collecting things, you can't die."

"Does that apply to art?" He quirked an eyebrow at me. "Do you collect paintings because it makes you immortal?"

He chuckled. "I collect it because it makes me rich. Art is an investment."

"I hear you have a Monet."

"One of his waterlily paintings. He painted something like two hundred and fifty views of his water garden trying to capture the light at various times of the day and year. Not all of them survive."

"What happened to them?" Harry shrugged.

"Monet was a perfectionist. When he wasn't happy with his work, he destroyed it."

"What about thefts? Are any of the survivors known to be stolen?"

"Yes. One very famous view taken from a Paris art dealer before the war." His words sent a tingling sensation up my spine.

"Harry! Wouldn't it be something if Ernst Hautamaki found the Monet? It would have been one of those modern paintings, right? An impressionist painting. Hitler and his henchmen wouldn't have valued it. Ernst might have saved it from being destroyed. Or he might have bought it cheap. "What if we could find it?"

He chuckled. "It would. But, remember, whatever Ernst found and sent to the Keweenaw, he has had seventy-five years to retrieve it. If your speculation is true, that painting is somewhere in Finland, or, more likely, it has been returned to the heirs of the original owner."

"What would something like that be worth? Any idea?"

"Upwards of sixty million."

I choked. "That's our local economy for about a century."

"Well, don't get your hopes up. Even if, by some miracle, we found it, the town wouldn't get to keep it. It would have to be returned."

"Yup. I know. Even so, it would be pretty cool to find it, though. And it would definitely put Red Jacket on the map."

"Meanwhile," he said, pulling a framed canvas out from behind a dresser, "we have here a lovely painting of Elvis on velvet. Think we should paint a swastika on it and tell Harry we think it's Hitler's work?"

That was as close as we got to anything German. I found a box of straw Finnish Christmas ornaments and plenty of books written in Finnish.

"This is hopeless," I said, finally, stretching my back. "I say we report our failure and take our lumps."

"Hold on," he said, calmly, "you're giving up too easily. Check this out." He crossed the creaking floorboards and showed me what he'd found. It was a little wooden box in the shape of a house with a peaked roofline. It had a flat metal catch at the top and stickers that said *Flor Fina* and *Fabrica de Tobaccos* on the sides. Etched across the slanted roofline was the mysterious phrase, "House of Idlers."

"An old cigar box?"

"Yes, but it's what's inside the old cigar box that is interesting. Go ahead. Look."

I opened the latch, peeked inside and lifted out a fairly hefty metal object that I could hold in my hand.

"A compass."

"Yes, my dear Cupcake, but look at it closely."

I held it up to the light and was able to read the letters engraved on the front.

"Marsch Kompass." I looked at him. Attic grime had seeped into the laugh wrinkles near his eyes and the vertical dimples on his lean cheeks. He looked weary but triumphant. "German. You think this compass ties the Finns to the Axis powers?"

"Of course not," he said. "It could be here for any reason, none of them having to do with World War II. The point is, it will make Vincent Tallmaster happy."

"And that's your life's goal?"

He paused for an instant and then hooted.

"I told you before. I think there's zero chance of any of this actually getting on the air but this little nugget will make Vincent think he's on the right track. And before you know it, we'll be out of your hair."

"But I don't want you out of my hair," I said. "I need you to help solve Cricket Koski's murder."

"And I," he said, with a mock bow, "am happy to serve."

CHAPTER 15

Elli had made her pumpkin-nut loaves and pickled whitefish for supper and Ronja Laplander, who owned the Copper Kettle Gift Shop, had whipped up a kettle of hearty potato-and-leek soup. Mrs. Sorensen's macaroni-and-cheese with the secret ingredient made a hit as did the raspberry applesauce I'd pilfered from my mom's pantry. And, somehow, Aunt Ianthe had found time to make a scratch apple pie.

It was a feast of comfort food and it worked for me. I experienced the first sense of wellbeing I'd felt since I'd gotten word of the murder and Lars's incarceration. I wasn't sure whether the warm glow was due to the flaky crust of the pie or the occasional glance I intercepted from Harry Dent. It felt good to have a partner-in-crime-solving. Good and supportive. And he was not just anybody, either. The man had worked for the FBI. We'd figure this out, come hell or high water. Together, we would defend the innocent and identify the guilty.

The pie was delicious.

When Vincent had finished eating, he wiped his mouth with his napkin, flung it on his plate and stood at his place to announce an all-hands-on-deck-emergency meeting in the parlor where the finds of the day would be reported. His smile reminded me of a cat that had successfully cornered a mouse. He was pleased about something and I wondered if Harry had already told him about the compass.

The group, in general, was jolly with lots of chattering and laughter. Everyone, I thought, except Mrs. Paikkonen whose long, narrow face was pale and tinged with green and whose lips twisted with tension. Was her obvious distress a result of translating the Hautamaki letter? But how was that possible. Both writer and sender must have died long ago.

Mrs. Paikkonen's gaze shifted to me and I read a question in her pale eyes. Whatever it was, it would have to wait.

Vincent had ordered everyone into the parlor.

"Let me begin by announcing that success has crowned our efforts." A smile appeared on his handsome face then almost immediately, it disappeared. He focused on his wife.

"My dear, please enlighten the staff with a description of what we uncovered this afternoon."

The staff? We were now Vincent's staff?

Helena Tallmaster, seated in Elli's re-upholstered armchair, with her legs elegantly crossed, looked remote and beautiful, an ice princess in a tailored white wool pantsuit with her hair perfectly coiffed in an updo fastened with a diamond clip. She represented a distinct contrast to those of us wearing old clothes and sporting dust in our hair. Had she really spent the afternoon searching the mortuary attic for treasures?

"Perhaps you should stand, my love."

Helena did not move.

"Vincent and I found an old stamp collection," she said.

A notch appeared between Vincent's eyebrows.

"Yes, yes, but not just any stamp collection." His voice contained a hint of irritation. "Tell everyone what was significant about our find."

Helena's cool gaze lingered on his increasingly agitated face.

"But you would tell it so much better," she said, in a bored voice.

Vincent ran a careful hand over his smooth hair and muttered something under his breath.

"We discovered stamps that had been released by the Finnish

government during the 1940s. They commemorate the Red Cross and the National Defense Fund." He produced a self-satisfied smile.

"Do the stamps bear any connection to the Third Reich," the Reverend Sorensen asked. He was leaning forward in his straight-backed chair.

"No," Helena said.

"Not as such," her husband admitted. "But the time period is perfect for our theme. It is a wonderful find and precisely what we have been seeking."

"Are the stamps valuable?" Harry threw out the question, casually.

"I'll take a look at them," Seth promised. "Stamps are like coins. Their value depends on how many were issued and whether they are hard to come by."

"This is an excellent start," Vincent boomed, as if to make up for the general lack of enthusiasm.

Kind-hearted Aunt Ianthe put down the striped stocking she was knitting and clapped her hands and Miss Irene followed suit. Mrs. Paikkonen, seated between the other two on the Victorian sofa, did not stir.

Seth got to his feet and produced an elaborate beer stein with a hinged metal lid.

"Elli and I found this here at the Leaping Deer," he said. "The relevance is the illustration on the side of the mug. As you can see," he held it up, "it's a soldier on horseback. He's wearing one of those spike-topped helmets."

"Ah, the Picklhaub helmet," the Reverend Sorensen said. "Those were worn by German soldiers in the Great War."

This time Vincent clapped his hands in excitement.

"Another wonderful find! Proof positive of the close connection between Finland and Hitler!"

"It's very nice and, historically interesting," Seth said, cautiously.

"What Seth is saying, or trying not to say is that the helmet was worn in the First World War, not the Second," Harry said.

Vincent stared at him for a moment and then, as if he'd found a loophole, he said, "Did Hitler participate in World War I?"

"Oh yes," the Reverend Sorensen said. "As a soldier. A corporal."

"Well, all right, then," Vincent crowed. "We'll use the pickle helmet in the show!"

"We found something else, too," Elli said, retrieving a brown paper bag from which she extracted and held up a long-sleeved pale gray shirtwaist dress with white collar and cuffs that were both frayed and yellowed. A silver badge, about an inch-and-a-half square, was pinned to the collar. Four heraldic roses had been carved into the four corners of the badge and the words *Lotta-Svard* were etched underneath.

In the center of the pin was another of those bent crosses.

"A swastika," someone gasped.

"*Voi kahua!*" The exclamation came from Aunt Ianthe.

"I don't understand," said Serena Waterfall. "What is the significance of this?"

"Perhaps you'll allow me to give you some background," the pastor said, in his low-key way. "*Lotta Svard* was a Finnish patriotic, auxiliary paramilitary organization for women. The *Lottas* were organized during the Finnish Civil War in the 1800s. *Lotta,* is the name of a fictional battlefield hero and *svard* is the Swedish word for sword. Many of the women who belonged wanted to fight for Finland but, as that was not possible in those times, they built a network of support."

He cleared his throat giving others a chance to speak but no one did.

"The volunteers did social work in the 1920s and 30s and then, during the World War II years, the women stepped into jobs traditionally held by men, such as hospital staff, air raid warning posts, and so forth. They continued in the effort to bring comfort to refugees and others who had been impacted by the violence. American Finns, here in the Upper Peninsula, supported the efforts with donations."

"Such brave ladies," Aunt Ianthe said, obviously moved by the recital of an old story.

"They had *Sisu,*" Mrs. Moilanen agreed.

"She is more precious than jewels. And nothing you desire can compare with her," Miss Irene said, somewhat obscurely. "Proverbs."

Harry hid a smile then asked the obvious question.

"Why the swastika?"

"I seem to recall," the Reverend Sorensen said, "that the swastika had been used as a symbol of luck on the first aircraft in the Finnish defense forces. You have to remember that before Hitler co-opted it the swastika was just a bent cross. It has been around for a long time."

Vincent waved a hand as if to dismiss the pastor's words.

"We don't have to go into all that. A swastika is a swastika." He clearly still had his heart set on exploiting the Finnish-Nazi connection.

"My turn," Harry drawled. "After an afternoon of backbreaking labor, Hatti and I discovered this." He held up the compass. "It appears to be German-made and we deduce that it was a souvenir collected from a battlefield and brought back by a returning G.I., probably a Finnish-American."

"An embarrassment of riches," Vincent crowed. "We shall start shooting the program in the morning."

"I have a few things to add," Serena Waterfall said, getting to her feet. She was, once again, a symphony of color in a fuchsia-colored peasant blouse that should have clashed with her carrot-y hair but didn't, and a broomstick skirt of forest green and hot pink buffalo checks. She smoothed the dancing ringlets away from her face and produced a folded quilt. "We believe this was constructed by Miss Ianthe's grandmother and her quilting circle during the 1940s. As you can see, it is a snowball quilt composed of blue squares topped by white snowballs. Very typical of the times but this one was done in traditional Finnish colors."

"That's very nice," Vincent started to say, "but, really, Serena, it doesn't tie into our theme."

"All the blocks," she continued, ignoring him, "are blue and white except for two, one in each of the lower corners. See the red one with the yellow star and sickle? The other is a typical snowball but someone embroidered it with a black swastika."

I'd been starting to feel anxious and this last discovery drove me over the top. Despite what Harry had assured me, it looked as if Vincent would be able to exploit Finland's connection to Hitler. I could feel my temperature rising and my heart working doubletime.

"The quilters must have been Nazi sympathizers," Vincent said. He was all smiles.

"I think it would be a mistake to infer that," Seth said. "There is a long tradition in quilting of incorporating important events. These quilters were, most likely, leaving an historical record of what was happening in their country at the time. Finland was in a deadly war with Russia on the one hand and, because of that, forced to become allies with Hitler. The quilt illustrates that dark heritage. No Finn or Finnish-American, as far as I've ever heard, was happy about the pact with Germany."

I threw him a grateful look.

"Serena, dear," Aunt Ianthe prompted, "tell Vincent about the newspapers."

"Of course." She disappeared into the foyer and returned a moment later with a short stack of yellowed tear sheets which she handed out to several of us, including the Reverend Sorensen, Mrs. Moilanen, Seth and me, while Aunt Ianthe explained.

"These are all copies of the Copper County Times which went out of print about ten years ago," Aunt Ianthe said. "My family collected what they considered historic issues. Henrikki, read the headline on yours."

"*Finland Declares War on Reds*, November 30, 1939," I said, holding it up.

Mrs. Moilanen adjusted her glasses and read the headline on hers.

"*Finland helps poles, Czechs*, Feb. 12, 1940."

"*Allies gain in Normandy*, June 6, 1944. D-Day," the Reverend Sorensen said, dutifully holding up his paper. Then Seth held his up, too, and said, "May 9, 1945: *Victory in Europe!*"

95

"Are the papers worth anything," Vincent asked Seth.

"They'll make a good timeline for the narrative," the antiques expert said. "In fact, we could make them into posters to decorate the set."

Vincent appeared to think about that for a minute.

"Speaking of historical context," Harry said, "Hatti and I found something else interesting during our search." His lips twisted in a wry grin and his eyes twinkled at me. "It's a postcard from a very famous event called the Degenerate Art Exhibition held in Munich in 1937."

"Degenerate art?" Elli looked confused. Harry smiled at her.

"Hitler held modern art in great contempt. He exalted German art and the Great Masters but he wanted to wipe out everything modern from the Impressionists to the Fauvists, to all the newest schools. He hated Monet and Manet, Matisse, Van Gogh, Klimt, Rousseau and Chagall. Part of it, we think, is that he himself had little imagination and his own work consisted of indifferent, photographic-type drawings of objects. He did not understand the concept of trying to capture a split second of life, an impression, rather than a realistic depiction, the new belief that what the eye perceives is different from what the brain understands.

"Part of it, quite frankly, was that Hitler had developed an intense hatred for Jews and therefore for Jewish artists. The degenerate exhibition was poorly mounted with the pictures crammed in against each other and Hitler's hope was to convince everyone to reject modern art.

"But didn't Hitler steal nearly all the art in Europe," Elli asked. "And didn't that include those Impressionist masters?"

"Certainly," Harry said. "He stole a fifth of the world's art treasures. Some of the modern art he sold, cheaply, to fund the war. Some he destroyed. He probably kept some as he was intending to build a fabulous museum in his hometown of Linz, Austria."

"Do you think there were stolen paintings stashed at Nazi headquarters in Munich?" The question came from Elli but a sudden movement from Mrs. Paikkonen made me look at her. All the color had drained out of her face and she looked as if she were about to be ill.

"Mrs. Pike," I murmured, "Are you all right?"

"A little tired. I need to go home and to bed. You must take me there, Henrikki."

I helped her to her feet but Vincent didn't allow us to leave.

"Hold on! What about the letter? What did it say? Was it anything to do with Nazi loot?"

Mrs. Paikkonen swayed a little and I spoke firmly.

"She can tell us tomorrow. Can somebody find her coat and boots?"

"Of course," Aunt Ianthe said, getting to her feet to help me.

"Just give us the gist of it," Vincent persisted.

Mrs. Paikkonen, looking like, as Charlie would say, death warmed over in the black dress with the high neckline and long sleeves, stiffened her spine.

"Ernst calls her his dear Aunt and hopes she is well. He talks about the weather."

"The weather? What about the loot? Did he mention a treasure?"

Mrs. Paikkonen looked down her long nose at him.

"He tells her he was a diplomatic officer who had been assigned to Germany, as he has a facility with language. He tells her he has chosen a gift for her birthday which he knows is some three months late and he says he is unsure whether he will be allowed to mail it to the U.S. from Germany.

It was clear to me that Mrs. Pike had become comfortable with both the letter-writer and his aunt. They were not shades of an earlier era but people who were alive for her.

He tells her he will send the package to his *aiti* to forward on to his aunt. He hopes she will like the gift and will keep it safe."

"*Aiti?*"

"Mother," the reverend translated.

Vincent stared at Mrs. Pike, then at Helena, then at Harry.

"So what is it? And where is it?"

The pastor sighed.

"I would have to say it sounds as if it is something Ernst wanted to smuggle out of Germany. Perhaps war plans."

"No," Helena said. "Not intelligence. If Ernst was housed in Munich, the central holding place for all that looted art, I think he found and rescued a painting. I think he shipped the painting to his mother in Finland with instructions to send it on to his aunt in Michigan for safe keeping."

"Huzzah!" Vincent could scarcely contain his enthusiasm. "That means there is a treasure, a priceless painting hidden here in one of the attics!"

"I hate to burst your bubble," Harry said, "but wouldn't Ernst have come to the U.S. to retrieve the painting after the war?"

There was a moment of silence while the mood plummeted and then Elli sprang to her feet.

"Hang on," she said, leaving the room. She reappeared a few minutes later with a huge, dusty, antique Bible. All eyes were on her as she sat on the step next to me and leafed through the front pages.

"Bingo," she said, after a minute. "I found her. Miss Bengta Hautamaki. She is part of my mother's family tree." Elli looked up and smiled at Miss Irene, who was a distant relation of Elli's mom. "She was born in a village called Kuoppala in 1860 and she died…" Elli's voice faded and she looked at me. "She died here. In Red Jacket. In the summer of 1942. Oh my gosh! She probably never even got the package."

"More than likely, Ernst Hautamaki visited here after the war and retrieved the painting," Helena said. I was both surprised and impressed at her contribution. And then I thought of something.

"Elli," I said, my heart thumping hard against my ribs, "what about Ernst? Is he listed in the Bible?" She ran her forefinger down the page.

"Yep. Here he is. Ernst Hautamaki, born 1920 also in Kuoppala. Died, July, 1942."

"Poor boy," Aunt Ianthe said. "To die so young."

"Where, Elli. Where did he die?"

She looked up, a grim expression on her face.

"It says he died in Germany."

"What does that mean? What does that mean?" squealed Vincent.

"It means," Harry said, "that either the young man was never able to mail the package or that he did mail it and Aunt Bengta was not here to receive it and it was returned to Finland. It means we have to forget about the alleged treasure."

"Or," I said, thinking aloud, "it means the package did get here and, in the confusion of Aunt Bengta's death, no one ever opened it. It could still be here."

Elli looked at me. "In one of our attics. But surely someone would have noticed it and investigated over the past seventy years."

While we digested that, Mrs. Moilanen spoke.

"I sincerely hope that young man's body was shipped home for burial in consecrated ground."

"If he was buried in Munich the ground was surely consecrated," the Reverend Sorensen said, in an obvious effort to comfort her. "The Germans are Lutheran, too."

"Missouri Synod," Mrs. Moilanen sniffed. The difference between the German Missouri Synod and the Scandinavian Evangelical Lutherans is considered a great divide within the church and, of no importance at all, outside of it.

As usual Vincent heard only what he wanted to hear.

"We have to find that painting," Vincent said. "I want all hands on deck!"

"I think we should slow down," Harry said. "The chances are slim that there is any kind of Nazi loot hidden in Red Jacket. But even if that is true, we could stir up a lot of trouble for this community by broadcasting it. There is a thriving black market for stolen art and we do not want to subject our friends here to a frenzy of treasure hunters."

"There may be some small risk," Vincent admitted, "but surely it is worth it to put on the best pilot possible. And Arvo Maki told me he wanted to put this burg on the map."

"I'm just asking that we be responsible about this," Harry said. "What if we agree not to mention anything about Ernst Hautamaki or his letter to his aunt unless we find the painting?"

Vincent looked undecided but Seth and Serena agreed with Harry and they carried the day.

"In the meantime," Serena said, "I'd really like to see your Rya Rug, Hatti. We can tape a segment on that."

Vincent gazed at me. "Please don't wear that sweatshirt. And you will have to do something about your hair."

CHAPTER 16

I woke the next morning to the nasal tones of Betty Ann Pritula and a new appreciation of Vincent Tallmaster's turn for publicity. He not only knew about Betty Ann, he'd fed her a press release.

"According to a little bird," Betty Ann said, coyly, "there really is a treasure in one of our attics. Rumor has it that, in the summer of 1942, a young Finnish officer assigned to Germany, rescued a stolen masterpiece right out from under the nose of the Nazis. The soldier packaged the painting, thought to be a Rembrandt, possibly, or possibly a Monet, and had it sent to his great aunt who is related to the Risto-Lehtinen-Aho-Maki families. Experts now believe the masterpiece is hidden somewhere on Calumet Street and, when found, will become the centerpiece of the soon-to-be-award-winning television show *What's in Your Attic?* Don't worry, though, there is plenty of air time for your own treasures. Come one, come all to the Red Jacket Opera House today to show off your World War II vintage finds and to become part of the program that everyone is talking about!"

I wondered whether it had occurred to Betty Ann that she was pretty much issuing an invitation for any Tom, Dick and Eino to break into our attics. I wondered, too, how Harry would react to the publicity. He had downplayed the possible find from the first and I figured it was because of his professional reputation. Chances were slim the painting was on the Keweenaw and Harry Dent didn't need his name associated with a fictitious report.

I rolled out of bed, pulled on a pair of jeans, a pale green turtle-neck that I'd outgrown in high school and slipped on a white sweat-shirt imprinted with the number *906* which is supposed to look intriguing to those who do not know it is the area code for the entire UP.

Betty Ann continued to talk about Finnish history, including the success enjoyed by the Finnish soldiers on skis as they faced off against the Russians in the Winter War. It was a story our commu-nity never tired of hearing. Or talking about. And I wondered why none of us had thought to try to deflect Vincent's Panzer initiative with that.

Both of the guestroom doors were closed and the corridor was silent as I slipped downstairs in my stocking feet to put on my boots, parka and gloves and to accompany Larry as he dolphin-ed through the drifts between our house and the Leaping Deer. The snow was falling softly now but those of us who grow up on the Keweenaw learn to read the sky and I knew it would get worse as the day went on. No matter. I was going to L'Anse today come hell or a foot of snow. And whether or not I had to go alone.

Harry still hadn't joined me when I'd finished a meal of Elli's hearty breakfast buns, the ones she made with molasses, currents and graham flour, and my second cup of coffee. I was reluctant to leave without Harry but, unless I wanted to get caught up in the day's drama or stuck on the road, that was the best move. I ambled toward the back door and felt a surge of relief when someone came through it.

The relief was short-lived. The newcomer was Eudora Paikko-nen. She had on the same black dress as the day before and both it and her shapeless wool coat that hung loosely on her on her gaunt frame and she looked, if anything, more unwell than she had the previous night. Great, dark circles underscored her eyes and her cheeks were as hollow as a death's head. My response was involuntary.

"Mrs. Pike! You look like you've seen a ghost!"

"I have seen a ghost." Her voice trembled. "Listen to me, Henrikki. You have to get these television people out of town. They are stirring up all kinds of trouble in *Tuonela*." *Tuonela* is the Land of the Dead.

"What do you mean?"

"The spirits are restless. It is all this talk of the Nazis and the dead boy and his aunt. First Maud left the mirror at the opera house. Now this other is haunting the funeral home. It is the girl who died on New Year's Eve."

My mouth went dry.

"Cricket? You believe Cricket Koski is haunting the mortuary? Why would she?"

"I don't think, Henrikki. I know. There is proof, physical proof. A message. And an ear witness, eh? I heard the footsteps last night. I climbed to the attic and found the message!"

Let me just say here that I don't believe in *Tuonela* or ghosts. Not officially, anyway. But it is hard to live in a small, ethnically-centered town without absorbing a lot of traditions and myths and my lack of belief in ghosts is not strong enough to propel me up to a dark attic alone in the middle of the night. I felt a rush of admiration for Mrs. Pike's courage.

"I think it's unlikely that spectral figures make footsteps. You probably heard Vincent and/or Helena Tallmaster prowling around the attic searching for the painting."

She didn't answer immediately and I was afraid I had offended her.

"No, Henrikki. I checked in their room. She was asleep in the bed. He was on the sofa. There was no one else alive in the house. But up in the attic, carved into one of the two-by-fours under the eaves there was a *karsikko* sign."

In Finnish mythology, a *karsikko* is carved into the trunk of a tree located between the home of the recently deceased and the burial ground. The sign, often a cross above the dead person's initials, is intended to remind the absentminded departing spirit not to return to its earthly home but to finish its journey to the Land of the Dead.

Pops says the custom has its practical aspects since having a lot of confused spirits sucking up all the air isn't really good for business or anything else in a community.

"The sign was an X made out of knitting needles," she said. "And the initials underneath were C.K."

I frowned at her. "Anybody could have carved a sign there at any time. And, anyway, Cricket can't be her real name. Why would a self-respecting spirit use a nickname in an official communication?"

The pale old eyes narrowed on me and I felt like a pupil who had gotten something wrong and disappointed her teacher.

"Use your head, Henrikki," she said. "Maybe her Christian name is Catherine or Christina."

I felt a mixture of sympathy and irritation. Mrs. Paikkonen was clearly upset by the sign which almost certainly was a hoax. Or, maybe not. I felt fairly certain it hadn't been left by a spirit but if it was a joke it wasn't very funny.

In any case, I was impatient to get on with my investigation. And that, ultimately, was my excuse for what happened next. I dismissed Mrs. Pike's concern.

And I was rude.

"If a spirit had decided to visit the mortuary and leave a message, why would she leave a picture of the weapon? We already know what killed her. That so-called sign could have been made at any time and most likely has nothing at all to do with any of this."

I was aghast as soon as the words were out of my mouth. I could only imagine what my mother would have thought. We are strictly brought up to respect the elderly. I stood very still and waited for Mrs. Paikkonen to give me a (well-deserved) piece of her mind. It didn't happen. Instead, the elderly lady spoke with a stiff dignity.

"Messages from the afterlife come in mysterious ways, Henrikki," she said. "This is something you would know that if you studied your Bible. I will not stay in the funeral home for another night and I thought it right to come tell you so you can make other arrangements to host the Tallmasters." She did not point out that, unlike me, she always remembered her manners. But then, she didn't need to.

"All right," I said, feeling penitent. "I'll switch places with you. You can stay at my house tonight and I'll stay at Maki's. Take the bed in my room. It's the first one at the top of the stairs. And, Mrs. Paikkonen, I'm sorry."

"Sorry is as sorry does. Remember, things are not always what they seem." And then she stalked out of the kitchen door that leads to the dining room. I grabbed my coat and headed out the back door. I welcomed the cold snow on my burning cheeks and offered a prayer of thanks that Harry had not gotten up to join me. I needed some time alone.

I let the Jeep warm up for a few minutes. Just as I started to crank it into gear there was a sharp knock on the driver's side window.

Harry Dent bent over to mouth some words at me. Geez Louise. I'd almost forgotten about him. Ungraciously I rolled down the window.

"What?"

"I brought you coffee." He handed over a traveling cup. He was wearing a leather bomber jacket and some kind of aftershave or cologne. He smelled clean, spicy, expensive. I'll admit my spirits lifted.

"You seemed preoccupied a minute ago, Cupcake," he said, after he'd slipped into the passenger seat and I'd turned the Jeep onto Tamarack. "Anything I can do to help?"

I shook my head but, after a few sips of coffee, I found I wanted to talk about Mrs. Pike.

"I'd like someone to explain to me how seemingly intelligent people can believe in the stories of God and Jesus from the Bible and pagan myths at the same time."

He sighed. "For one thing, they are both attempts to explain the inexplicable. How did we get here and why? Is there a higher power or are we just a product of evolution? Do we have an imperative other than the continuation of the species or not? When you think about it, Hatti, religion and mythology are pretty much the same thing."

I was aware that my mother and all the rest of the members of

St. Heikki's Finnish Lutheran would consider those words blasphemous but I could see his point.

"Okay, I'll be more specific. This is about Mrs. Paikkonen."

"The elderly lady who looks like an aging Morticia Addams? The one who is staying at the funeral home with the Tallmasters?" I nodded.

"She heard footsteps in the attic last night. She went to investigate and found a *karsikko* sign drawn onto one of the struts under the roof."

"A *karsikko* sign?"

I explained the pagan belief.

"Somebody could have doodled it any time in the last one hundred years but Mrs. Pike is convinced it was left by the ghostly spirit of the young woman who was murdered on New Year's Eve outside Red Jacket."

"The one with the insect nickname?"

"Yep."

"What makes her think so?"

"Instead of a Christian cross there's a pair of crossed knitting needles." This required more explanation, of course. "I made the mistake of claiming the fatal wound had been made by a knitting needle."

"Why?"

"Good question. I don't know. It was a round hole with no real tearing of the skin around it. It just looked neat and tidy and, I guess, since I now sell knitting supplies, I was thinking along those lines. Anyway, Mrs. Paikkonen believes Cricket left the sign and she's afraid to stay at the funeral home tonight."

"A ghost," he said, lightly, "with a sense of humor." I frowned. "Look, Cupcake," he said. "Pagan myths aside, the real question here is who did make that drawing in the attic? It sounds to me as if somebody, some flesh and blood person, wanted to scare the old lady."

Of course. He was right. The issue that was bothering me wasn't Mrs. Paikkonen's superstitious beliefs. It was the actual fact of the sign. It seemed so threatening.

"Anyway, Mrs. Pike refuses to stay at the funeral home tonight, so she and I are switching places."

"You aren't worried about the sign-making spirit?" I shook my head.

"I don't believe in them." Mostly.

We drove in silence while I thought about that. He finished his coffee and turned sideways.

"Has it occurred to you," he asked, his voice more serious than I'd ever heard it, "that the murder of this Cricket occurred hours before the Attic people turned up on your doorstep?"

My fingers slipped on the steering wheel and, for a few harrowing moments, I veered onto the shoulder of the road. When I had the Jeep under control, I glanced at him.

"You're trying to say that one of your colleagues killed Cricket Koski? But why? None of you except Seth has ever been in the UP and I'm ninety-nine percent sure Cricket never left the Keweenaw in her twenty-eight years. How would any of you even know about her or Lars's cabin? Besides, you didn't arrive until Sunday morning. I saw you arrive."

Harry shrugged. "Point taken."

"But why would you even raise the question, Harry?"

"One of the things I learned as a professional investigator is that, when it comes to major crimes, there are very few coincidences."

"Now you sound like Sherlock Holmes." I shook my head. "I can't see any possible connection between this blighted television show and a dead barmaid." I waited. "Can you?"

"Well, no. Not immediately. But, don't forget, things aren't always what they seem."

His use of the same phrase I'd just heard from Mrs. Paikkonen shook me. And yet, there was such a thing as coincidence. Just not in a crime novel.

"This the way to L'Anse?" He asked the question as I turned off the two-lane road that leads to Frog Creek.

I explained that I wanted to check in with Lars at the county jail and he was obliging enough to offer to pick up some breakfast for us. I suggested stopping at the Lunch Box Café and did not point out the fact that I'd already eaten.

"By the way, I checked with one of my old sources in the world of stolen art. He said there's been no chatter about a piece of Nazi loot hidden on the Keweenaw."

I wasn't sure whether I was relieved or disappointed to hear that.

"So this is a bunch of malarkey?"

"It's wishful thinking based on desperation. Think about it. There's no real indication that Hautamaki was even talking about art. He probably sent his aunt a handkerchief of German lace or a brooch or something that got lost years ago. The leap from the letter from Munich, to the recovery of a stolen Monet, is like trying to jump the Grand Canyon. Vincent will have to be happy with the other Nazi artifacts we turned up. To tell you the truth I was surprised to find as much as we did." I shrugged.

"I thought you said this pilot would never get on the air. Have you changed your tune?"

He grinned. "No. Tune is the same. But I'll admit I never thought we'd come up with so much Nazi stuff."

"Harry," I said, as a thought occurred, "if this is a pilot, where are you planning to videotape the next show in the series?"

"Hibbing, Minnesota, birthplace of Bob Dylan."

"You know that's right in the heart of Iron Range."

"What does that mean?"

I glanced at him. "It means that community is Finnish-American. Maybe Vincent can find more Nazi treasure there." He groaned.

"Bite your tongue."

I parked in front of the one-story, cinderblock building that is our sheriff's department, jail and morgue.

"The Lunch Box is down there. Do yourself a favor and ask Vesta for Trenary toast."

WAINO MET me at the front door.

"You can't come in, Hatti. Sheriff says for you to keep your nose out of the murder, eh?"

"He makes me sound like a Labrador retriever."

"He's still ticked off about those last murders. And because your sister won't talk to him."

"Okay. I don't want to get you in trouble," I said, in my most persuasive voice, "I just need five minutes with Lars."

Waino shook his massive head. "No can do."

"Look, Waino, you owe me," I said, desperate to get past his guard. "What about the cloak closet? What about Spin-the-Bottle?"

The blue eyes focused on me.

"I've paid you back a million times for that," he said. And, of course, he was right. Anyway, I'd been at least as interested in the kissing experiment as he.

"Okay, okay, but this important, Waino. I've got news for Lars. Important news." I'd made up my mind to tell Lars about Sofi even though I knew it was totally not my business. But desperate times called for desperate measures. Lars was sitting in jail and Sofi was holed up in her bedroom. Their hands were tied until they talked to each other. Each needed reassurance that the other had not killed Cricket Koski.

"Tell me. I can tell him."

I studied the sea-blue eyes for a minute. Waino wasn't heartless, just clueless. I moved close to him.

"All right, Waino. Here's the deal. Sofi's pregnant."

I may have lived a sheltered life on the Keweenaw but I'd seen plenty of male reaction to that kind of news. It was invariably some-where on the scale of uncomfortable to panic and I figured Waino would be no exception. I was right.

"Geez zow!" He jumped out of my way. "Five minutes, Hatti. Sheriff could be here any time, eh?" He melted out of my way like a popsicle on the summer pavement.

I found Lars slumped in the same position where I'd left him the day before but he looked even worse. He was still wearing the same clothes. A dark beard had sprouted on his cheeks and chin and sleeplessness had left dark circles under his eyes that made him look like a raccoon. His dark skin was stretched tight across his high cheekbones and the green eyes held no expression at all.

"I should have brought you some fresh clothes," I murmured. "Are you at least eating?"

He sat up straighter but ignored what I'd asked and he began to pepper me with questions of his own.

"Why are you here? Is Sofi all right? Charlie?"

"Charlie's still in Florida with my folks. Sofi's been laid up with the flu. The sheriff's chomping at the bit to see her though and he's got some damning evidence."

Alarm flared in Lars's eyes. He jumped to his feet, jammed his hands into the pockets of his jeans and paced as well as he could in the tiny cell.

"What evidence?"

"He's got a ladies size-six boot print from the snow under the pines out at the cabin. Some of the confetti from our celebration at the Leaping Deer is frozen into the prints. He figures that's proof that Sofi was out at the cabin that night. I think he's just trying to make up his mind whether she killed Cricket or you killed Cricket or whether you guys did it together."

"Sofi wasn't out there."

Under the burgeoning facial hair, his face was chalk white.

"You mean you didn't see her. I think she was there, Lars. I think she drove out there to talk to you and she saw something that scared her so much that she hightailed it back to Red Jacket and hid under the covers."

He shook his head.

"Why would she have driven out there at that hour? She could've called me."

"She needed to talk to you in person."

He must have heard the urgency in my voice because he stopped pacing and stared at me.

"About what?"

I knew I didn't have much time but I needed to light a fire under my ex-brother-in-law and I needed some answers.

"She thinks you lied to her. You told her you hadn't seen Cricket in three years but apparently you left a pair of jeans at Sofi's place and she found Cricket's phone number scribbled on a napkin in one of the pockets." He looked away from me and my heart sank.

"I can explain that."

"Can you also explain why I found your new phone number on an envelope in Cricket's bedroom?"

Lars jammed his fingers into his already disheveled hair and muttered a soft expletive as he dropped back onto the bare mattress.

"Yeah, all right. I was in contact with her. It's not what you think but I wanted to keep it hidden. Sofi and I were on the path to reconciliation and this could have derailed it."

I must have had a horrified expression on my face because he hurried to explain.

"Cricket called me in mid-December. It was right after the St. Lucy murders. I should have hung up but, for whatever reason, I didn't."

I understood. We were raised to be polite. Witness my distress at my incivility to Mrs. Paikkonen.

"She wanted to get together?" He nodded.

"Not because of any personal interest in me. She wanted to hire my services. She'd heard I was a P.I. and she needed some information."

"Well, for cripes sake, Lars, why didn't you turn her down?"

"I did. More than once. She said she was desperate. She'd lost her job at the Black Fly and she was trying to get her life on track. She said she didn't need much, just a simple, local job and she'd be out of my hair forever. I don't know, Hatti. I just couldn't keep saying no."

"I get it," I said, and I did. Yoopers value independence but we are reared in a tradition of pitching in to help one another regardless of the inconvenience to ourselves.

"There was another reason I agreed to do the job, too. Cricket wanted background on a local family. She wanted an expanded family tree, you know, where people lived during the last century, who they married, what the connections were. I figured if anyone was going to dig that stuff up it had better be me."

"Whose family was it?" I asked, but I knew. A ripple of unease made its way down my spine.

Lars shrugged.

"Yours. All the branches. The Lehtinens, the Ristos, the Makis, your mother's people, the Ahos, the Suutulas, the Makis. Cricket wouldn't tell me why she wanted the info just that if I didn't find it someone else would. I had to make sure she wasn't going to find anything she could use for blackmail."

I sat still for a moment.

"Did you get it for her?"

"I got it. I never gave it to her. I think that's why she was at my cabin on New Year's Eve. I think she came out there with her partner-in-crime. I think they broke in to the cabin and when they didn't find what they were looking for, he killed her and left her in my bed."

"He?"

Lars shrugged. "It's a pretty good guess. I can't see Cricket hooking up with a female. She was excited about the guy and she was jacked about her ship coming in. She was like a kid, Hatti. She believed in Tinkerbell and Cinderella and fairytale endings." He seemed to remember then what had happened. "She finally paid the price."

I thought about that for a minute.

"It doesn't make any sense, though. Who would benefit from Cricket Koski's death? She didn't have any money or connections. I can see someone using her as a pawn to get what he wanted but it would be much easier to pay her off or make a promise he had no intention of delivering than to risk killing her."

"Unless the promise was marriage and he either didn't want to marry her or couldn't. Killing Cricket would get that monkey off his back and shut her up at the same time. And the cherry on top was being able to pin it on me."

"But you hadn't seen her in three years," I said.

"You're forgetting I'd seen her recently and we'd exchanged phone numbers. You and Sofi figured that out. How long do you think it will take the sheriff to do the same?"

I could hear the front door opening and figured we were about to get interrupted.

"Did you find anything in your investigation of the family?"

"Nothing worth writing home about. A few divorces. Your dad took off when you were a baby. No criminal records or suspicious deaths. Nothing that would benefit a blackmailer."

"What about Ernst Hautamaki?"

"Who?"

"A young Finnish military diplomat stationed in Munich in 1942. There's speculation that he retrieved a valuable painting, a piece of Nazi loot, and had it sent to his aunt who was visiting here at the time."

"That's new to me," Lars said, rubbing his bristly chin. "Think it's relevant?"

I shrugged.

"Look, you could have avoided all of this by leveling with Sofi, you know."

"About my contact with Cricket? Are you crazy? She'd never have understood. You know your sister. She's not big on forgiveness."

I thought about the baby.

"You should talk to her, Lars," I said, as I slipped out of the cell. I'd have to exit out the back and circle the block to get back to the Jeep. "She loves you, you know. And she's got some news."

I FOUND Harry Dent behind the wheel gnawing on a bit of Trenary toast.

"You got a dentist out here," he asked. "This stuff is hard enough to crack a tooth."

"You're supposed to soak it in coffee."

"Well, hell. Vesta didn't tell me that."

"Why are you behind the wheel?"

"I figured you'd like a break. And I'm good in snow. I live in the Hudson Valley."

"That up in New York?" I was intrigued. He nodded but said

nothing else. "Is that where you keep your art collection?"

"I've got a small, climate-controlled gallery in my basement."

"So you have to go down there to look at the paintings?"

He glanced at me and smiled.

"Masterpieces, like the Waterlilies, don't usually hang on the living room wall where someone just walks by them a hundred times a day. If you are lucky enough to have that kind of art, you devote a lot of time to it. I can spend hours just sitting on a bench in the gallery gazing at the work. It absorbs my soul."

I felt a sudden, fierce envy. What would it be like to have something extraordinary that would take you out of yourself?

"It must be like meditating. Or praying."

He nodded.

"How did you get it? Are you independently wealthy?"

He chuckled. "Yeah. My old man was a vice president in one of the major auto companies. But I'd never have had enough to buy a Monet. This one was uncovered in a bust the art theft squad did. The owner was an old man, alone in the world. The painting had gone missing twenty years ago. He didn't want it to go to a museum where people would just walk by. He wanted someone to own it, to cherish it. For some reason he took a liking to me and wound up leaving it to me in his will."

I gave him the directions to the interstate and L'Anse.

"How'd your talk go?"

"It was kinda weird." I told Harry about Cricket contacting Lars to provide information on my family. "He didn't find anything very interesting. Just the same old, same old, that we're all related if you go back far enough."

"One of the original tight-knit communities, huh?"

"Hm. So tightly night that we've all lived within a few blocks of each other for generations. In fact, we've all wound up living on Calumet Street. Aunt Ianthe and Miss Irene, Elli's B and B, the Maki Funeral home and my folks' place. Four houses and four attics." I looked at him. "There's another coincidence. Attics. I mean, that's the name of your television show." I grimaced. "I must sound crazy."

"Not crazy. I think your instincts are right but I don't know yet what they're trying to tell us." Harry said stared through the snowflakes at the road ahead. No lane lines were visible, neither were the shoulders.

I shifted around in the seat until I was staring at his profile.

"What are you thinking?"

"Just that while the five of us got to the B and B at the same time, we didn't travel together. We joined up at the Hancock airport and took the shuttle to Red Jacket, but we were coming from different places.

"Seth flew from Detroit Metro to Petoskey then took the morning puddle-jumper to Hancock. Vincent and Helena Tallmaster left from Flint's Bishop Airport and spent the night in some motel or other in Escanaba." He was easily negotiating the snow on the road but his brow was furrowed in an effort to remember. "Serena wanted to stop at a couple of textile shops in Ohio and southern Michigan so we drove together out from New York. Started on December 26th."

"You rented a car?"

"Yeah. Some kind of SUV."

"And where did you stay on New Year's Eve?"

"Some little no-count motel on M-28. The proprietor said we were lucky we didn't hit anybody because we were at a magical section called the Seney Mile and on New Year's Eve drunken revelers like to see if they can make it across before they get hit by a car."

"It's called the Dreaded Dash of Death," I said, diverted.

"We didn't see a damn soul. Not even a deer."

"It sounds like you've thought about this before. I mean, you know all the details of all the travel arrangements."

"I'm a professional detective. Given a situation, like a murder, my mind automatically starts making connections."

"Why would any of you want to hurt Cricket?"

"I don't know the answer to that, but if there's one thing I've discovered in thirty years of investigating, the truth will emerge."

CHAPTER 17

The L'Anse Bay Ojibwe Reservation, located at the base of the peninsula, is divided into two non-adjacent tracts of land that hug the Keweenaw Bay. It is a total of some three-and-a-half square miles, an area twice the size of the Copper Eagle Reservation that is home to my grandfather-in-law, Chief Joseph Night Wind.

The L'Anse Bay community has its own school system, council, fire department and tribal police and, like the Copper Eagle, it has, for some years, owned and operated a casino.

"I thought the casinos were supposed to line the pockets of the folks on the reservations," Harry said, as we drove along a curb-less street, past a bank of shabby looking businesses, including a laundromat and a pawn shop and a couple of empty storefronts. "Where are all the riches?"

"The UP casinos face the same problem of other tourist attractions up here," I said. "Not many people want to drive a few hundred miles to play slot machines. And there are restrictions on how the tribe can spend any profit it makes. The biggest advantage to having a casino is that it provides some jobs." He looked at me.

"You're an expert on Indian casinos?"

"My husband represents tribes and individuals in law cases. A lot of them have to do with casino issues."

"He's an Indian?"

"Half. The clue is in the name: Night Wind. His mom was from the rez near Red Jacket. She left as a teenager and Jace and his half brother grew up in Canada. Oh, pull over there, will you," I asked, as I spotted a tiny post office. "Somebody will know where Cloud lives."

I was laughing when I returned to the Jeep.

"What's so funny?"

"There are approximately 1,200 people living on this reservation and thirty of them are named Cloud but I think we got it narrowed down to the right one."

"Let me guess, Cloud Two Crows."

"Miller," I said, correcting him. "Cloud Miller. Take a right up at that corner. She's at number 52, about half way down the road."

Number 52, like the other dozen houses on Rural Route 12, was a mobile home. The structure looked shabby but tidy with a huge, thick blanket of snow covering the yard.

"One reason there are so many mobile homes on reservations is because the land is communally owned. A family owns the home itself but not the land it is on which means they can't borrow using that land as collateral. And there's less incentive to invest in the property when it doesn't belong to you."

"And so all this poverty is as simple as communally owned land?"

"No. It's more complicated. It's not easy for non-Indians to set up businesses on the rez because the normal regulatory practices are different here, as are the police and courts. Generally speaking there's no economic base."

"The same problem you have on the Keweenaw for different reasons," he said, pulling up in front of Cloud's house and turning off the Jeep. "It can't be easy to scratch out a living here. Why do people stay?"

"We stay because it's home," I said.

"You say that as if home is the Holy Grail. What is home compared with adventure and riches and excitement?"

I grinned at him. "C'mon, Harry. You're just playing devil's advocate. You know you have a home in New York." He shook his head.

"It's just a place to hang my hat."

"And your Monet."

"The point is, I don't miss it. I don't miss any place."

"How about people?" He shook his head.

"Don't miss them, either."

I felt a sudden stab of compassion and I reached over to touch him on the forearm.

"You know what I think? I think you need a family."

"Hmmm," he murmured, noncommittally. "You may not be the first person to have mentioned that. But you know what I think? I think we'd better talk to Cloud Miller and get back up the interstate before we get snowed in down here. After all, you promised Mrs. Paikkonen you'd switch places with her tonight."

The woman who opened the door to us was about my age, on the short side and solidly built. Her moon-shaped face was framed by thick, black hair pulled into a braid and she wore a flannel shirt open over a worn-looking but clean white tee shirt. She had on jeans and a pair of fawn-colored moccasins. A sleeping baby was hiked up on her shoulder and her dark eyes were soft but serious.

I introduced myself and Harry and told her why we were there.

"Please come in," she said, stepping back so we could crowd into the small, rectangular-shaped living room where two small boys sat cross-legged on a thin carpet watching cartoons on a tube television with foil-covered rabbit ears. One of the kids turned to look at us and, as if our arrival was some sort of signal, he jammed his elbow into his brother's side and the room rang with the sounds of cries and punches as they wrestled, seemingly to the death. My heart leapt into my mouth but their mother remained perfectly calm.

"Calvin, Jack, get your snowsuits and boots," she said, quietly. They stopped fighting, apparently more interested in going outside than in killing each other, and Cloud handed me the baby while she zipped and buttoned them.

"You should have seen your face when Calvin let out the banshee cry," Harry whispered. "You looked like you were on the verge of a panic attack."

"I don't spend much time around kids."

He eyed the picture I made with the baby on my shoulder.

"You look pretty natural to me."

The baby squirmed against my neck, made a little burping sound and settled back to sleep. I grinned at Harry.

"This is the easy part. When my niece was a baby and I was ten, I was in love with her when she was asleep. When she was awake, I was always tempted to fling her out the window. It takes more patience than I've got to be a mom."

"Or," Harry said, "more patience than you had at age ten."

The baby was still on my shoulder, when we three adults sat at the scarred wooden table in Cloud's kitchen and sipped herbal tea. He smelled wonderful, like clean laundry, and he was keeping me warm, too. I was so relaxed I was in danger of falling asleep. Harry seemed to know it and he took over the questioning.

"Thank you for talking to us," he began. "It's obvious you have your hands full." He indicated the sleeping baby. "This one a boy, too?"

"Yes. Three boys." She sounded proud. "They keep me busy. Luckily, my mother lives next door on one side, my sister on the other. When these guys are outside, there are eyes on them all the time." He laughed, appreciatively. "Do you have any children?" He shook his head, regretfully.

"I'm afraid my marriage didn't last long enough."

"It's not too late."

Harry grinned at me. "Hear that Cupcake? Play your cards right and you could have one just like that."

The words struck me hard, not because they'd been spoken by the charming Harry Dent but because I was on track to miss the whole motherhood experience. And because he was right. If my marriage had worked out better, I might have a dark-haired, creamy-skinned baby just like the one on my shoulder. And I might have the patience to deal with him. I shifted the child into my arms and focused on why we had come.

"We're trying to find out who killed Cricket Koski," I said. "I found your name on a Christmas card she'd kept under her pillow and thought you might be able to tell us something about her family and her childhood."

"I knew she'd died," Cloud said, a sad expression on her kind face. "Thank you for telling me she kept the card. We didn't see each other but we talked on the phone once in awhile. She really wanted to be done with the rez but things just didn't work out for her." She settled back in her chair. "You want to know her background? I'll tell you what I can. Mainly, she's alone. No family. She was fostered with an elderly Ojibwe couple during high school. They were kind enough but she didn't fit in at the rez high school. A few of us tried to be friendly with her but she resisted."

"You must have tried harder than anybody else," I said.

Cloud smiled. "I'm stubborn. And my mom pushed me. She felt sorry for Cricket."

And then I remembered to ask her about Cricket's real name.

"It was Caarina," Cloud said.

Caarina. With a "C".

Caarina. Dearly beloved. Someone, sometime, had loved Cricket Koski.

"Both of the foster parents died during our senior year and Cricket moved in with my family. There were seven of us squished into a trailer smaller than this one but we made do. After graduation though, Cricket took off. She worked at different restaurants and bars in the UP and ended up at the Black Fly. She came to visit three times and each time she only stayed for an hour. I spoke with her on the phone a few times over the years, too." Cloud sighed. "I was always worried about her."

"Did she ever mention any friends," Harry asked.

"Not really." The young woman hesitated. "Just one. It was a guy. She called him her Prince Charming."

The name hit me like a blow to the chest. *Prince Charming?*

"What can you tell me about him?"

Cloud looked at me with her opaque, dark eyes.

"Not very much. I never heard his real name. He was a guy she met at camp." She paused and backed up. "That last summer in high school, the Little Mooses were able to get Cloud a scholarship to a Finnish camp, one of those where they teach about Finnish culture and stuff. She was there for six weeks and when she got back she said she'd met her destiny, her Prince Charming. She was in love and she said he was in love, too, but he was older. He told her he'd come back for her when she was grown up and he had gotten out of his marriage."

"He was married?"

Cloud nodded. "I know, I know. Bad news."

"I'll say. Sounds like he was a con man."

"I thought that, too. But then he never contacted her. He never showed up. So I figured there was no harm done. In fact, I never heard about him again until last Saturday."

I stared at Cloud. "Saturday, the day she died?"

"She called me. In the afternoon. She was so excited. So manic. She said it was all happening. Everything she wanted. The guy, the money, a ticket off the Keweenaw."

"Did she," I asked, almost breathless with excitement, "tell you who the guy was? I mean, was it the one from camp all those years ago?"

"I don't know," Cloud said. "She called him her love but she never said whether she'd known him before."

I sensed the uncertainty in her.

"Cloud, if you have to guess, would you think it was the shyster from ten years ago?"

She considered her answer carefully.

"I would. There was something about the way she spoke of him. And then, she called him her prince."

I stared at Harry.

"We need to get a list of campers from that year."

"It was called Camp Kaleva and it's near Ontonagon." Harry

slipped his phone out of his pocket and called information. The camp, he was informed, no longer existed.

"Damn," he said, disconnecting the phone. He looked at Cloud. "Did Cricket ever give you any clues about the guy? Did she describe his looks?"

"No. Like I said, he was a bit older and," she broke off. "Oh, excuse me for a minute." She left the room and was gone several minutes. The baby stirred on my shoulder.

"Oh! I hope he isn't hungry."

"Or wet," Harry said, with a wink.

It turned out he was both. Cloud came back to an agonized screech. She took the child and, at the same time, handed me a photograph. It was one of those large, group shots taken with a wide-angled lens. The subjects in the front two rows, all of them blond and blue-eyed, were easily identifiable but those in the back rows were much smaller and harder to discern. The photo paper had been folded and creased and, if I was any judge, had spent many nights under Cloud's pillow.

"Which one is Prince Charming?" Harry asked. I could hear the excitement in his voice. We were on the verge of a major breakthrough.

"I don't know. She wouldn't tell me. I think he had warned her not to tell anyone. Excuse me, again. Time for a diaper change." She disappeared and the room got quiet again. Harry and I stood at the table hovering over the photograph.

Suddenly Harry dropped back into his seat and drew a hand across his forehead.

"What? What is it?"

"Do you see Cricket? Second row just to the right of center."

I had to squint. I'm supposed to wear glasses for reading and driving but I nearly always forget them. He pointed a finger and I noticed it was trembling.

"Oh, right. There she is."

"Look at the boy next to her."

"They must have been friends. She's smiling at him. He's in

three-quarter profile but his cheek is crinkled, as though he's smiling back at her."

"Anything else?"

I stared at the picture.

"Geez Almighty Louise," I breathed. "That's Seth Virtunen."

CHAPTER 18

By the time we got back to Red Jacket it was after twelve so we parked in the alley behind Calumet Street and headed straight over to the Bed and Breakfast. I was glad to get there and not just because of the howling wind and the swirling snow on the interstate. Harry and I had argued nonstop during the sixty- minute return trip and things between us were tense the way they get when people who have been on the same wavelength, suddenly are not.

"The mere fact that Seth attended a camp on the Keweenaw ten years ago does not make him a murderer," Harry maintained. Whereas I could not imagine anything else that would account for this coincidence.

"It's not like I want him to be the killer," I'd argued. "But they were clearly friendly ten years ago and here he is on the Keweenaw just after she's been killed. You said he came up here by himself. He could have lied about when he arrived. Heck, he could have been here all the time. Face it, Harry. If this were an episode of *Law and Order,* no one on the force would question Seth's guilt. The fact is, he was the Prince Charming of long ago and, without a doubt, he's the Prince Charming of now."

"Seth's only about thirty. Cloud said the guy was older and married."

"That's a two-year age difference which can seem like a decade to a teenager. And who says he wasn't married?"

Harry blew out a breath.

"All right. Take it from a different angle. Why would Seth have killed her?"

"He was after a treasure. He wanted her help to find it but he couldn't let her live afterwards."

"A treasure? You're talking about the mythical Nazi loot?"

"We don't know that it's mythical."

"Okay, say he used Cricket to find out which of the attics housed the painting. Then he found it and killed her. Why the hell's he still hanging around in Red Jacket?"

"Oh, come on, Harry." I knew my exasperation had as much to do with my disappointment in Seth as anything else. He looked like every boy I'd gone to Sunday school with. He could have been my brother. I didn't want him to have killed Cricket Koski. "Seth's cover for being on the Keweenaw is the television pilot. How would it look if he just disappeared? He has to stay until the rest of you leave. Then he can slip away and enjoy his ill-gotten gains."

Harry shook his head. "I can't believe this rush to judgment. There's no proof that he did anything wrong. I'm assuming it's not illegal to go to Finnish camp."

We were not on speaking terms when we entered the back door of the B and B. Elli was stirring a pot on the stove and Harry took an exaggerated sniff.

"Something smells extraordinarily good," he said. His heartiness sounded forced.

"Pea soup," she said, absently. "Perfect for white-out conditions. Help yourself. There's fresh banana nut bread, too."

My cousin turned to look at me. "I'm worried about Mrs. Pike."

"She told you about the *karsikko* sign?"

Elli shot a quick look at Harry who was busy ladling the fragrant soup into one of her blue-rimmed bowls.

"Don't mind him," I said, with more disdain that was strictly necessary. "He's helping with the investigation." Elli grinned at the former art theft cop.

"Bet you weren't expecting to deal with murder and ghosts when you signed up for this gig."

"Surprises," he said, after tasted a spoonful of soup, "are the spice of life. Speaking of spices, what did you put in the soup? It's amazing."

"Marjoram. And a dollop of hot mustard." She turned her attention back to me. "I think there's something else bothering Mrs. Pike. She popped in about fifty times this morning, looking for you. She wouldn't stay, wouldn't leave a message, just said she'd speak with you later."

"Where is she now?"

"She was going next door to put clean sheets on your bed then down to the opera house with Seth."

"Seth?"

Neither my voice nor Harry's was raised but the name came out of our mouths simultaneously and Elli's eyebrows opened up like a drawbridge. An explanation was required but I could hear voices in the hall and it wasn't the time to get into the story of Cricket and the Finnish camp.

"Just the two of them?" She shook her head.

"Serena Waterfall went too, and Diane Hakala. They were going to do an impromptu séance. They heard about the *karsikko* sign and they figure that Maud's their best bet to communicate with Cricket's spirit."

"That makes a certain amount of sense," Harry said, grinning at me, "if you believe in the afterlife."

It's odd how someone's clever comment can rub you the wrong way. Yesterday, I'd probably have laughed at the joke. Today it just sounded offensive. No doubt because I was unhappy with Harry Dent.

"Oh, I almost forgot to tell you," Elli said, as she turned from the stove to the island countertop. As she spoke, she deftly removed half a dozen loaves of the fresh bread from their pans, sliced them and arranged them on serving dishes. "Serena asked if I thought you would mind videotaping the segment about the Rya Rug down at Bait and Stitch. She thought using the yarn shop as background would add to the ambiance."

"That's fine," I said, automatically.

"There's more." She gave me a quick, ironic smile. "Aunt Ianthe got to talking about the knitting circle and how, at least on Thursday nights, the shop seemed like the center of the community. The comments inspired Serena who spoke to Vincent and, the long and the short of it is, they want to videotape the knitting circle at the shop this afternoon. Aunt Ianthe's not too happy about it."

"Why not?" Harry asked, reaching for a slice of bread. "Seems like it could be good publicity for the shop and the town."

"The name of the group," Elli explained, "is the Thursday Night Knitting Circle and today is Tuesday. We Finns are very literal. I can't imagine what Einar will have to say about it."

Einar Eino, a short, bald, gnome-like octogenarian has been the assistant at the bait shop since before I was born. He is the repository of all the Finnish male eccentricities from *Sisu* and a strong work ethic to a well-hidden, soft heart. He guards both his privacy and his words, sticking to a regimen of uttering as few syllables as possible each day. He is an acknowledged expert on the local weather and fishing and, to my everlasting relief, he is always willing to handle the live bait. He is fond of Sofi and Elli and me but he is not a fan of change and I have to admit I was pleasantly surprised when he put up no real resistance to my plan to sell yarn in the bait shop.

"He's not gonna like turning his store into a stage set," Elli said. "And then there's the very real possibility that Vincent will try to tie you in to the Nazis. Maybe you should give him the afternoon off. He can go take a sauna."

The reference caused Harry's and my eyes to meet. I remembered how much fun we'd had the previous afternoon both in the sauna and in the attic. I remembered why I liked him. I supposed it was only natural that he defended Seth who was, after all, a colleague. I realized that the distaste in my mouth and the uncertain sensations in my stomach were not because Harry and I were feuding but because I was upset by Seth's apparent involvement in the murder.

We heard the front door, followed by voices and footsteps.

"Here comes the cavalry," Elli murmured, as the ladies, Aunt Ianthe, Miss Irene, Mrs. Moilanen and Mrs. Sorensen trooped into the kitchen. Each was carrying a plate, a bowl or a pan of home-cooked food. A few minutes later the smorgasbord was set out again as the Tallmasters, Serena, Diana Hakala and Seth arrived. After he'd stomped his boots on Elli's well-placed mat, hung up his coat and rubbed his reddened fingers together for warmth, Seth sought me out. He was wearing his usual friendly smile.

"Mrs. Paikkonen wants to see you, Hatti. She wanted to get the sheets out of the dryer and onto the bed next door, then she'll be over."

We filled our plates and sat at the long farm table. It was a cozy scene, with half a dozen different conversations going on, silverware clinking, bursts of laughter. The view outside the arched, latticed window looked like a snow globe and the inside felt warm and cozy. At least it did if you could forget about the murder.

I listened with half an ear to Miss Irene's discovery of a box of antimacassars crocheted by some distant relative and, until this morning, neglected in the duplex's attic but most of my focus was on Seth. He was making himself useful by refreshing the coffee and replacing empty serving dishes with full ones. I saw him follow Elli through the swing door into the kitchen and watched as she laughed over her shoulder at something he said. It was obvious she liked and trusted him and that was unusual for Elli, who usually avoided eligible men. She would be sick when she found out about the Camp Kaleva picture.

I could only imagine how vulnerable Cricket Koski had been. After years of living in other people's homes, she'd been at a camp, swimming and sailing, running and folk dancing. She hadn't been the only blond in a high school of Native American kids. For once in her life, she'd looked like everybody else. And a guy had liked her. It must have felt like a magical summer. No wonder she'd fallen in love.

I was a million miles away from Elli's dining table when someone said, "you gonna eat that bite, Cupcake?" I realized there was food on my fork and Harry Dent's fingers, too. Before I could respond, Aunt Ianthe's shriek split the air and everyone froze.

"*Voi kahua*! You are trying to poison Henrikki, then?"

I closed my eyes. This had happened many times before but never right after an actual murder. I set the fork back on my plate as Miss Irene quoted the book of James.

"But the tongue can no man tame; it is an unruly evil, full of deadly poison."

"Deadly poison?" Harry sniffed. "That's vinegar cabbage."

I set the fork down and pulled myself together.

"I'm fine, Aunt Ianthe," I called out. "I wasn't going to eat it." Talk broke out up and down the table which gave me a chance to explain to Harry.

"Years ago my face swelled up after a church potluck at which Aunt Ianthe claimed I'd taken a bite of Mrs. Moilanen's vinegar cabbage. My mom explained that I'd caught the mumps from the Hautala twins but Aunt Ianthe never believed it. She's convinced I have some unique allergy to the cabbage. The whole thing is ridiculous, of course. I never tasted the stuff as a child and I've never tasted it since." I shuddered. "I can't stand the smell."

"Then what, may I ask, was it doing on your fork?"

It was a good question and I had no answer.

"Search me."

"Now that we know Hatti is going to live," Elli said, pleasantly, "please help yourselves to dessert. We've got strawberry snow, chocolate pudding, applesauce meringue, almond log bars and dark chocolate caramel bars. And, of course, fresh coffee."

After lunch I bussed the dishes out to the kitchen, filled the dishwasher then went to work on the serving pieces of Arabia crockery. I never minded doing the dishes because it made my finger nails clean and, more importantly, it gave me a few minutes to think. And there was a lot to think about at the moment.

It was Harry who had suggested the murder was connected to the cast of *What's in Your Attic?* Now it was Harry who was insisting the killer could not be one of the cast members, Seth Virtunan. Why was he taking polar opposite positions on this? What did he really think? I felt a sudden, vicious longing for the days of the St. Lucy murder when I'd had all my friends around. And Jace. Especially Jace.

I felt that annoying prick of potential tears behind my eyeballs. Dang. There was no time for self-pity. I hung up the towel, grabbed my parka and headed for the door.

I needed to talk to my sister.

A few minutes later I was climbing the steps to Sofi's door and letting myself in.

The lights were off and this time there was no ribbon of light under the bedroom door. After a quick, fruitless search, I fished my phone out of my parka pocket and punched in Sofi's number, prepared to leave a message. It turned out not to be necessary.

"Main Street Floral and Fudge," she said, "Specials of the day are forced bulbs and maple coconut."

"Maple coconut?"

"It's an experiment."

"You're at work?"

"Of course I'm at work, Hatti. Mom and Charlie are out of town and Lars is in the pokey. Someone has to earn some money here. Why did you call?"

I've known my sister a long time. She doesn't suffer fools gladly but she's not usually short tempered with me. On the other hand, she had a lot of reasons to be upset.

"I wondered if you were feeling better."

"Of course I'm feeling better." I pictured the little notch between her sky blue eyes. "I told you it wasn't the flu."

"All right, all right. Do you need some help? I've got some time on my hands."

"I thought you were investigating the murder."

"I am, but…" I paused and she interrupted, irritably.

"Never mind, never mind. Yes, you can help me. I've got a special order from one of your television people." I didn't bother to remind her that they were not my television people. "Vincent Tallmaster. He wants twenty-four flower arrangements by tomorrow morning to be delivered to the opera house. I need you to go to Shopko. Bring me all the carnations they have. And then drive down to the hobby shop at Lake Linden for the pipe cleaners and spray paint."

"Pipe cleaners?"

"The order is red and white carnations with black swastikas." She ignored my groan. "Maybe you'd better pick up some daisies and lilies at the market, just in case anybody dies in the next few days."

I knew she wasn't referring to the murder. Finns prefer to use white and yellow flowers for funerals and she just wanted to be covered. But the comment sent a shiver down my spine.

"On the double, Hatti. I've got to go."

"Wait," I said, "I need to ask you something about New Year's Eve."

"I told you. I got home a little after eleven and went to bed."

"Waino found confetti under the lodgepole pines out at Lars's cabin. It was frozen under the print of a size six boot."

"I don't know anything about that," she snapped. "Hurry up and get the supplies. Chop. Chop."

"I'm heading to my car as we speak," I said, "and this is important. You were out there, Sofi. I know it. Tell me why."

"Not to kill Cricket Koski."

I kept my voice calm and steady even as I wondered why she'd lied.

"I never thought that. Just tell me what happened after you left the B and B."

"I can't tell you, Hatti."

"You followed him out to the lake, didn't you," I said. "You saw something there, how? Through the cabin's window? If he'd been out in the clearing, he'd have seen your car."

"He wasn't there." Sofi is normally as straightforward as an arrow and it was indicative of her state of mind that she kept toggling back and forth between protests and narrative. "The cabin was dark when I got to the lake and there was no one parked in the clearing. I figured he was dawdling, maybe stopped for a drink or something. I decided to wait but parked the van deep in the pines so it would be hard to see."

"Why?"

"I don't know. I've been asking myself that. It was almost like I knew there was something wrong. Hell, Hatti. I did know something was wrong. Lars wouldn't stop for a drink. He's been on the wagon for three years. I was worried." She paused. "I was angry, too. I thought we were getting back together and then I'd found the Insect's phone number in his jeans."

"What happened next?"

She was silent for a moment and then she must have made a decision to trust me because she stopped waffling.

"Lars's SUV showed up about eleven-thirty. He parked it near the cabin and got out of the driver's seat."

"Did you call to him?"

"No. He looked, strange. Furtive. Like he was sneaking around. After a minute, I understood why." I waited. "He came around to the driver's side door, reached in and helped a woman out of the car."

"Sofi!"

"I know. My blood was boiling. I think my eyes were crossed because my vision blurred. I thought about making a scene right then and there. He had his arm around her, like they'd been out on a romantic date and had every intention of extending that date into the bedroom. I saw them go in the cabin and then the light came on in the front room but I couldn't see anything else because the curtains were closed."

I made a mental search of my memory. Hadn't Lars said he'd left the lights off when he got home? Of course, he'd also said he come home alone.

"Did you go in after them?"

"No. I just couldn't do it. Not after he scooped her up in his arms and carried her over the threshold. It looked just like a groom with his bride, Hatti. He never carried me over the threshold."

A Double Pointed Murder

"Well, in all fairness, he was seventeen and weighed about a hundred and twelve and you were seven months pregnant."

"Even so. It felt like he was married to someone else."

My heart ached for her.

"Was the woman Cricket Koski?"

"I couldn't tell. They both had on knitted hats and their hoods were up. I can't imagine who else it would be given she was the one Waino found there."

"Right. You saw Cricket alive at eleven thirty-ish and Waino discovered her dead at about one fifteen. So at least we've narrowed down the time of death."

"The autopsy should do that. Besides, all this does is make a watertight case against Lars. Not that I care," she added.

"Lars didn't do it," I replied. "He's not a killer."

"Who knows what someone will do when they're desperate?"

"Why should he be desperate? Tell me something. If Cricket Koski had contacted you to say that Lars and she had taken up again and Lars had denied it, which of them would you have believed?"

She heaved a sigh. "I don't know."

"Sofi, Sofi! You've nurtured a grudge about this a long time. If you want to help Lars in this situation you have to decide whether you're going to trust him. Hell's bells, girl. If you plan to resume your marriage you have to trust him. Look at the facts. He cheated on you once and he didn't even lie about it. He told you."

"He lied about being in contact with Cricket recently."

She was right.

"Okay, nobody's perfect. Maybe he left the phone number in his pants pocket so you'd find it. Maybe he was afraid to tell you just like you're afraid to tell him about the baby."

On that coup de grace, I disconnected, parked the Jeep and headed into the Shopko.

133

CHAPTER 19

An hour later I carried four buckets of white, red and yellow carnations into the work room of Sofi's shop then I dug the pipe cleaners out of my jacket pocket and laid them on the plastic-covered work table.

Sofi's thick, straight wheat-colored hair was twisted into a knot on top of her head and she wore a pale green cobbler's apron over her sweatshirt and jeans. Her short, powerful fingers pulled the bunches apart and stripped the leaves. There were still dark crescents under her eyes but her cheeks were pink and she was back to her normal business-like self.

"You'd better let me spray paint the carnations," I said. "You shouldn't inhale the fumes."

"Fine." She had spread newspapers on her work table and now she laid the stripped stems on it "side by each," as Pops would say, like prisoners positioned before a firing squad.

I thought, not for the first time, how much being a shop owner suited Sofi and how she'd never have taken the plunge if it hadn't been for the divorce. She'd worked for years as an assistant to Lauri Hyypio who had owned the flower shop. Lauri had been ready to sell two years ago and Sofi, newly divorced, had gotten a loan from Miner's Bank to buy the place. She'd tightened up Lauri's somewhat lackadaisical business practices and she'd diversified by offering her customers not only floral arrangements but mouth-watering fudge. Fudge had been a natural addition. Sofi had always loved experimenting in the kitchen and the fudge making gave her a natural outlet for her creativity. In addition to seasonal favorites like eggnog and peppermint, she'd experimented with apple, pineapple and lingonberry fudge, all of which sound gag-inducing, but were actually delicious.

"I've lost four pounds," she said.

I hid a smile. Even in the midst of a crisis such as the threat of a murder charge, she was aware of the numbers on her scale. And I knew, very well, that she was not alone in that.

"Morning sickness?" She nodded.

"And I'm doing a land rush business. There's nothing like a scandal to bring out the shoppers." She nodded toward the curtain that leads to the front of the shop. "I borrowed Astrid Laplander from Ronja since Charlie's out of town." Astrid is the eldest of five daughters all of whom help out at the family owned Copper Kettle Gift Shop. "She can't cut an even square to save her life but she's good at the cash register."

"What are people saying about the murder?"

She laughed.

"They're a lot more interested in *What's in Your Attic?* Lots of talk about whose treasures are the most valuable and which of the locals will be spotted by some talent scout and whisked off to Hollywood." She shot me an ironic look. "Who says Finns don't have any imagination?"

"It gives people something to get excited about."

She shook her head. "I predict a lot of disappointment. Clara Tenhunen plans to bring that blue-and-white pitcher of hers because it looks like Dresden china. Trouble is, I remember when she bought it with wedding money at that K-mart that went out of business. It was made in Japan."

"That could work. Japan was also one of the Axis Powers in World War II."

"At least she has a good reason for not letting the host turn it upside down to see the bottom. At the moment, it's housing her *mummi's* ashes."

"Yikes."

"Willa Marsi found some marks made in East Germany. They were issued in the 1970s but she figures that, if there hadn't been a war, there wouldn't be any East Germany so the marks have some relevant historical value." She uncapped a can of spray, shook it and handed it to me.

"Ready to shoot?"

I stood back and pointed. I felt like one of the playing cards in *Alice in Wonderland*, tasked by the Queen to paint the roses red.

The air was thick with the detritus and scent of the black spray when the door from the shop opened and Ronja Laplander chugged into the room. No one knows why Ronja and her husband, Benne, named their souvenir shop as they did. So many tourists have stopped in there for fudge that Ronja's taken to purchasing it daily from Sofi.

Both Ronja and Benne are descended from Sami reindeer herders in Finnish Lapland and, unlike those of us with a Swedish-Finnish heritage, they are dark-haired, on the short side and squarely built. Ronja always reminds me of a heavy-bottomed, Great Lakes freighter and today was no exception.

"Hatti!"

I winced at the shrill tone. "Yes?"

"Diane Hakala just told me the television people are going to film a scene at the bait shop this afternoon. Is that true?" She planted her fists against her sides even though her waistline was no longer in evidence. Characteristically, she did not wait for me to answer. "That is very unfair. We should all have been given a chance to be the venue, then. My shop has the advantage of the copper pots and pans to remind people they are in Copper Country. Plus we have flags and posters and sweatshirts with maps of the UP as well as books and *Sisu* mugs. You have nothing but yarn and worms."

"You have a point," I said, diplomatically. "I think the point is to hold a knitting circle which is supposed to remind viewers of tradition. Also, Serena Waterfall is going to do a segment on the Rya Rug."

"I suppose there is no chance of making a change to the Copper Kettle." She didn't wait for an answer. "In that case, I will be happy to attend the knitting circle. I'll bring Astrid so the viewers can see that we are teaching the craft to the next generation. The important thing then is for Astrid to be seen. You remember how good she was in the St. Lucy pageant."

Sofi and I exchanged a look. We both knew Astrid had never picked up a pair of knitting needles in her life. Ronja, as starstruck as the next Yooper, wanted Astrid to have a career in Hollywood.

"Ronja," Sofi said, playing devil's advocate, "what would you do if Astrid went out to California? You'd have to leave the Keweenaw. You'd have to sell the Copper Kettle."

"Oh no," she said, taking the comment seriously. "That's where you're wrong. Benne can stay here and run it while I am in Hollywood. The other girls can join us when they graduate. I'm sure Astrid can find parts for them in her movies. I'll see you at three. Be sure Astrid combs her hair before coming over and Hatti," she tsk-tsked, "your head looks like a haystack. You are probably too old for the silver screen but you might want to get a better husband."

"Thanks for the tip," I said. "I'll bear it in mind."

CHAPTER 20

W hen our downtown blocks were built, more than a hundred years ago, shop owners invariably lived above the storefronts. In more recent years, those second story flats, accessible by staircases along a back hallway, have been used for offices, rental apartments and, more often in recent times, left vacant. Thanks to our harsh winters, the red brick of the downtown blocks has darkened, the metal cornices have tarnished and the wooden columns have been re-painted many, many times.

Hakala's, Patty's Pasties and the Hardware store take up the west side of the street while the Copper Kettle, Main Street Floral and Fudge and Bait and Stitch anchor the east side so I only had to take a couple of steps to get from Sofi's shop to mine for the videotaping. The little bell over the door tinkled merrily as I entered. Ever since I'd installed it, the sound had triggered a feeling of wellbeing and relief. It reminded me that at some point, I'd gone from being a law school drop-out and marriage failure to respectable UP shop owner. It seemed like a step in the right direction.

This afternoon the relief was short-lived. I was too aware that I now possessed a story (Sofi's) that implicated both her and Lars. I also had special knowledge that implicated Seth Virtunan. Did I owe this information to the sheriff? What if he found out some other way? Wouldn't that look worse for everybody involved? And what was the truth? Who had killed Cricket Koski?

As soon as Einar spotted me he hopped down off his high stool, put away the bits of wire and string he was using to tie flies and shrugged into his heavy parka and the flannel hat with the ear flaps that we call a stormy kromer.

"You're leaving?" I said, pointing out the obvious. "What if somebody wants live bait?"

"Won't."

That was probably true. It was the first week in January and too snowy for ice fishing.

"What will you do this afternoon?" I really was curious. Einar spent all his time at the bait shop.

"Sauna," he said, pronouncing it correctly.

When he left, I spent a few minutes straightening the shop. I'd bought some small accent lamps and they provided a soft glow that balanced the bowl light in the tin ceiling. There was a round gray rug on the floor to define the work area and the walls were white as were the wooden wine racks I'd bolted to the wall with Pops' help to display the yarn. The yarn itself warmed the scene with the variety of color from baby blues and pinks to the rich ruby, emerald and sapphire jewel tones of the worsted wools. Even though my customers were mostly proficient at the colorwork knitting technique called Fair Isle, I had stocked some of the newer striped yarns, the ones in which the pattern is generated by a computer.

My glance moved to the shop's centerpiece, the white Rya Rug with a tree of life design embroidered in red. It had hung in Pops' study at home all my life but when I got the idea of adding knitting supplies to the bait shop, he gladly handed it over to me. I'd considered washing away the grime of years but had gotten it dry cleaned instead and I had to admit the results looked good. The story was that it had been woven for an engaged couple from a small village in Finland by one of the Lehtinen relatives. Before the marriage could take place, the young man was killed in the war and the rug, considered a bad omen, was shipped to a relative in the United States.

Mom and Pops discovered it when they moved into the home that had belonged to his family.

I went to the work room and brought out the old wooden chairs I'd bought and painted to use during knitting circle and I arranged them in a semi-circle opposite the upholstered loveseat and the antique dressing table I'd restored and used to display samples of sweaters, scarves, hats and mittens. I happened to glance at the carousel of packaged knitting needles. The rod that held the size six DPNs was empty. My blood ran cold. Someone had bought the DPNs since the last time I was here. Was it the murderer? Was I complicit in Cricket Koski's tragedy?

I abandoned the chairs and hurried over to the cash register. Most people paid with credit or cash cards these days and there would be a number and a name. I dug through the receipts and found the transaction. It had been made with cash and, anyway, the needles were part of a larger order that included three skeins of multi-colored sock yarn, a stitch holder and a package of stitch markers. Something inside of me unclenched. The purchaser had intended to knit a pair of socks not stab a barmaid. A quick look at the date of the sale, though, gave me pause. It was Saturday, December 31. The very day of Cricket Koski's murder.

Hell's bells. Here was one more piece of information I didn't know what to do with. The acid from my stomach started to work its way into my throat, a sure sign of an incipient panic attack. I sucked in a series of deep breaths and tried to calm down.

By the time Seth and Serena arrived a few minutes later I'd gotten myself under control. Seth was charming and polite as always and Serena very complimentary about the shop. I tried to put all suspicion of the former out of my mind. Then I remembered the séance and asked about it.

"Were you able to make contact with Maud?"

"I think so," Serena said. "There was a green glow in the mirror. When I pointed it out, the others saw it, too." She smiled, a trifle self-consciously. "That happens a lot. When someone thinks you have psychic powers they are very suggestible."

I found her honesty disarming.

"But you saw a green glow, right?"

"Green-ish. Nothing is very clear cut in the spirit world."

"Except the *karsikko* sign."

Serena hadn't heard about that so I told her. Afterwards, though, I was curious.

"I'd have thought Mrs. Paikkonen would have told you all about it when you gathered for the séance."

"Oh, she didn't stay. She said she wanted to get back to your house to wash and change the bed sheets so Vincent drove her back in the van. I was worried about her, you know. She looked kinda green around the gills. I guess staying overnight at a funeral home isn't everybody's cup of tea."

It occurred to me that, despite my plans, I never had talked to Mrs. Paikkonen. I'd make it up to her this afternoon. Mrs. Pike loved to knit and she loved to pontificate. I'd position her in a central location for the videotaping and be sure she got air time to talk about her craft.

"I hope she has a way to get down to the shop."

Serena nodded. "Don't worry. Elli asked Harry to bring all the old ladies down here. Ooh, I love the Rya Rug. It's a real work of art. Beautiful! But it isn't going to work to interview you about that now. Too much commotion in here. Can I have somebody take it over to the theater later on? It'll make a great backdrop for the show."

Vincent, Helena and Harry, along with a gaggle of old ladies arrived just after the camera crew and the little shop was suddenly Grand Central Station. I was in the midst of trying to answer questions from half a dozen people when Vincent sidled over to me.

"Get me a bottle of Artesian mineral water out of that cooler, will you?"

I hid a smile.

"We don't stock much in there at this time of year. Just waxworms and maggots. Sometimes, honey worms, but we're out of those at the moment."

He shuddered but, somewhat to my surprise, he recovered quickly enough.

"Oh. Bait. Anyway, I was researching on Wikipedia last night and discovered that Hitler was an avid fisherman. Let's find a way to work that into the narrative. Have you got any antique fishing rods?"

I was spared from answering by the ringtone of my cellphone. It was my cousin.

"Hey, Hatti. I have to stay at the inn and do laundry. Any chance you can send somebody up here to pick up Mrs. Paikkonen? She was lying down when Harry collected the other ladies and I wouldn't want her to miss the afternoon's excitement."

Before I could answer, Aunt Ianthe and Miss Irene, followed by Harry Dent, arrived at the door. I waylaid him, asked if he could go back and pick up Mrs. Pike, and then the other knitters arrived and it was time to organize the circle. Normally we started with a blessing from Miss Irene or Mrs. Sorensen and then we discussed something new in the world of knitting while we worked on our individual projects.

Today, though, it was hard to get in a word edgewise. The ladies chattered as Pops would say, nineteen to the dozen and it took quite a while to bring the group to order.

"Hatti!" It was Vincent and he sounded exasperated. "Sit down, will you? We're ready to begin. Say something to the camera about the town or the knitting circle or something."

I felt like an idiot. Luckily bits of a speech I'd heard somewhere popped into my head.

"One of the things that is important to a small town like Red Jacket," I said, "is tradition. We have traditions for everything, from coffee for visitors to cake after church to knitting. The knitting circle goes back in time to the old country. It is one of the practices that helps us keep our balance up here in the north. Because of our traditions, everyone knows who she is and what God expects her to do."

"Cut!" Vincent shrieked at the cameraman then glared at me.

"What?"

"You are quoting from *Fiddler on the Roof*," Vincent said. "Start over," Vincent commanded. "And for God's sake, talk about the war." When he nodded at me, I started again.

"The gathering in this room today might have taken place ten years ago or twenty or even seventy years ago. Finnish-Americans in Michigan spent many hours making stockings, hats, mittens and sweaters for the refugees created when Russia attacked Karelia during the Winter War."

"Not that war," Vincent hissed. "Hitler."

I looked around the circle and help came from an unexpected source.

"In those days," Mrs. Sorensen said, "the ladies would have met in the church social hall or, more likely, in someone's home. Fuel was rationed, you know, and shops were not open at night or on the weekends."

"I wouldn't be surprised if they met in the biggest sauna in town," Mrs. Moilanen said. "That would be warm enough."

"Someone would have provided refreshments," Diane Hakala said.

"More than likely it would have been the kitchen committee of the Ladies Aid," Mrs. Moilanen said, with the confidence that came from her position as head of the St. Heikki's Finnish Lutheran Church Ladies Aid, the most powerful position in town. "They would have provided *Joullutortu* at this time of year and cloudberry meringue in the summer."

"And coffee, Edna," Aunt Ianthe said. "Don't forget that."

"Women aren't supposed to make coffee," Miss Irene said. "The Bible says He-brews."

"Cut!" While Vincent fumed the rest of us went off into peals of laughter.

"You are supposed to be talking about the connection between the Finns and the Germans." He motioned for the camera but before I could get my thoughts together, Aunt Ianthe spoke.

"There are some misconceptions to clear up. When World War II started, Finland was at war with Russia and since the Soviet Union was a member of the Allied Powers, Finland could get no assistance from

England or America. As a result, the Finns became co-aggressors with Germany but there was never any allegiance to Hitler or any of the Nazi precepts." She looked around. "And Finland paid its war debt."

"Today," I said, responding to a frown from Vincent, "I thought we would talk about a knitting technique that is very popular in Finland. It is called *Entrelac*." My pause for breath was a mistake.

Astrid Laplander, a younger version of her mother right up to and including the scowl on her face, hunched her shoulders and shot a dagger look at her mother.

"You told me there wouldn't be any French."

An ugly flush appeared on Ronja Laplander's face and her dark eyebrows met in an expression that mirrored that of her daughter. I hastened into the breach with a huge smile.

"Astrid is absolutely right. *Entrelac* is French and it means interlaced. It is a knitting technique that has become very popular in Norway, Sweden and, especially, Finland where it is called *konttineule* which means a backpack woven out of a sturdy material." Luckily, I had a pair of socks with the basket-weave pattern in green and orange and I held them up for the knitters.

Both Aunt Ianthe and Miss Irene (bless them) ooh-ed and aah-ed as if they'd never seen anything so miraculous, so delightful, so unique. I was well aware it was a put-up job since the sample socks had been knitted by Miss Irene but I dismissed the irony. This was, after all, a television show, right? They were acting.

I invited Miss Irene to explain the technique that involves starting with base triangles then working short rows and turning. A couple of the ladies (Diane Hakala, usually a good sport, and Mrs. Sorensen, always the same) pulled needles and fresh yarn out of their knitting bags and followed Miss Irene's precise instructions which was more challenging than it needed to be because they were interlaced with Bible verses from Colossians 2 and Psalm 139, respectively.

"That their hearts may be comforted, they being knit together in love," and "For you created my inmost being; you knit me together in my mother's womb."

The second offering was too much for Mrs. Moilanen. She drew herself up with all the majesty of her high office in the Ladies Aid, looked over the tops of her granny glasses and said, with spoke with some asperity.

"Good gracious, Irene, however did you find Biblical references to knitting?"

Aunt Ianthe grinned. "She is a wonder, isn't she?"

And then three things happened simultaneously. Well, four.

Vincent yelled, "Cut!"

Harry Dent lounging against Einar's counter lifted his hands in the universal gesture of helplessness signaling that he hadn't been able to find Mrs. Pike.

Astrid, heading out the door, hissed at me, "You do know you can buy socks at the mall, right, Hatti?"

But it was the fourth thing that took away my breath.

The front door slammed open hard enough for the little bell to become unmoored and bounce across the room. Arvo Maki, big and barrel-chested with a thick carpet of white-blond hair burst into the room. His patented smile was gone and he glared at the group like a hibernating bear who'd been poked.

"Henrikki! Another murder? And what is this I am hearing about Nazis and hidden treasure?"

Even though the words were addressed to me, I wasn't listening. All my thoughts, all my focus, was on the second man who entered the shop.

Jace looked good enough to stop my heart even though his handsome face was screwed into a scowl aimed at me. Not that there was anything new in that.

He crossed the crowded room with the skill of a tracker. I felt his strong fingers around my wrist then heard the low growl of his voice.

"Hello, wife. Got a minute? I'd like a word."

CHAPTER 21

I was so happy to see him and so irritated with myself for feeling that way that it never occurred to me to resist. I let him pull me outside into the falling snow.

"We forgot your coat," he said, surprising me. I didn't even feel the cold. "But Arvo's got an industrial-strength heater in here. You'll be fine." He opened the passenger door on the vehicle parked along the curb. "This baby's got amazing traction."

"Why are you driving the hearse?"

He dangled something in front of me.

"Daddy gave me the keys."

I didn't know what to say to that. He'd said it with a hint of mockery but still, it was a sign that Jace had begun to accept the man who really was his natural father, Arvo Maki.

"Have the two of you been spending time together?"

Jace nodded. "He came to D.C. to visit. We talked some. When we got back to the Leaping Deer Elli told us about Lars's incarceration and about the television people and the existence of Nazi Loot on the Keweenaw. You know Arvo. Any publicity is good publicity as long as it doesn't link us with the world's most evil empire. So what's really up with that? Is there really a priceless Monet hidden in one of our attics?"

I wanted to kick up my heels at his use of the plural pronoun. At the same time, I wanted to scream in frustration. Was he all-in or no? I wanted an end to this emotional no-woman's land. But talk of our future would have to wait. I gave him a thumbnail sketch of what had been happening for the last few days, including the discovery of that Pandora's Box, Ernst Hautamaki's letter.

"So this is a sixty-million-dollar fantasy based on a seventy-five-year-old letter."

"Yes. And no. It turns out there have been academics studying the contact between Finland and Nazi loot. Harry Dent, who worked as an art theft expert on an FBI squad, says there's been no chatter about a painting hidden on the UP but maybe the scholarship just hasn't caught up with it. The possibility we're looking at is that Ernst rescued a piece of art, sent it home to Finland with instructions to send it on to Red Jacket."

He looked unconvinced.

"It could have happened. Ernst was stationed in Munich where the stolen art was kept. He told his aunt he was sending her a special birthday present and to watch out for it."

"That's it? This soon-to-be-televised treasure hunt is based on that?"

"The letter was sent in the summer of 1942. Both Ernst and his Aunt Bengta died that same summer. If he sent the package it would still be here."

"Or, someone would have opened it seventy five years ago and noticed then that it was a stolen masterpiece."

"That's possible, of course." I shivered. "I'm not sure I want to find it, to tell you the truth." I told him about Cricket Koski's Prince Charming and her murder. I told him about finding Seth Virtunan in the ten-year-old camp picture with Cricket and I told him about Harry's refusal to believe Seth was involved in the murder. I started to tell him about Lars but he stopped me.

"That can wait. Tell me more about this so-called art expert." I looked up into the gray eyes and caught a glimpse of something. Jealousy? My heart leapt and I was immediately filled with self-disgust. What kind of a marriage runs on the fuel of jealousy?

"Harry knows a lot about art," I said, lamely.

"Is that why he came up here? To look for the painting?"

"No. I told you. He says there are no rumors about it. He decided to do the television pilot because his ex-wife asked him to do it."

"Sure."

I eyed him, unsure of how to take that.

"We've all been searching the attics for any treasures at all, and, specifically for the missing Monet."

"How do you know it's a Monet?"

"I don't. I was using the artists name in the generic sense. Harry has another version of the waterlilies in his home in the Hudson Valley."

"I'll bet he does." This time the sarcasm was unmistakable. "I imagine it hasn't escaped your notice that these television folks showed up within hours of the murder, right?"

"It does seem like a pretty big coincidence," I admitted.

"You can't trust them, Umlaut. You have to walk away from this."

"I can't do that. The body turned up in Lars's bed. He's in jail. Sofi was out there at the lake right around the time it happened. My family is implicated, Jace."

He cursed, noticed my shiver, then cursed again, unbuttoned his jacket and put it around my shoulders.

"Thanks."

"All right. Tell me what you know about the dead girl."

I filled him in on every last detail I could remember having to do with the murder. Jace has an orderly, logical mind with flashes of brilliance and I knew that if anybody could make sense of this whole thing, he was the best bet.

"Why did Sofi go out to the cabin that night? Jealousy?"

"She said it was to confront him about the paper she found with Cricket's phone number but I think she wanted to tell him about the baby."

"What baby?"

"Sofi's pregnant." And then, to my total shock, I burst into tears.

Jace lifted me across the bench seat and onto his lap. He tucked my head under his chin and rocked me while I sobbed.

"That's not exactly bad news, is it," he asked, finally. I shook my head.

"It's good news. It's just that they're in so much trouble."

The tears continued to come but Jace Night Wind is a good man in an emergency. He produced a handkerchief with which he dried my cheeks and let me blow my nose and when I'd finished, he pulled me even closer and kissed me.

The kiss lasted a long time.

WE DECIDED to skip the smorgasbord at the B and B.

I made a fresh pot of coffee then found sliced ham and a loaf of *pulla*, a kind of bread, in the freezer. I dug out some Provolone, too, and made grilled ham-and-cheese sandwiches. They went well with another frozen offering, a container of roasted tomato soup.

"Comfort food," Jace said. "Tastes like heaven."

"Tastes like home," I agreed. He shook his head.

"Tastes like heaven."

WHILE WE ATE Jace told me about a case he was working on for a tribe in the southwest, one of the many that had tried to improve its financial standing with the construction of a casino only to find itself enmeshed with organized crime. I listened to his animated voice and stared at the clear gray eyes between the long, dark lashes and thought about how committed he was to his work, how much I admired him because of it and how little chance there was that he would ever want to settle down in Red Jacket.

When he'd finished talking he just looked at me for a long minute and my heart jumped around inside me like popcorn in a microwave. Here it comes, I thought. Time for a follow-up kiss. This is where he tells me (I thought, against all logic) that he's made up his mind to become a small-town lawyer, to commit himself to our marriage and potential family. And also that he's sorry he didn't call me on New Year's Eve. I was so enmeshed in my fantasy that his words caught me flatfooted.

"You don't want it to be Seth, do you?"

"What?"

"You don't want it to be Harry Dent or Lars or Sofi or anyone else you know and care about. You felt the same way during the St. Lucy murder investigation. You couldn't bear to think the killer was someone you knew."

"I hope I have an open mind," I said, somewhat stiffly. "But you have to admit there's a big difference between normal people and a person who has crossed the line. A murderer is a monster."

"Murderers are just men. Or women. We are what we are. Remember the words of Hercule Poirot: The sun shines, the sky is blue. But you forget *mon ami,* everywhere there is evil under the sun."

"Why didn't you call?"

There was no segue. There was no context. It certainly wasn't what I'd meant to say but I decided I wasn't sorry.

He looked at me.

"On New Year's Eve? Why didn't you call to say Happy New Year?"

The gray eyes were clear and intense.

"I thought we were past that kind of game-playing."

The back door opened and I jerked my hand away.

"Oh, sorry, Cupcake," Harry said, entering the room and stomping his snowy boots. "Am I interrupting anything?"

"No," I said.

"Yes," Jace replied. "But we can bookmark our place." He stood and offered his hand. "I'm Jace Night Wind, Hatti's husband. And you must be the art theft detective."

Harry grinned, shook his hand and apologized again. Then he took a seat at the table, pulled a flask out of his inside coat pocket and poured it into the cup of coffee I'd put in front of him. Wordlessly, he offered the flask to Jace who slid his own mug close enough for Harry to pour.

"The videotaping down at your shop ended in a shambles," Harry said to me. "We decided to disband for the evening and the rest of them are over at the inn stuffing their faces with some kind of fish stew. I told you this project is doomed."

I supplied Harry with a ham sandwich and listened as Jace asked him a series of questions about *What's in Your Attic?* And Harry's own thoughts about the missing Monet.

"A couple of academics identified a Finnish connection with Munich and have postulated that Nazi loot may have made its way to Finland or even the Upper Midwest," Harry said. "Chances are slim that it's here."

"But you came up to find out."

It wasn't a question and Harry Dent grinned at me.

"Smart guy, your husband."

"You told me you joined the TV company because Serena asked you to. You said you did it as a favor to her."

Harry's grin widened.

"I didn't lie. She wanted to come."

My eyes narrowed on him.

"Look, Cupcake, it's a sixty-million dollar masterpiece. I'd have been a fool not to look for it."

I felt a chill run down my spine.

"The search for this painting precipitated Cricket Koski's death."

"That's possible. Probable, even."

"Are you saying that Cricket was just collateral damage?"

"In a sense." He repeated himself, this time with more emphasis. "It is a priceless, irreplaceable piece of art and begs the age-old question, is it right for someone to die for culture? What else was World War II about?"

Jace was staring at him. After a moment, he said, "where is the Hautamaki letter?"

"The old lady has it," Harry said. "The one who's afraid of ghosts."

The mention of Mrs. Paikkonen acted on me like a shot of adrenalin.

"Geez Louise! I forgot. You were supposed to pick her up this afternoon, Harry. What happened?"

He shrugged. "Nothing at all. I stopped at the B and B, Elli told me to come over here and get her and when I knocked on her door she didn't answer it."

"She wasn't there?"

"No. I misspoke. She wouldn't open the door. She spoke through it. Told me she was exhausted because of her sleepless night, that she'd taken a sleeping pill and just wanted to be left alone. I said okay."

I frowned and Jace searched my face.

"What's the matter, Umlaut?"

"It's not like Mrs. Pike to take a pill. Folks in her generation believe that everything can be cured by sauna or Vicks VapoRub. And she was nervous. Why would she want to stay here alone all afternoon?"

Neither of the men had an answer to that. I hurried up the back staircase to the second floor and my room. The door was closed and there was a neatly printed note taped on the outside.

PLEASE DO NOT DISTURB

I pictured the old lady's reaction if I forced my way into her bedroom and found I didn't quite have the *sisu* to do that. I obeyed the sign.

CHAPTER 22

Serena, covered in snow from the thirty-foot walk from the B and B, arrived half an hour later, bringing Larry, my parka and the message that Arvo had helped her and the cameramen close up Bait and Stitch.

"The folks around here are nice," she said, yawning. "For the most part. What's the story with that Ronja woman? After you left she came back with a different kid. That one didn't knit, either."

"Ronja's got five daughters," I explained. "She's hoping at least one of them will be spotted by a talent scout and offered a Hollywood contract."

"Why would she want that for her girls?"

"Delusions of grandeur. In the end they'll probably all marry boys from Copper County High and she'll be perfectly content."

"It's tough for them that they have to marry or leave the area. I can see there aren't many jobs here."

Serena's thoughtful comments pleased me. The lack of employment opportunity was a very real problem for families that wanted to stay together.

"We're trying to promote tourism," I explained, "but there are problems with that. It's beautiful country with an intriguing back story but we're too far away from the population centers.

Convincing you guys to come up here to videotape your pilot was one of many, endless attempts by Arvo to increase our profile. I'm sorry it's not really working out for you." Or us, I wanted to add.

"Why do you stay in Red Jacket, Hatti?" Serena's hazel eyes were focused on my face. "Surely you could go somewhere else, get a job, get married, whatever."

I wanted to grin at her and tell her it was complicated but I couldn't speak freely, not with Jace and Harry in the same room. I settled for a version of the truth.

"It's home."

Serena nodded and yawned. It was one of those huge, uncontrollable yawns that involves the stretching of arms and making of faces.

"I think I'll go up to bed," she said. "I'm exhausted."

"You should go up, too, Hatti," Jace said, surprising me. "Maybe Harry and I can grab some guy time, play a little euchre."

Harry's light brows lifted but he didn't disagree. I got up from my chair and remembered I was supposed to sleep tonight at the funeral home. Unfortunately, I couldn't grab my nightshirt and toothbrush without disturbing Mrs. Pike. And then I remembered that Arvo was back in town. I could stay home. Up on the third floor.

"I'll be on the sofa in Pops' study," Jace said. "Feel free to join me if your agoraphobia kicks in."

"Or you can join me if you'd prefer not to use the chamber pot," Harry said, with a wink.

I made a face at each of them.

"I'll be fine in the attic."

A short time later I crawled under the heavy quilt and listened to the snow hitting the window over my head. It was cozy under the slanting eaves and I should have been, in my late *mummi's* words, as snug as a bug in a rug. And I was. I was also hyper aware of the fact that my husband was under the same roof for the first time in more than a year and that we had plenty of unfinished business between us. And three floors.

I tried deep breathing. I tried shallow breathing. I tried breathing in with my left nostril and breathing out with my right. Or was it vice versa? One way was supposed to be relaxing and sleep inducing, the other, energizing. Since I couldn't remember which was which, I tried to think about Lars and Sofi. But that just led to anxiety. I thought about Seth. More anxiety. Inevitably, I thought about Jace. Maximum anxiety.

He hadn't called me on New Year's Eve but he was here now. He hadn't made any promises but he'd kissed me as if he'd meant it. What did he want from me? What did I want from him? What about Max? Where was Max? For that matter, where was Sonya, my midwife friend? Then I remembered she'd gone to New Mexico to visit her family. Had that been only two days ago? It felt like a year since we were melting ingots and casting them into a bucket of cold water to tell our fortunes.

Sofi's had looked like a baby carriage. I couldn't remember mine. I was getting drowsy.

When I opened my eyes it was to see light filtering in through the attic window. Light, of course, is a relative term. On a January morning in Red Jacket, the sun rises behind snow clouds and the light is a soft gray, at best. I'd slept in a tee shirt and underwear and, as I stepped out of bed onto the ice-cold wooden floor, I shivered as I pulled on my jeans and sweatshirt.

The good news was that the agitation and uncertainty of the night before had disappeared. I felt ready to make decisions about my life, to be in charge of my own destiny.

The bad news was heralded by the series of sharp, hysterical shrieks that pierced the door to the stairwell. I flung myself down the stairs and onto the landing. Serena Waterfall, wore a woolly, purple robe that made her look like a grape. Her red hair flared out in all directions, like the crown on Lady Liberty. Her face was so white she appeared to have drowned and her voice just kept blasting out screams that were so loud they made my ears throb.

"Geez Louise, Serena! Quiet down! You'll wake Mrs. Pike!"

She must have heard me because the screaming stopped and she said in a trembling voice, "Nothing will wake Mrs. Pike. Not ever." I followed the finger she pointed toward the window-seat at the end of the corridor.

Eudora Paikkonen, dressed in the familiar black wool dress that reached from just below her pointed chin to her wrists and then to her ankles, was propped against the window like a life-sized marionette. She was very still and she was seated at just the right angle for me to see that there was something protruding from her torso, just under her left breast. It was short, narrow and made of bamboo.

A double-pointed needle.

I froze, too shocked to even scream. What was she doing here? What had happened? Why were her spectacles riding low on her nose? Why were her eyes open? I knew, on some level, it was because she was dead, that someone had killed her with the double-pointed needle, but it didn't make sense. Why had she been killed? When? And, as always, my thoughts came around to myself. Was this my fault? Was Mrs. Pike dead because I'd failed to find her yesterday or to check on her last night?

Had she been stabbed, like Cricket Koski, because she knew something that represented a danger to someone?

It came to me with a crystal-clear clarity. Of course she knew something.

She knew the contents of Ernst Hautamaki's letter to his Aunt Bengta. She knew that there was a priceless piece of Nazi loot on the Keweenaw and what's more, she knew where it was. And, now she knew who had murdered Cricket.

Or, rather, she had known.

Hell's bells.

My mind was a whirling dervish of guilt and grief and that curious clarity. I was aware of Harry Dent, wearing only a pair of jeans and a tee shirt taking his ex-wife into his arms but it was background noise. Even when Jace slipped his arm around me, I couldn't really feel it. All I could think about was Mrs. Pike, how she'd learned something important and how that knowledge had led to her death. Someone had valued her life less than a work of art.

"Another knitting needle murder," Harry murmured, looking at me over Serena's head. "It must be the same killer or a copycat."

"Why Mrs. Paikkonen?" Jace asked. "Was this about the letter from Munich?"

Serena let out a howl. When she'd finished I spoke in a low voice.

"It had to be the letter. She'd translated it but she hadn't told anyone what was in there. That's why she wanted to get ahold of me yesterday. This is all my fault."

Jace didn't waste time trying to comfort me. Not with words.

"There couldn't have been anything in the letter to threaten anyone after three-quarters of a century. It must have been confirmation that the painting exists, that it is hidden somewhere on the Keweenaw."

"And," Harry agreed, "it may have revealed the painting's whereabouts."

Tears pricked the backs of my eyes. I was a bit surprised to feel a wash of grief. I hadn't liked Mrs. Paikkonen very much. No one liked her, except possibly Mrs. Sorensen. But she was a member of our community and she'd been dedicated to that community. And for her dedication, she'd been trussed up on a knitting needle.

I heard Jace's voice and realized he was talking to me.

"Get dressed and we'll call the sheriff. And don't forget your socks."

He'd remembered about my perennially cold feet. I smiled at him, showed him my phone, and headed back to the attic to dress and to call the emergency number.

Waino answered the phone at the sheriff's department and I remembered that the receptionist, Bertha Lamko, was still with her grandkids downstate.

"*Hei,* Hatti. You wanna talk to Lars Teljo? Because you can't."

"No, no. I'm calling to report a murder."

"No need. I already know about it."

I felt a jolt as if someone had thumped me between the shoulder blades.

"Another anonymous tip?"

"Yah. On the telephone."

Another indication, if one was needed, that these deaths were linked.

"When will you be over?"

"Over where?"

I was used to glacial reaction time from Waino but even so he was trying my patience.

"To my house. On Calumet Street. To take a look at the crime scene and examine the body. And remove it," I added, in case that didn't immediately occur to him.

"No need, Hatti. Body's here in the morgue."

I covered my face with my right hand. Branding Waino as slow was like me calling the kettle black.

"There's been another murder," I said. "A second one. Some-body stabbed Mrs. Paikkonen with a knitting needle."

"Holy wah! I'll pick up the chief down at the diner. Hatti, if you want to get rid of the body you have to call Arvo Maki for his hearse. Sheriff drove the Corvette today."

Clump was just lucky that he had Arvo to fall back on. The hearse, big and heavy with its snow tires and chains, was often used for municipal tasks which allowed the sheriff to stay within his budget.

The sheriff clearly wasn't thinking about the sports car or the hearse or the budget when, half an hour later, he huffed and puffed his way up the main staircase at the Queen Anne. He glared at the corpse and then at the rest of us.

"H-e-triple hockey sticks," he gasped, after he'd caught his breath. "What in tarnation is goin' on in this town?" His narrowed eyes turned to me. "This is your fault."

"Hold on, sheriff," Jace said. "You can't say that to her."

"Oh, I dunno," Clump replied. "The Koski girl was killed at her brother-in-law's. This one in her own house. The weapon's a damn knittin' needle and who in town sells knittin' needles?" He pointed a fat finger at me. "She does."

By now Elli had arrived. She suggested that Waino examine the crime scene and interview the witnesses while Clump accompanied her next door to help himself to Scotch eggs and coffee. She didn't have to twist his arm.

Jace, Harry, Serena and I told Waino everything we knew about the previous night and that morning. Waino spent most of the time trying to figure out where we had slept.

We gathered at the wicker table in the kitchen while Waino consulted his notes.

He asked me, for the third time, why I'd slept in the attic.

"Because Mrs. Paikkonen was using my room."

"Don't she have a house just down the street?"

I sighed, inwardly, and explained, again, that Mrs. Pike had spent the previous night at the funeral home as hostess for the Tallmasters who were staying there.

"Yesterday she told me she did not want to spend another night there so I offered to swap with her and I gave her my room."

"Why did she refuse to stay at Maki's?"

So far I had avoided getting into the business with the ghost and the *karsikko* sign. It really had nothing to do with the murder and I knew it would confuse Waino.

When I hesitated, Serena solved the problem for me.

"Mrs. Paikkonen thought she heard footsteps in the attic last night. It frightened her."

Waino turned his baby blues on me.

"So why didn't you sleep at Maki's?"

"Because Arvo arrived home yesterday. There was no need for me to go over there. And since Mr. Dent and Ms. Waterfall were occupying my folks' bedroom and the guestroom and Mrs. Pike was in my room, I decided to catch some z's in the attic."

"Where'd Night Wind sleep?"

"Downstairs in the study," Jace repeated. "Like I told you."

"Thing is," Waino said, "that's kinda weird, you know? Seein' as you guys are married."

It wasn't a stupid question but it wasn't relevant. I didn't answer it and neither did anyone else. Then he asked to see each of the bedrooms before he reported to the sheriff.

I led the way and we climbed the narrow, uncarpeted stairs to the attic. At the top I pulled the string of the overhead lightbulb and the spill of light illuminated something that caught my eye. It was a *karsikko* sign.

A new one.

I glanced at it, briefly, then directed Waino over to the area by the bed. I didn't want to have to explain about the sign. Not, anyway, until I'd had a chance to think about it. Not that I had to think about who had put it there. It was a message from beyond the grave but not left by a ghost.

This sign, I was certain, had been left by our latest murder victim. It was not directions to Tuonela. Mrs. Pike had been trying to tell me something.

Emotion swept through me as I imagined her hurrying up to the attic, out of breath, out of time, knowing that death stalked her. She'd known too much. That letter, the one from Ernst Hautamaki had revealed something, most likely where the painting was hidden. Mrs. Paikkonen, forbidding, unlikeable and remote, had used the last minutes of her life to leave me a coded message. What was it? The location of the Nazi loot or the identity of the killer?

I realized Waino was staring at me. I'd been quiet for too long. I forced myself back to the present and groped for something to say.

"At least this time you can't suspect Lars," I said.

Waino shrugged his massive shoulders. It was like watching a mountain move up and down.

"Depends on what time she was killed."

"Hold on, hold on. Lars was locked up. He's been locked up since early Sunday morning." Then I remembered the sheriff's honor system. "He was and is incarcerated."

Waino shook his head.

"Not since ten-thirty last night. I went out to the beer depot and when I got back he'd made a break for it. Damn shame, too. I'd been winning at poker."

CHAPTER 23

J ace and Arvo took the remains of Mrs. Paikkonen to the morgue in Frog Creek while the rest of us joined Sheriff Clump and half the population of the town at the B and B.

I sat in a kind of stupor as the lawmen questioned everyone gathered there. Well, Waino took statements while the sheriff stuffed his face with Elli's freshly baked almond cake. Gradually I began to realize that the deputy was doing a good job. He asked a few questions then let people talk. He didn't interrupt Mrs. Moilanen as she relayed, in intricate detail, what she'd done the previous evening, from whipping up a new batch of vinegar cabbage to watching *Jeopardy!* Then reading three chapters in Leviticus before going to bed.

He didn't make fun of Aunt Ianthe when she said she'd woken up at exactly midnight with the sudden fear that something terrible had happened.

And when Serena Waterfall said she'd gone down to the kitchen of the Queen Anne around one a.m. to get a glass of milk, he didn't even ask whether she'd seen anyone, including Mrs. Paikkonen posed in the window-seat.

I was impressed with my old friend's detecting ability but also alarmed by it. I thought I could read his mind pretty well. Waino was convinced that Lars had killed both Cricket Koski and Mrs.

Paikkonen. He had nailed down method and opportunity. All he had to do to pin it on Lars was to find a motive.

And, unfortunately, there was a motive. Waino just didn't know it yet. But I did.

Cricket had asked Lars to research our family tree and even though he never turned over any results to her, he almost certainly would have run across rumors of the Nazi loot. Lars, like everyone else on the Keweenaw, needed more income and he was planning a big reconciliation with his family which included another mouth to feed even though he didn't know that part yet. Anyway, what was to stop him from finding the Monet and selling it on the black market?

For all I knew Cricket may have asked for the family tree because she knew about the painting. And she may have confided that to Lars. He'd have every reason in the world to get rid of her. And then these blessed television people had turned up like a fistful of bad pennies, the Ernst Hautamaki letter was discovered and Mrs. Paikkonen was in on the secret. Lars (this is in my version of Waino's thinking) would have had no choice but to kill Mrs. Pike, too.

Except it was all nonsense. Lars wasn't a killer. He was a man, Sofi's once and future husband, who'd always held himself to the highest ethical standards. Except when he'd cheated on Sofi three years ago with a barmaid. And, except when he'd lied to Sofi about that barmaid during the past few weeks. He wasn't a murderer. I had to keep reminding myself of that.

I felt a flutter of anxiety in my stomach and, in an effort to avoid a full-blown panic attack, I tried an old strategy. I stopped listening to the conversations in the dining room of the B and B and focused on something else. The *karsikko* sign. The one left by Mrs. Pike. She'd been trying to tell me something, but what?

Like the sign at the funeral home, the one left in my attic had dispensed with the Christian Cross, and in its place, had substituted a fish. It could have been the Christian symbol or it could have been something else. We, on the Keweenaw, have a lot of truck with fish. Underneath the fish were the initials *R.R.* I was fairly satisfied that the *C.K.* under the crossed knitting needles at the funeral home were for Cricket Koski but I couldn't think of anyone named *R.R.*

Mrs. Pike had been in fear of her life. Had she meant to leave a clue to the murderer and gotten in wrong? It was certainly possible. Maybe she'd wanted to write *B.B.* and hadn't closed the loops. I couldn't think of a *B.B.*, either.

I tried going back a little further. Mrs. Pike had felt uncomfortable at Maki's. Was it because she'd suspected Vincent Tallmaster of killing Cricket Koski? Or Helena? Surely she hadn't suspected Harry or Serena since she'd been happy to move into the Queen Anne with them.

She'd collected her belongings from the mortuary and officially moved some time around mid-day. I hadn't seen her since the early morning but Elli had seen her, and Serena and Harry had seen and talked to her. She'd been so tired she'd taken a sleeping pill during the afternoon. Except if she'd been sound asleep, how could she have left the *karsikko* message? She'd have had to be quick, agile and fast thinking to leave a coded message. It didn't make sense.

"HATTI!"

I jumped at the sound of Waino's voice. He nodded his head to indicate Sheriff Clump whose egg-shaped head was covered with perspiration and whose cheeks were flushed a dull red and whose too-close-to-his-nose eyes were narrowed on me

"Deputy here says the old lady was killed because of a letter." I could tell by his tone and his body language that he didn't believe the story and worse, he hated that he had to appeal to me for information. I explained, as best I could, about the Hautamaki letter and why it was important.

Clump extracted a giant handkerchief from his pocket and wiped his head.

"You tryin' to tell me this gal was kilt because of a painting stolen from the Nazis seventy years ago?"

"Stolen by the Nazis," I said, unsure how much Clump knew about the events of World War II. "The Nazis took artwork from galleries and private homes because Hitler wanted it for the museum he planned to build. It's said they stole about a fifth of the world's treasures. We think one of them wound up in Red Jacket."

The beady eyes focused on me.

"So where in the H-E-double-hockey sticks is the letter at?"

"I WOULD LIKE to know that myself," said Vincent Tallmaster. "As you may know, sheriff, we intend to use the heretofore unknown relationship between Finland and Hitler as the theme for the world premiere of *What's in Your Attic?* The letter from the Finnish soldier in Munich is to be the *chef d'oeuvre* of our program and thus, we need to find it. And frame it. I think something in the Nazi colors of red and black."

Helena Tallmaster shook her head and then she surprised me.

"We can't just continue down this road, Vincent. Mrs. Paikkonen was killed because the letter must have revealed information about the looted painting. It would be very bad taste to make any sort of profit from her death."

"Bless you, dearie," Aunt Ianthe said, her eyes moist. "Eudora wasn't an easy woman but she was a good Lutheran and does not deserve to have her unfortunate death exploited then."

"An unjust man is an abomination to the righteous," Miss Irene said, adding, "Proverbs."

No one had anything to say to that. After a moment, I answered the sheriff's original question.

"We don't know where the letter is. I imagine the killer took it."

"Not that it would do him or her much good," Harry Dent put in. "Since it was written in Finnish."

My eyes turned, involuntarily, to Seth Virtunan. He looked pale and depressed. Perhaps he'd liked Mrs. Paikkonen. Or, perhaps, he'd killed her.

"Lars Teljo is Finnish," Clump said. "He coulda read the letter. Anyways, we know he kilt this one, too."

I was prepared for that and it still shocked me. Everyone else looked thunderstruck.

Into the ensuing silence, Waino spoke.

"What were your movements last night, Hatti?"

It occurred to me that I didn't have to tell. I'd gone up to the third floor and gone to bed and in the morning I'd wakened to find Serena screaming on the second floor landing. Jace would never tell. No one would know. The delay didn't last long. I knew I couldn't do it.

"I went to bed about nine, I think. Mrs. Paikkonen was in my room so I sacked out in the bed up in the attic."

Waino kept looking at me.

"You stay there all night?"

"Why not?" Harry spoke in a teasing voice. "Hatti's got a perfectly good chamber pot up there under the bed."

I felt the color come up in my face but there was no help for it.

"I came down once during the night," I said. "I couldn't remember whether I'd let Larry out and wanted to check on him."

"What time was that," Waino asked.

"Two o'clock. Maybe a little later."

"What time did you get back to the attic?"

I swallowed hard. "Jace Night Wind was sleeping in Pops' study. He heard me in the kitchen and we talked for awhile."

Waino didn't bother to repeat the question. He just waited until my conscience kicked in enough for me to give him the answer.

"It was probably about four when I got back to the attic."

There was another of those pregnant pauses and if there had been doubt in anyone's mind about what had been going on for those two hours, Miss Irene dispelled it.

"Therefore shall a man leave his father and his mother; and shall cleave unto his wife: and they shall become one flesh."

"Indeed," Harry murmured, under his breath.

"So I take it that you and your spouse have reconciled," Harry said, after Clump and Waino had left.

I shrugged. I no longer felt the same comfort with the ex-FBI agent that I'd felt during our trip to L'Anse. I still liked and trusted him. I just did not want to hear any humorous or sardonic comments about my marriage. Besides, I hadn't had a chance to analyze what that late-night encounter with Jace had meant. I didn't know whether we were really back together or if that had just been a détente, like the Christmas truce in World War I when the combatants called a cease-fire and British and German soldiers crossed the trenches to wish one another season's greetings. Harry seemed to understand because he changed the subject.

"Tell me something. When you came back upstairs did you see the old lady in the window-seat?"

"No." I was chagrinned. I'd been too absorbed in my own business to have noticed anything else. To excuse this lapse, I decided to tell him my theory that Mrs. Pike had been killed early in the afternoon and not in the evening. Naturally, he wanted to know the reason behind my thinking.

"Nobody saw her after she left the Bed and Breakfast. You stopped by the house to pick her up, right? And when you knocked on the door she didn't answer?"

"She'd been given a sleeping pill."

"I don't think she took it."

He eyed me, strangely.

"What makes you think that?"

I shrugged. "The folks in that generation just don't take pills. Ask Aunt Ianthe or Miss Irene. If she was tired, she'd have put her feet up for awhile."

"Ah, but you forget, Cupcake. She told me she'd taken the pill. Do you think she lied?"

That was even more unlikely than that she'd taken a pill.

"No. I can't account for it. But I think she died sometime in the afternoon."

THE *ATTIC* PEOPLE went off to talk over their plans or lack thereof, and that left Aunt Ianthe, Miss Irene, Mrs. Moilanen and me to help Elli clean the kitchen. When we'd finished Elli poured cups of fresh coffee and we sat at the end of the farm table. My mind was like a skein of yarn that once tangled was almost impossible to straighten out. I took a sip of the reviving drink and found myself reaching out for help.

"Mrs. Paikkonen left me a message. A *karsikko* sign." I didn't examine the feelings that prompted me to share the information with the ladies when I'd been reluctant to talk about it with Harry. This just felt right.

"A *karsikko* sign," Mrs. Moilanen said, thoughtfully. "Eudora must have left it on her way to *Tuonela*."

Aunt Ianthe nodded. "A farewell, perhaps? Or something she'd forgotten to say while she was alive."

Not for the first time I marveled that these women steeped in the tenets of the Lutheran church for scores of years, could simultaneously believe in the pagan myths. Or, maybe they were just comforted by the old traditions.

"I'm pretty sure she drew it before she died," I said. "I believe she was trying to tell us something."

I explained about the location of the sign on a strut under the eaves in the attic. I described the simple drawing of a fish underscored with the initials *R.R.*

"The trouble is that I don't know what she was trying to tell me."

"The fish could stand for the church," Aunt Ianthe said, helpfully. "You will recall that the early Christians adopted the symbol as a code to other like-minded folks."

"Come follow me, and I will make you fishers of men," Miss Irene put in. "The gospel according to Mark."

"But why would Eudora reference the church then," Mrs. Moilanen asked.

"Edna!" Miss Irene sounded scandalized.

"I understand what Mrs. Moilanen is saying," I said, hastily. "By my calculations Mrs. Paikkonen didn't have much time to leave the message. She'd have wanted to convey the most important information quickly. If the fish refers to the church it may be the actual physical place."

"Then what are the initials, Henrikki," Aunt Ianthe asked. "Do you think they belong to the killer?"

I frowned. "I can't think of anyone with those initials except for Elli's dad, Reino Risto, and he's down in Lake Worth."

"R.R.," Aunt Ianthe said. "Ricky Ricardo? No, no, that can't be right. Rudolph the Red-nosed Reindeer? Rudi Ryti?"

"Oh, no, dear. Rudi Ryti died years ago," Mrs. Moilanen reminded her. "He was quite an old man."

"Our Rudi died, too," Miss Irene said, with a sigh. "Raffi, too. It was very sad but I suppose it always happens with canaries. Remember you were always so disappointed they never produced any eggs?"

Aunt Ianthe smiled, reminiscently. "I remember saying something to Carl (my stepdad) one day and he was very comforting. He patted me on the shoulder and said, I think, we will have to conclude they are both males. After all, they have beautiful voices."

Her words triggered a thought.

"I saw a gold-colored cage in a corner up in the attic yesterday. Was that home to the canaries?"

"Oh yes. Carl was kind enough to take it off our hands after they died. We couldn't bear the memories."

Elli and I exchanged a look of mutual understanding.

"Did Mrs. Paikkonen know about Rudi and Raffi," I asked.

"Oh, yes. Remember, Ianthe?" Miss Irene sounded very animated. "We invited her to tea one day and the birds were singing so beautifully."

"She said she couldn't imagine keeping wildlife in a house."

"Let's say Mrs. Pike was hiding in the attic. She'd have known she couldn't escape the stalker below but she wanted to leave us some kind of message. What if she spotted the bird cage and she left the initials so that only someone with long roots in Red Jacket would understand?"

"Understand what, dearie?"

"Understand that she hid the Hautamaki letter in the birdcage," Elli said, on a squeal of excitement.

We left the older ladies behind as we flung on our jackets and raced through the falling snow. By the time we'd climbed to the third floor we were both out of breath with red cheeks and damp hair.

The bird cage was perched on an old highboy that hadn't been used for several generations. When I pulled it down, dust flew in every direction which was not a promising sign. And it made Elli sneeze. Still, I refused to lose hope. I ran my fingers over the spindles, opened the little door and pushed the swing.

"Come on, Hatti," Elli urged. "Check the bottom."

As with all birdcages, there was a kind of screen on the floor to allow the droppings to fall through.

"There's some kind of paper in there," I said. My heart was thumping hard and I could hear Elli's labored breathing. I turned the contraption upside down and released a set of clamps. The paper slid out into my hand.

It was a sheet of newsprint from the Mining Gazette, dated June, 1995. In fact, it was the funnies. It reminded me of the confetti we'd thrown on New Year's Eve. Disappointment about the possible clue mixed with anxiety about Lars and Sofi and the murder investigation. My voice wavered.

"The clue isn't Rudi and Raffi." I knew I sounded as disappointed as a child.

"I know. We'll figure it out, Hatti. You'll figure it out. You always do."

I shook my head. This time I was not so sure.

CHAPTER 24

E lli and I found Jace in the kitchen. He was slumped in one of the wicker chairs, staring off into space. He looked like I felt; defeated.

"Jace," Elli said. "Good to see you." He got to his feet, as if he'd just remembered his manners, and she gave him a brief but sincere hug. A moment later she was gone and we were alone.

"We have to talk," he said. There was no flicker of a smile on his face. My heart thundered against my ribs. Maybe this wasn't about the murder. Maybe, after our little tryst last night, he was having second thoughts about continuing our marriage.

My stomach rumbled, not with hunger but with anxiety. Were we about to have the big conversation? Was I ready for it? I'd given a lot of thought to relationships during our twelve months apart and one thing I'd learned (or thought I'd learned) was that when something's over, it's over. That is to say, that when one person is no longer interested, the relationship, in this case, a marriage, is finished. Of course, the events of the previous night could be interpreted as encouraging but I was no Cricket Koski. I no longer believed in Happily Ever After.

However, I was willing to be convinced.

Unfortunately, the mood just seemed to worsen. My sense of

doom increased with every silent second. He was going to say he was sorry about last night. (And a week ago.) He was going to say it was time to call it quits.

"I'm sorry," he said. My heart seized up and I told myself it was for the best. What was he sorry for? I was tired of living in the uncertainty. "I should have called on New Year's Eve."

Well.

"So why didn't you?" I was proud of myself for remaining calm.

"The truth? I figured you were in the midst of a celebration." He paused. *Not good enough.*

"I thought there was a good chance you were with Guthrie and it didn't seem fair to interrupt that." *Better, but still lame.* He shrugged.

"I'd abandoned you for a year and you'd moved on. You'd found a decent guy and I didn't want to intrude."

Worse and worse. Time to cut through the B.S.

"Okay, so let me get this straight. Were you jealous or not?"

"Jealous. Guilt-ridden. Conflicted. All of the above."

"Why conflicted?" But I thought I knew.

"The time apart from you confirmed what I'd always suspected, that I'm too messed up to be a good partner. This marriage isn't fair to you."

OMG. This was one of those, it-isn't-you-it's-me break up arguments. I didn't even try to argue. I'd learned something, too, in the past year.

"We got together so fast. It was such a whirlwind. And then the first thing that came along turned it into shrapnel."

"For you. Not for me." He nodded.

"I know, I know. The commitment freaked me out. You deserve better. But I'll tell you this. I can live without you. I can compensate just as a colorblind person can figure out the traffic light by position rather than color. But life without you isn't vivid. It isn't joyous. I missed you, Umlaut. Everything, from the trail of freckles across your nose to the *Joullutorttu* to that belly laugh that bursts out of you and makes everybody in the vicinity turn around and grin. I miss your zest for life and your conviction that there is no problem too large or too small for you to solve for someone else." He sucked in a breath. "I miss hearing *Geez Louise* ten times a day."

He'd pulled me onto his lap. I hadn't realized I was crying until he wiped my wet face with a napkin.

"I've missed everything about you," he said. "Especially this."

We managed a long, magical kiss, in spite of my dripping nose. When we came up for air I knew there was something I had to say.

"I love you."

"But?"

"I love the Keweenaw, too. There was a time when I'd have done anything to leave. Now, though, being back here, I realize it's where I belong. This community is my tribe, Jace. It needs me. And I need them."

He nodded.

"And my office is in D.C. So are you saying you want to try a long-distance marriage?"

"Not really." I sucked in a deep breath and put my cards on the table. "I want you to live here." I noticed the way his long lashes closed but tried to ignore it. "I want you to confront your own conflicts about your background, both your Ojibwe half and your Finnish half and I don't think you can do it without spending some time here."

"So this ultimatum is for my benefit."

"I'm being honest with you. It's not an ultimatum."

"But you won't go back to D.C. with me."

I looked at his handsome face, the confident mask that hid so much emotional damage.

"I don't know."

He lifted me off his lap and touched my cheek. The silver gray eyes were unreadable.

"I love you, Hatti," he said.

My phone rang and it was Einar.

"Come," he said.

One word. Einar had exceeded his own record in economy.

"That was Einar," I said to Jace.

"I know. Let's walk down to Main Street."

We decided to take Larry. There was a stiff wind that swept the fallen snow up into our faces but it felt good. It was a relief to get outside away from the twin issues of murder and the future of our relationship. The Christmas wreaths, still hanging from the lamp posts, and the twinkle lights in the shop windows gave the downtown a festive air but it was three days into the New Year and time to take them down. I slipped my hand through Jace's arm.

"Do you remember Claude?"

"Ollie Rahkunen's reindeer?" I nodded.

"He's going to be a dad. It seems that Ollie borrowed a female reindeer from a guy down in Toivo for the Christmas pageant and, while the angels and shepherds were reciting their lines in the front yard of the church, Claude and Porot were getting friendly in the backyard."

"Poirot?" I laughed.

"The female deer is name Porot – which is Finnish for reindeer. I guess the Toivo guy isn't as creative as Ollie. Anyway, it turns out a calf is expected in a few months."

Jace shook his head. "I haven't spent much time with Claude but he doesn't strike me as much of a family man."

"I think he'll rise to the occasion. Most men do."

He pulled my arm closer against his side.

"You seem happy, Umlaut."

"I'm trying to enjoy individual moments, you know? Anxiety occurs when you think too far ahead. And I guess I'm growing up. There are few absolutes in life but the one thing you can count on is change.

"There's a character in the *Moomins* which, as you know, was my favorite series growing up. It's about a family of creatures that kind of look like hippopotamuses but are very small. One time, when Moomintroll, the child in the family, comes out of hibernation too early, he's upset. He feels alone in the world and it wasn't what he expected.

"Too-Ticky is a wise woman who tries to comfort him with the truth. She says, all things are very uncertain; and that's exactly what makes me feel reassured."

"Are you reassured by that?"

"Oh, no. I hate it. I want everything in writing, in black and white and assurances that we will all live forever in health and good will." I grinned at him. "But life isn't really like that, is it? All we really have is today."

"This is what's happening today," he said, his voice a low growl as he pulled me closer for another pulse-pounding kiss.

CHAPTER 25

Bait and Stitch, for once, was full of customers. The death of Cricket Koski had been shocking because murder is shocking, especially here on the Keweenaw, but no one in Red Jacket had known her.

Mrs. Paikkonen's murder in a respectable house on Calumet Street was a red flag to a bull. Folks were on high alert. Something was terribly wrong in Moomin Valley and everyone had his or (mostly) her opinions about what it was. Not surprisingly, they blamed events on Vincent Tallmaster and the rest of the television people although, at the same time, everyone was jazzed at the prospect of finding Nazi loot on the Keweenaw. Humans are not always as logical as Moomins.

Lydia Saralampi, recovered from her injury, met us at the shop door. She was full of theories about the hiding place of the stolen masterpiece.

"Have you looked in the crypt at St. Heikki's? Or the old vault in the library?" I could tell the moment she caught sight of Jace. Her eyes widened and her tone softened and she reached out to put a hand on his arm. "You must be the Prodigal husband," she purred. "Welcome."

For once I didn't react to Lydia's blatant flirting. For one thing, I didn't think Jace would fall for it. For another, I didn't have time. There was too much at stake here to worry about Red Jacket's resident vamp.

I could see Einar perched, as usual, on a high stool behind the cash register and I started to make my way across the crowded room. It wasn't a fast voyage. I was stopped by several ladies who, like Lydia, wanted to suggest possible hiding places for the missing Monet or who sought details on Mrs. Paikkonen's death.

"*Hei*, Einar," I said, when I finally reached him. "Where did all these folks come from?"

The blue eyes twinkled at me. "Altar Guild."

Of course. It was Wednesday which meant the women who served on the Altar Guild at St. Heikki's had spent the morning cleaning and polishing the pulpit, the lectern and the baptismal font, sweeping the floor and changing the paraments, or linens. The white cloths traditionally used for Christmas would have been replaced with green ones. Technically, the next church season didn't start until Epiphany, which was January 6, still a few days away, but the ladies of the guild invariably decided to be head of the game, a practice with which I was familiar as my mom had served on the guild for many years.

In recent years they'd wound up their Wednesday session by gathering at Sofi's shop for coffee and fudge. Sometimes they wandered next door to see the latest yarns.

Today's gathering had nothing to do with knitting.

Ronja Laplander planted her short, thick-set body in my path.

"This is your fault, Hatti," she said. "You should never have agreed to this television pilot."

"It isn't Henrikki's fault," Aunt Ianthe said, stoutly defending me as usual. "Arvo set it up and then he wasn't here to control it. They never should have brought in the Nazis."

"Woe to them that devise iniquity! And work evil upon their beds." Miss Irene said. "Micah."

"Work evil upon their beds," Lydia Saralampi said, turning the Bible verse into a tantalizing suggestion. I noticed she was still clinging to Jace's arm. "We could discuss that," she said, turning to him, "while you help me search my attic for the treasure." She turned to me. "I can't search alone because of my concussion." She began to tell him about her fall from the opera house stage.

"Sorry to interrupt," I lied, "but Einar needs Jace's help with something. See you later, Lydia." I stepped toward her to detach my husband's arm from her fingers but he had already done that. He put his hand on my lower back and piloted me through the rest of the throng and we followed the old man into the work room.

"What's up?"

Einar shook his head and responded with a directive.

"You go upstairs."

I was mystified but didn't argue. I led Jace out the back of the shop into the narrow corridor that runs behind the entire block. We climbed the old staircase to the empty apartment above. As I unlocked the door, the scent of sawdust and mold triggered memories of the months I'd lived up here. It had been six months into our separation. After spending the first period with my folks, the time alone in the apartment had been what I needed. I'd only moved back to the Queen Anne after Pops's snowmobile accident to take care of Larry and the house while he and my mom were up at the Mayo.

There was no heat in the apartment and the curtains in the front window were drawn but, somehow, I was not surprised to see a familiar figure approach us as we came through the door.

"Hey, Jailbreak," I said.

"Cripes, Squirt," said the fugitive from Justice. "Where've you been? I thought you'd never get here."

"I'm here now. What's with the blackout? And the lack of heat? It feels like Siberia in here."

I could see Lars's white teeth in the dark. It was sort of like the Cheshire cat, just a smile and nothing else.

"I'm on the lam, remember? I didn't want any sharp young deputy to notice signs of human habitation above the bait shop and put two and two together."

"Speaking of that," I said, dropping into an easy chair whose springs had been broken since the Korean War, "what were you thinking? If you'd stay behind bars you'd have had an alibi for Mrs. Paikkonen's murder."

"Well, I didn't know someone was going to kill her, did I? And I needed to talk to, uh, you. What did you learn from Cricket's friend down in L'Anse?"

I hesitated. Not because I didn't trust Lars but because, oh, I don't know. Because it didn't seem fair to lay the blame for the murders on Seth Virtunan. I needed to remember that it was not my job to protect the guilty. Seth could have done the murders. He could have done them both.

"Cricket attended a Finnish camp ten years ago when she was seventeen. She met someone there. A guy. She called him Prince Charming. According to Cloud he was older and married but he promised to come back for Cricket when he'd gotten a divorce and she'd grown up."

"That sounds exactly like something Cricket would believe."

I nodded. "Cricket called Cloud on New Year's Eve day. She said Prince Charming had finally returned and that they were going to live happily ever after." Lars groaned. "Oh, and that they were going to be rich. If this stuff is all connected, and I think it is, we can deduce that Prince Charming found out about the Nazi loot. He intended to use Cricket to find out the location of the hidden painting. I imagine he always intended to kill her when she'd outlived her usefulness but the opportunity to implicate you in the murder led him to do it on New Year's Eve."

Lars had turned on a desk lamp which provided a small, intimate light in the dusky living room. In the semi-dark his face looked carved in stone. A glance at Jace showed a similar expression of concentration.

"I think Hatti's right," Jace said. "Prince Charming used Cricket then killed her to shut her up and to frame Lars. It was a brutal, but efficient plan. Everyone knew about the long-ago, one-night stand with Cricket. And everyone knew about your planned reconciliation with Sofi. We're working with a diabolical sociopath here."

"Agreed," Lars said. He leaned toward me. "So all we need now is to identify Prince Charming."

Again I hesitated.

"Cloud gave us a photo of the staff and campers. Most of the faces are hard to distinguish but Cricket happened to be sitting next to a boy who was familiar. His name is Seth Virtunan. He's an antiques dealer in Royal Oak and he's here this week with the *What's in Your Attic?* people."

"On top of that, we think Prince Charming killed Mrs. Paikkonen because having translated the Hautamaki letter, she knew the location of the painting. Seth Virtunan had the time to kill the old lady before he came down to the bait shop yesterday."

Lars studied me.

"That seems pretty open and shut." Lars said. "So why am I sensing you're not happy with it, Squirt?"

I shrugged. "I like Seth. He just doesn't seem like a killer."

There was a moment of silence and I shut my eyes waiting for them to heap ridicule on my head. I deserved it, too. Criminal cases are built on evidence not instinct. Lars next question surprised me.

"Where's the letter now?"

"We think the killer swiped it when he killed Mrs. Pike." I remembered my misguided conviction that she'd had the time and forethought to hide the letter. "She did leave a message." I told them both about the *karsikko* sign.

"No one can think of anyone involved with the initials R.R. so I started to think she was trying to tell us where she left the letter."

Lars nodded, absentmindedly. "Or, it could refer to the hiding place of the painting."

The comment went over my head.

"Why don't you seem surprised about all this?"

"Jace filled me in when he picked me up in Frog Creek last night. Oh, not about the *karsikko* sign. He told me that when he brought me breakfast."

I glared at my ex-brother-in-law and at my husband.

"You didn't need to speak to me at all, did you?"

"Hatti, I broke out of jail because you told me to talk to Sofi."

"Well, then, why aren't you talking to her? Did she refuse to meet you?"

"No. I didn't refuse to meet him." Sofi came out of the bedroom. She had a blanket wrapped around her and her hair, no longer confined by a pony tail holder, streamed down her back. Her expression was soft though and, even in the semi-dark, her face seemed to glow. "We've been talking about Cricket's phone number. I overreacted, of course." Her smile widened. "And we've been talking about the baby."

Lars had stood up when she'd entered the room. Now he put his arms around her and I felt a lump form in my throat. At least one good thing had come of all this mayhem. After a minute, they both sat down.

"I heard what you said just now," Sofi said, "and I think I know why you can't believe in Seth's guilt. He looks like every kid we went to Sunday school with, right? I know it's sometimes hard to remember that Lutherans are normal people with the same temptations as everyone else. Seth told us business is bad for antiques dealers. He told us he'd agreed to do the television show in order to get some publicity for his shop. Maybe he heard about the long-lost painting and joined Vincent and company because they were coming up to the Keweenaw and he thought he'd get a chance to look around. By my calculations, he had means, motive and opportunity for both murders, plus he's obviously Cricket Koski's Prince Charming."

I knew she had a point. A good point.

"The *Attic* cast members came up here separately. Seth supposedly spent the night in Petoskey. His name is in the motel's registry."

"That proves he checked in and paid for the night," Jace said, "not that he stayed there. He could have left at any time. No one would have checked."

"The same is true for the others," I pointed out. "Waino checked up on the two couples, too. Vincent and Helena Tallmaster checked into a B and B near Escanaba which is only three hours away. They could have easily driven to the Keweenaw, have killed Cricket and driven back."

"What about Harry Dent?"

"He and Serena stayed in a motel near Paradise. That's more than six hours away."

"So they could have done it," Lars said.

I shook my head.

"Harry couldn't have done it without Serena knowing. She was hysterical when she discovered Mrs. Paikkonen propped on that window-seat. She'd never have agreed to murder Cricket."

There was a moment of silence in the room and then Lars spoke.

"It's not that I don't believe you, Hatti. But I don't think we can rule anybody out yet. Any of these guys could have done it."

"But not all of them could have been Prince Charming," Sofi said. There was a note of regret in her voice.

"What we need to do," Jace said, "is figure out the meaning of R.R., and find the letter. Or the painting."

"But, first," my sister said, "Hatti needs to drive Lars back to Frog Creek before he gets dinged for jumping bail. Use the flower van so he can hunker down in the back."

CHAPTER 26

From his position behind the front seats, Lars questioned me about Harry Dent.

"He's a former art theft detective who agreed to do this television gig because his ex-wife asked him to do it. He's been helping me with the investigation."

"I know all that. What I'm really asking is your impression of him."

"I like him. Anybody would. He's kind of a bon vivant with a dry sense of humor. He's smart and good company with the ladies from Aunt Ianthe to Elli to me. He was very sweet with Cloud and her little boys."

I paused and he said, "in other words, he'd make a good con man."

I glared back at him over my shoulder. "Why would you say that? Con men are sleazy. Harry's genuinely nice."

"You would have no way of knowing this, Squirt, but all the best shysters, drug dealers and swindlers are charming. The butter-wouldn't-melt-in-your-mouth types. That's how they pull their victims in. Not that Dent is necessarily a con man or a killer but look at the facts. He's a sophisticated guy, the guy who knows the most about valuable art. He's the one who'd have been in a position to know there was a war-looted painting on the Keweenaw."

"I take your point," I said, trying to be fair, "but I don't see how he could have done the murders without involving Serena."

"She's the ex who is still in love with him, right? Don't you think he could have gotten around her scruples?"

Was that possible? I didn't know.

"Maybe. But, in my experience, people who work with fabric and wool tend to be practical and straightforward, you know?"

"I think you're right, in general. There are always exceptions. It would be interesting to see an academic study on the profiles of murderers. You know, find out what their hobbies are. I imagine few are weavers or knitters." He paused. "And yet, someone plunged knitting needles into Cricket Koski and Mrs. Paikkonen. Go figure."

"Lars, what about Vincent Tallmaster?"

"What makes you think it was him?"

"I don't. But talking about Harry committing murder with help from Serena made me think about Helena Tallmaster. I'm not sure she'd shy away from murder if it could help her get what she wants."

"Which is?"

"Out of her marriage. Maybe she agreed to help Vincent recover the painting for a percentage of the take when it was sold. Seth told me Vincent's the one with the money and Helena signed a pre-nup when they married."

We had pulled up on the street behind the sheriff's office.

"It's something to think about," Lars said as he let himself out the back of the van. I knew he could have pointed out that Seth was our number one suspect and if he'd killed two women, he wouldn't have balked at lying about Helena Tallmaster's alleged pre-nup. "Thanks for everything, Squirt. I want you to go carefully now. We're dealing with a cold-blooded murderer here."

I was touched by the warning.

"And one other thing. You might try to find out what Vincent Tallmaster and Harry Dent were doing that summer, ten years ago. There's got to be a tie-in to Camp Kaleva."

After Lars disappeared through the back door of the morgue, I sat still for a few minutes just to clear my head. So I was still in Frog Creek when Doc Laitimaki called on my cell and asked to see me.

"Perfect timing," I said. "I'm only about a block away."

Doc's office is in his house on Frog Creek's Main Street, three blocks down from the sheriff's office, jail and morgue

The place is a quaint cottage, tiny and picturesque, a fairy's dwelling, an enticement to his young patients, of which I was one. The front windows were arched with red shutters that matched the front door. Doc's wife had always served as the receptionist and she always met us with fresh cookies unless we were there because of the stomach flu.

The house seemed to have been created for Mrs. Doc, who measured under five feet tall but Doc himself was built like Pops, a Paul Bunyan of a man whose shoulders were permanently stooped from living and working in the cottage.

As usual, Mrs. Doc opened the door, gave me a hug and a cookie and ushered me into Doc's postage-stamp sized office.

"You're looking well," he said, deliberately (or so I thought) ignoring my hair.

"So are you," I replied, although Doc always looked the same to me. "How was Lake Worth?"

"Great, eh? Warm weather. Nice people. A perfect spot for a vacation. We took the grandchildren, you know."

"I'll bet you were sorry to leave."

He grinned at me. "Did you hear what I said, Henrikki? We were sharing the house with four children under five. Believe you me, I was ready to get back home. Your folks looked good. I think they are considering a permanent move."

I nodded. "It would make sense. There's no reason to stay here anymore now that Pops is retired."

"Eh. They will miss their grandchildren."

I thought about that.

"Charlie's down there now, as you no doubt noticed. Sofi will make sure she visits often."

"And what about your children?"

It's not like I hadn't thought about children. Stressed about it. Still, Doc's easy assumption that now that I was married children would naturally follow hit me hard and he could tell.

"I'm sorry, Henrikki. I don't mean to interfere."

"It's all right. It's complicated," I said, not knowing what else to say. "Have you done the autopsy on Mrs. Pike?"

"*Joo*. I have, then. That is why I called. The needle in her chest pierced her lower left ventricle which stopped her heart. It seems especially cruel because the killer must have been looking into her face just before the attack."

I flinched. "I believe she knew it was coming even before then. She was alone in the house, heard the killer arrive and knew he or she was stalking her."

"There were no defensive wounds. Why didn't she try to stop him?"

"She did what she could." I felt tears gather in a lump in my throat. "She knew she had no chance in a confrontation, no chance to hide the letter the killer wanted. She ran up to the attic and left me a sign on one of the struts. I believe the sign is meant to tell us where the letter is hidden but I haven't yet figured it out."

He put his big hand on my shoulder.

"I can relieve you about one thing. Mrs. Paikkonen was able to hide the letter." He chuckled. "A very resourceful woman, that one."

"What do you mean?"

"I found it. Inside her corset." He walked over to a cabinet by the window and indicated a piece of paper drying there. "It was soaked in blood and some of the words blotted. I translated what I could."

"Geez Louise," I said, breathless with excitement. "What did it say? Did it tell you the hiding place of the painting?"

Doc shook his head.

"The young man told his aunt he was sending her a gift and inside that gift was another gift. He asked her to take care of both until he was able to get to America."

So. Not much more than we already knew.

"It turns out he never got here," I said, with a sudden rush of sadness. "He died in Germany. Bengta died that summer, too. She may not have even received the gift. And now it seems like we will never find the stolen painting."

"I am sorry, Henrikki."

I nodded. I looked at the letter he'd found.

"Were you able to decipher any of the writing under the blood stains?"

"Only ordinary words here and there. They did not mean much, eh? *War* and *summer* and *wedding gift*. There was something about a dead dog. It did not make sense to me but my Finnish is not too good anymore."

I nodded.

"Doc, do you think both women were killed with the same kind of weapon?"

"You mean a knitting needle? There's no way to tell about Ms. Koski. It could have been a skewer or anything long, thin and pointed. It could have been a needle."

"Do you think they were killed by the same person?"

The old man nodded.

"The wounds were almost exactly the same depth, in the same position under the breast and at the same angle. The killer was either very strong, strong enough to force the victims into the desired position or clever enough to convince the victims to do as he said."

"He? You think it was a man?"

Doc nodded. "I think so. Whoever it was had to move the bodies, eh?" His kindly blue eyes reflected concern for me. "You must be very careful, Henrikki. This killer is not just strong and clever. He – or she – is ruthless, too, eh? And may not be finished."

"You think someone else is at risk?"

"He will not like to get caught. You and your sister and Elli must be very careful." He paused then spoke again. It was as if he'd read my mind. "And there could be an accomplice, willing or unwilling. That person may be at risk, too."

I thanked him and left with a new sense of resolution. I could no longer afford to treat Seth or anybody else with special consideration. It was time to finish this up.

It was time to talk to Seth Virtunan.

CHAPTER 27

I found Seth at the opera house with the cameramen and technicians. As soon as he spotted me he hurried down the carpeted aisle and took my hand.

"I'm so sorry about Mrs. Paikkonen, Hatti. So damned sorry. This television show thing has turned out to be disastrous for the Keweenaw."

I was touched by his concern even though (some people believed) he was turning into the leading candidate for both murders.

"Thanks," I murmured. "Seth, do you think these deaths are connected to *What's in Your Attic?*"

He shook his head but in that I-don't-know-what to think manner. "One way or another. The search for treasure has stirred everything up. I can't help but feel it's time for us to get out of Dodge, you know? We need to let the community here mourn in peace." I couldn't help but wonder if he was laying the groundwork for a quick exit. Had he found the painting? Was it, even now, hidden in his room at Aunt Ianthe's?

I gazed at the stage. My rug was hanging from a clothesline that had been run from one wing of the stage to the other and Sofi's Nazi-flower arrangements decorated nearly every surface.

"It looks like you're getting ready to do more shooting."

"Yeah." He laughed, humorlessly. "Vincent's orders, of course."

"You think he's being insensitive not to just cancel the whole project?" Seth sighed.

"I think he's just being Vincent. He brought us up here to make this pilot and by the great horn spoon, he's going to make it."

This time my laugh was genuine.

"I haven't heard that expression since my *papa* died."

He grinned at me. "It's an oldie but a goodie."

I realized we'd gotten sidetracked and I needed some answers. I asked him to come with me into the green room for a minute where we sat together on the ancient, comfortable sofa. I studied his face. The blue eyes, flushed complexion and blond hair were so familiar. He looked like a male version of myself.

"You implied these deaths had something to do with the television show," I said, carefully. "Do you think someone in the cast is responsible?"

He didn't answer right away. Instead, he put an arm up on the back of the sofa and dropped his head as if he were thinking. After a few seconds he looked at me.

"It seems impossible, doesn't it? I mean, I know these people. Vincent is vain and a little stupid. Helena is vain and very smart, smart enough to know she married the wrong guy. Serena's a talented artist with a soft heart and no real sense of self preservation when it comes to her ex. And Harry, well, he's a law unto himself."

I looked at him sharply.

"You think Harry did this?"

"There's no evidence to prove he did, but there wouldn't be, would there? I mean, Harry Dent is a risk taker. He's an adventurer. If you ask me, there's nothing he wouldn't attempt and there's probably not much he hasn't done in his life. And art theft, well, it's not a well-regulated field. When a rich man or a museum loses a picture, who cares? Think of the movies that have been made about it, *The Thomas Crown Affair, How to Steal a Million, The Grand Budapest Hotel, Ocean's Eleven.* They all sound like lighthearted romps. Even the real-life thefts in 1990 from Boston's Isabella Stewart Gardner Museum that included a Rembrandt and a Vermeer didn't result in anyone's death. The guards were just tied up. Except that this time someone did die. Two someones."

"You've thought about this a lot."

"Sure." He leaned toward me, lowered his voice a little and surprised me. "I knew Cricket Koski, you know. A long time ago."

"At Camp Kaleva?"

His pale eyebrows lifted in surprise.

"You know about that?"

I nodded. "I talked with Cricket's childhood friend. She told me about camp and the relationships she made there."

"I didn't mention it," he said, stating the obvious. "To tell you the truth, I'd forgotten all about it. Ten years is a long time. It wasn't until we got up here and someone mentioned the name of the victim. Even that just rang a tiny bell. But it was the same girl, I'm sure of it."

"You were friends?"

"Yup. At first, anyway. She got involved with someone else after awhile and I didn't see her so much."

I sucked in a breath.

"Seth, does the name Prince Charming mean anything to you?"

"You mean the one from Cinderella? I always thought he was kinda of stupid. I mean, what if some other maiden in the kingdom wore the same size as Cinderella and the glass shoe fit her? He could've married the wrong chick."

I laughed.

"I meant in connection with camp. Cricket's friend said she came back with stories of someone called Prince Charming. Someone who was a bit older but who promised to come back for her when she'd grown up."

It occurred to me that I'd revealed the few cards I had in my hand. Seth would either implicate himself (unlikely) or someone else. Or, he'd claim ignorance of the whole thing.

"I don't know who it was," he said, disappointing me, "but I was pretty sure she was shacking up with someone. One of the counselors, maybe, or one of the guests. They used to bring people in to talk to us about possible careers. Most of them were Finnish," he added, answering my unasked question, "but not all."

Now for the sixty-million-dollar question.

"Could it have been anyone associated with *What's in Your Attic?*"

"You mean Vincent or Harry?" I didn't reply and he continued his thought. "It seems unlikely. Vincent's the right age but I can't imagine him concocting such a daring plot. Harry is nearly fifty. He's too old."

I nodded, accepting his answer, but I wondered.

Greed can make even a plodder daring. And charm, as I was well aware, was ageless.

"Frankly, I think Harry is too smart to involve someone as flighty as Cricket in any kind of a plan," Seth said. I just looked at him.

"Even if he knew he was going to kill her?"

Helena Tallmaster opened the green room door bringing our conversation to an immediate halt.

"Seth. There you are. I've been looking all over for you. Vincent wants to start taping. Ollie Rahkunen, the guy who shot the proscenium the other day? He's got an antique rifle with a swastika scratched into the stock. Oh, and he asks that his reindeer be included in the segment."

Seth stood and held out his hand to help me up.

"We'll talk later," he said before he left. I thought Helena would follow him out the door but she surprised me by lingering. She surprised me even more with her observation.

"For what it's worth, I think we should shut this operation down and leave and not just because this place gives me the creeps."

"Why then?"

She shrugged her graceful shoulders.

"Respect." I nodded.

"Helena, do you have any idea who killed Cricket Koski and Mrs. Paikkonen?"

"Certainly not. They have nothing to do with me."

"Their deaths seem to be linked to the presence of the television company in Red Jacket. And to the search for the painting."

"The mythical painting?" Her disbelief was palpable.

"Do you really think two women would have been killed for something that never existed? I think that, if nothing else, those murders are proof there's something up here worth killing for."

Her face was as pale as the white wool sweater she was wearing.

"Let me ask you another question. Did you know about the rumored painting before you chose the Keweenaw for your pilot?" She shook her head. "Did Vincent know?"

"It's unlikely. Vincent doesn't know much." She turned to leave as I asked what I really wanted to know.

"How long have you been married?"

"To Vincent? For three years." So they hadn't been married ten years ago. But something about her answer made me probe further.

"What about before that?"

"I was married to someone else." Her tone was light. She headed for the door. When she got there she turned around and answered the question I hadn't asked.

"Harry Dent. For about two minutes. The two most exciting and terrifying minutes of my life."

Geez Louise. I headed back up to the Leaping Deer to help with lunch, unable to process what Helena had just said. I wasn't sure I believed her, for one thing. Or it might have been a joke. But what if it was true? What was going on with this television company? Musical marriages? I tried to think through the implications as I arranged sliced beets, pickles and cole slaw on a plate, carried it out to the dining room to add to the smorgasbord of a hotdish of creamed whitefish, mashed potatoes and turnips and several plates of bars.

Even though we'd just had our second murder this week, I knew everyone would show up to eat. If there's one thing we are known for it is practicality. No matter what happened, life went on and three meals a day were served.

I did notice a plate of egg salad sandwiches and another of Cheez Whiz on rye, both of them staples of the funeral spread.

The conversation at the table was gloomy.

"You know the timing on this is really unfortunate," Aunt Ianthe said, between bites of Mrs. Sorensen's mustard ring salad. "What with the two events last month and Eudora and the Cricket girl, the vault is nearly filled up."

Mrs. Moilanen nodded.

"No one else can die before the thaw."

Harry Dent, arriving late, had taken a vacant seat next to me.

"Do you know what they're talking about, Cupcake?"

I swallowed what was in my mouth – I think it was whitefish – before I answered.

"No one can be buried when the ground is frozen. So there's a brick vault out at the cemetery."

"Like a holding pen?"

"Except they aren't animals. And they aren't alive."

"So more like a body depot."

I knew he was teasing but it felt a little like ridicule. I didn't answer.

"The Lord giveth and the Lord taketh away," Miss Irene said, predictably quoting the Book of Job.

Aunt Ianthe shook her head.

"You know, Eudora was younger than Irene and I." She sighed. "At least she got to enjoy one last Christmas."

It was a common sentiment expressed after a death near the holiday. I tried and failed to get an image of Mrs. Paikkonen enjoying Christmas.

After she'd eaten, Miss Irene sat down at Elli's old upright piano and softly played Sibelius's funeral air *Be Still My Soul.* Aunt Ianthe asked me whether Sofi would have enough yellow and white flowers for the service and Mrs. Moilanen asked what about Cricket Koski since she apparently had no family. I reminded her that Arvo had been kind enough to handle the arrangements for the victims of our previous murder.

"Of course there was a family connection in that case," Diane Hakala said.

No one pointed out that the connection had been to the murderer.

At the end of the meal, after the coffee and bars were served, the Reverend Sorensen stood. Although he'd offered a fairly lengthy blessing before we'd broken bread, he apparently felt called upon to do more, he said, in honor of the late Eudora Paikkonen, a pillar of the community and, more importantly, of God's church. He recited, in a slow, sonorous voice, the entire Twenty-Third Psalm.

When he finished Vincent Tallmaster spoke.

"Are you finished?" When the reverend nodded, Tallmaster got to his feet and pinged his water glass.

"On behalf of Helena and myself, Serena, Harry and Seth, I would like to extend our condolences to the family and friends of the late Mrs. Paikkonen. Her passing was a sad thing."

"Sad, criminal, whatever." I hadn't realized I'd said the words aloud until Harry sent me an amused glance.

"Mrs. Pike, as she liked to be called, was a stalwart member of this community and one of its greatest cheerleaders. She was the first person we met upon arriving in Red Jacket and I think it is safe to say she was one of the strongest supporters of *What's in Your Attic?* Who will forget that she offered, no, *insisted*, upon translating the letter from Nazi Germany?"

"I shouldn't think anyone would forget that," Harry whispered for my ears only, "since that is apparently why she was killed."

"I believe we can honor Eudora best by carrying on, by making the best pilot in television history and by dedicating it to her memory. The show," he said, with a dramatic pause, "must go on!"

The words fell into a deafening silence. Finally, Seth spoke.

"I don't mean to rain on your parade but the two recent deaths are linked directly with our program. I'm not sure it would be respectful or honorable or in good taste to continue with this project."

Harry cleared his throat.

"It seems to me the troubles have been linked to the theme we've chosen, specifically the hunt for the Nazi-looted painting. Perhaps we could substitute Finnish-Americans or focus on the beauty of the Keweenaw Peninsula."

"I know!" Aunt Ianthe got to her feet. "You've already shot some footage of our knitting circle at Hatti's shop. Why not make that the theme for the pilot? Knitting circles have been around a long time. They have warmed hearts, and fingers and toes, through lots of cold winters. We could talk about patterns and how they've evolved."

Vincent's eye twitched and his lips twisted.

"What about the Nazi-themed flowers? I just paid for them."

"If we take off the swastikas they can do double duty," Helena said, drily. "After we've videotaped the pilot they can be used at the funerals."

"*Voi kahua!*" Mrs. Moilanen uttered the mild expletive on behalf of everyone at the table. Red and black flowers would never be used at a Finnish-American funeral.

"Let's face it, Vincent," Harry said. "If these deaths are connected in any way to the pilot, the best thing we can do for this community is get out of town. Let's shoot a little more footage today then do the editing in Detroit. I'm sure a proper theme will emerge."

"I agree," Seth added. "It's time to throw in the towel to make sure no one else is hurt. The prospect of Nazi loot was enticing but we're no closer to finding it and two people are dead."

I felt a combination of relief and regret. If the television people left now we might never catch the murderer but the trouble on the Keweenaw might cease.

"Oh my land! I have it!"

I groaned. Aunt Ianthe was always full of ideas. "I don't know why I didn't think of this before."

"You have it?" Vincent's face lit up. "You know where the painting is hidden?"

"Well, not yet," Aunt Ianthe admitted. "But I know how to find out. We can consult the Ouija Board!"

"Good Lord," Harry whispered. "We're back to the spirit world."

"And he made his son pass through the fire, and observed times, and used enchantments, and dealt with familiar spirits and wizards." Miss Irene said. "Second Kings and also Second Chronicles."

"But, dear," Aunt Ianthe said, "you know there is more to the verse. Those enchantments were meant to provoke the Lord to anger."

"I did a little editing," Miss Irene said. "It seemed a pity to add fuel to the fire."

"All right," Vincent said. "I bow to the pressure. Gather up the folks with the antler lamps and beer signs, the broken toboggans and old bathtubs and meet down at the theater. This will be the final curtain call!"

CHAPTER 28

Like all the best laid plans, Vincent's were dashed when a sudden eruption of thundersnow hit Red Jacket. The whiteout storm caused by our proximity to Lake Superior and accompanied by thunder, lightning and hailstones, meant everyone had to stay indoors. There would be no trek down to the opera house.

"This seems like one more excellent reason to never again set foot in this godforsaken place," Helena Tallmaster muttered to Serena Waterfall.

Not everyone viewed the storm as a calamity.

"Such a silver lining," Aunt Ianthe said, clapping her hands. "Now we can spend the afternoon consulting the Ouija Board."

"I don't know," Vincent said, clearly conflicted. "It might be more useful to go through the inn's attic again. Or, maybe the cellar. On the other hand, if the spirits are willing to reveal the painting's hiding place, that would be even better. I really think this storm is an omen. We are *meant* to find the painting. Serena, you have an excellent rapport with the netherworld. You take charge of the séance."

There was a short silence in which, I suspected, Aunt Ianthe struggled with her pride. The Ouija Board had been her idea. I could see the uncertainty on her face and I knew the moment when she became reconciled to letting Serena Waterfall take the lead.

Serena seemed oblivious to the struggle. In fact, she didn't seem herself. She was wearing a multi-hued caftan and her hair danced around her face but the wrinkles in that face were more defined and there were small, grim lines near her mouth. Finding Mrs. Paikkonen's body in the window seat had clearly traumatized her. I felt a pang of compassion.

Nevertheless, she made the effort. She directed Jace and Seth to move the farm table back against the wall in the dining room and to set a round table in the center of the floor, along with two chairs, one on either side of it.

At Serena's request, Elli produced a white table cloth, a candle and the game-set and I lowered the blinds in the dining room to block the light from the snowstorm.

"First," Serena said, "I want you to stand in a circle and hold hands. Then I'll go over the rules."

I felt my hand scooped up in a bigger, warmer hand and then I heard Harry Dent's voice in my ear.

"Who came up with the rules? Hasbro?"

I shushed him but Serena answered as if it had been a serious question.

"The spirit board dates back to twelfth century China. It only became a parlor game in 1890. The scientific community explained the planchette's responses as a result of unconscious muscle movement on the part of the participants. So it is very important that the participants are without an agenda."

She looked at the man on my other side, the one who was glowering at Harry.

"Jace Night Wind," she said, "I would like you to be my partner, to sit opposite me at the table. The rest of you tighten your grip on the hands you are holding and build energy and tension. Miss Irene?" She nodded at the old lady. "Will you read the letters from the board?" I was surprised she hadn't picked Harry as her partner, especially because it would have necessitated his letting go of my hand. A moment later I understood.

"Hatti, you write down everything Miss Irene says."

"Sure," I murmured, frankly glad to break the contact. I

wondered what was wrong with me as I took up a pad and pencil and prepared to record.

"There are a few rules. Never taunt or goad the board. Only one person can ask the questions. Me. If you want me to know something, you can whisper it in my ear. Remember, be respectful. Spirits are notoriously thin-skinned and they have it in their power to lie. One last thing. Never ask the board when someone is going to die."

A chill ran down my spine at those words and, from the murmur that whispered through the group, I figured others had had the same response.

Serena and Jace took their places at the table. He followed her lead in placing fingertips on the plastic planchette and closing his eyes.

"We are creating this circle of acceptance," she said, after a moment. "All who are present are seekers. We seek the wisdom that only the incorporeal beings can give us. We welcome any astral presence who wishes to come among us." She paused, then, "we await a sign of your presence."

The silence in the room seemed to be magnified as outside the window, the frantic wind died down. It was quiet enough in Elli's dining room to hear a pin drop. The sudden, loud clang of *Straight to Hell*, made us all jump.

"Sorry," Elli murmured, reaching into her pocket to turn off her cellphone. "Charlie programmed the ringtone. I'm sorry."

Only Serena and Jace seemed unaffected by the interruption. They continued to sit at the table, their fingertips in place.

"We wish," Serena said, in a high, floaty voice, "to invite the spirit of Ms. Eudora Paikkonen who has recently crossed over. Will you speak to us?"

The planchette trembled, moved a centimeter to the right and another to the left and then shot up to the top of the board and landed on the word *yes*.

There was an audible gasp from Aunt Ianthe.

"Thank you, Eudora," Serena said. "First, how are you? Have you had a peaceful crossing?"

The planchette trembled and spun and wound up in the space between the *yes* and the *no*.

"So-so," Serena interpreted. "We have come to you," she continued, "because we need an answer. We believe you know the location of the stolen painting, Monet's Waterlilies. Will you tell us?"

Nothing happened. Not even a wiggle. Maybe Mrs. Paikkonen didn't know where the painting was hidden. I found myself thinking that if I were controlling the planchette, I'd ask for the identity of the murderer.

The stillness on the board continued for a long time.

Finally the plastic pointer with the viewfinder at its center, began to slip and slide. It swooped and soared like a skater on an ice rink and both Serena and Jace had to concentrate hard not to lose contact with it.

After what seemed like a long time, the planchette stopped. Miss Irene peered at the board through her reading glasses and pronounced the letter *R*.

An instant later the planchette began to rocket back and forth. Finally it stopped abruptly. It occurred to me that the spirit of Mrs. Paikkonen was enjoying the limelight and didn't intend to give it up in a hurry.

"It's *R*," Miss Irene said. "Another *R*."

"My stars," Aunt Ianthe said, catching the significance before I did. "*R.R.* The initials from the *karsikko* sign."

Geez Louise.

"Ask her to spell it out," I muttered.

"It doesn't work like that," Serena said, quietly. "It's like twenty questions. One question, one answer."

"Ask her," Harry said, urgently, "about the Hautamaki letter. Where is that?"

It was an excellent question and a good strategy for getting around the one-answer dictate. Serena posed the question and, once again, the planchette began to move. It slowed over four letters. Miss Irene called them out and I wrote them down.

"What is it, Hatti," Aunt Ianthe asked.

"SAEF."

"That's not a word," Mrs. Moilanen pointed out.

"She meant SAFE," Serena clarified. "Spirits are notoriously bad spellers."

"She's telling us the letter is safe," I said. And it was true. The letter, though covered with blood, was safe in Doc Laitimaki's office.

Suddenly Serena lifted her hands off the planchette and slumped in her chair. Jace removed the plastic pointer from the board.

"That's it, folks," he said. "The show's over. Could someone get Serena a drink of water?"

"That was a big nothingburger," Vincent groused. "Not worth the time."

"And yet," his wife said, "better than getting lost in a snowstorm."

I said nothing but I didn't agree with Vincent. I thought it had been worth the time. The Ouija Board answer reflected the *karsikko* sign. Did that mean that one of the participants knew the meaning behind R.R.? It couldn't be Jace. That meant it was Serena. And, if she knew, it also followed that she had killed Mrs. Paikkonen. No wonder she looked haggard today.

Murder is not a laughing matter.

CHAPTER 29

Someone turned the lights on. Someone else got Serena a drink of water. She had gotten to her feet and was leaning against her ex-husband. Everyone seemed sort of at a loss. The Ouija had responded but we didn't know what to do with the answer. And then a loud pounding exploded in the room. My heart jerked, as Elli answered the back door to an angry-faced, very rotund, snow-covered Sheriff Clump and his equally snow-covered deputy.

"Awright now," Clump barked. "Where in the Sam H-E-double-hockey-sticks-hill are all these damned suspects?"

"Come in," Elli said, hurrying them inside. "What are you doing out in this blizzard?"

"The law," Clump said, loftily, "cannot be stopped by wind or rain or sleet or snow."

"Like the postman," Waino added. "We were down to the opera house but it was locked up tight. So we hiked up here. Sheriff says if we gotta interview the suspects again we might as well do it with coffee and cake."

Clump glared at his deputy.

"Haven't you already talked to everyone, sheriff?" Helena Tall-master's voice dripped with disdain.

"Yes, ma'am I have. And I'm damn sure gonna talk to everyone again on account of the autopsy results."

"There was a surprise?" Harry sounded mildly curious. "I imagine something has changed in the timeline."

Clump's beady eyes narrowed on the taller man.

"You got a good imagination," he said. "Anything else you wanna say?"

"No, no. Forgive me, sheriff."

"The old lady was killed in the afternoon," Waino said, helpfully. "That means Lars Teljo didn't do it."

"Hush up, boy," Clump growled. "I'll handle this." He sniffed the air, for all the world, like a basset hound. Elli responded immediately with offers of fresh coffee and *omenakakku* or Finnish apple cake made with granny smith apples and slivered almonds.

"You got any manila ice cream," Clump asked when Miss Irene set his plate before him. While Elli fetched the ice cream, Aunt Ianthe and Miss Irene took seats at the table and, within minutes their double-pointed needles were clicking merrily as they worked on a pair of color-stranded socks for Charlie. Over the years they had cooperated on hundreds of pairs of socks for dozens of people. The socks were always beautifully knit, if slightly mismatched as Aunt Ianthe's knitting tension was loose and Miss Irene's was not.

Not that we minded. We all loved them and we loved the socks.

"I volunteer to go first," Aunt Ianthe said. "Ask away, Horace."

"Shoot-a-mile," Clump said and frowned. He probably didn't like the familiarity but since Ianthe Lehtinen was old enough to be his mother and since he'd been in her third grade class at Red Jacket Elementary, he couldn't object. "I don't need to hear from you, Miss Ianthe. I know you were at the knittin' thing at the bait shop until suppertime. I'm here to question those others." He glowered at the Tallmasters, Seth, Serena and Harry.

"We are more than happy to cooperate, sheriff," Vincent said. "We have nothing to hide. Helena and I were at the Bait and Stitch shop shooting footage of the knitters. Our intention is to show how time has stood still up here in Northern Michigan. The same sort of knitting circle was going on seventy-five years ago. I think we captured the essence pretty well although we haven't yet looked at the daily rushes."

Clump stared at him for a moment.

"What time did you leave Main Street?"

"I'm afraid I couldn't give you an exact time. I'm not the kind of person who looks at his watch all day. I believe it was dark. And snowing."

"It's always snowing," Helena said.

Clump gazed at her.

"Where'd you go after that?"

"Right back here," Vincent said, jovially.

"It's not," Helena put in, "like there was a lot of choice. Another day, another smorgasbord."

"I think I can save you some time, sheriff," Harry said, smoothly. "We were all down at Bait and Stitch from the middle of the afternoon until just before supper. Mrs. Paikkonen did not join the other ladies at the shop and Hatti sent me back to the Lehtinen house to pick her up. It must have been about three p.m. When I knocked on her bedroom door she told me she wanted to stay there and rest."

"She'd taken a sleeping pill," Serena reminded him.

"That's right."

"Anybody see or talk to her after that," Clump asked. There was a chorus of negative replies.

"Guess that makes you the last one to talk to her," Clump said, his eyes squinting.

"Except for the murderer," Harry murmured.

"Sheriff," Jace said, his eyes on Harry, "what time did Mrs. Paikkonen die?"

For awhile I thought he wouldn't answer but he finally did.

"Doc's best guess is mid-afternoon. No later than four p.m."

Everybody at the table stared at Harry.

"I guess I was the last to talk to her," he said. "A damn shame, too. I must have just missed the murderer."

I closed my eyes and pictured the shop that afternoon. Vincent had been there and Helena and Serena and, of course, I'd sent Harry back to the house to pick up Mrs. Paikkonen but he was back by a little after three. What about Seth? As if he'd read my thoughts, he volunteered the information.

"I took Hatti's rug over to the theater and hung it up," he said. "I think I got back to the shop around four-fifteen or four-thirty, but I wouldn't swear to it."

It felt like a stunningly, self-incriminating confession and for a moment no one spoke. And then Clump surprised me again.

"Where were you all on New Year's Eve?"

Harry spoke up first.

"Serena and I stayed in a motel out on the Seney Mile near Paradise. We had a rented car, an SUV actually, and we had hoped to get closer to the Keweenaw that night but we stopped for a burger at some place called the Pine Stump and after we'd eaten we realized we were exhausted. We're not spring chickens anymore, you know? So we found something called Dan's Cabins, checked in and lights out."

It was a lot of detail, a lot of words. It was also consistent with what Harry had told me before. I noticed Serena was staring into her coffee. When Harry finished speaking he said, "That the way you remember it, Serena?" She nodded.

In fact, all the alibis matched what Harry had told me. It almost seemed as if they'd been rehearsed but that was ridiculous. How hard was it to remember where three sets of people were only a few days earlier? Each of the actors spoke of their travel that weekend. None of them, naturally, had been anywhere near Lars Teljo's cabin on Dollar Lake.

Clump glared at each of them in turn.

"Well somebody sure as hell stuck a knittin' needle into that old lady and something a lot like it into the girl. Somebody here ain't tellin' the truth."

Elli, correctly surmising that his sugar high had worn off, got up to cut him another piece of cake.

"What was she doin' at the Lehtinen house, anyways?"

"She thought she heard a ghost at the mortuary," I said, hoping I wouldn't have to try to explain the *karsikko* sign to the sheriff.

"Geez, Hatti," Waino said, "maybe the deadly knittin' needle was meant for you."

I sighed. It was obvious we had to fill in the blanks for the lawmen. "We found a letter up in the attic sent from Nazi Germany. The letter mentioned a piece of Nazi loot recovered by a young Finnish diplomat and sent to the UP for safe-keeping. Mrs. Paikkonen was the only one to have read and translated the letter. We think there's a chance she was killed because she knew where the loot was hidden."

Waino looked at me as if I had grown elk horns.

Sheriff Clump canted his head to one side (not an easy thing to do with his lack of neck) and said, "just what do you mean, Missy, by loot?"

Seth answered.

"It would be a painting. Most likely, a painting of waterlilies by the French Impressionist Claude Monet."

I sensed a lack of appreciation so I told them it was worth sixty million dollars.

"If it exists," Sheriff Clump said.

"There's no question that it exists," Harry said. "There are still many thousands of works of art and cultural artifacts listed in the international Art Loss Register. Other Nazi looted artwork has been found in attics and basements of American cities. The Monet could be on the Keweenaw but it seems unlikely as we haven't been able to find it."

Clump stared at him.

"Somebody believes it enough to murder two gals."

I felt a sudden, grudging respect for Horace Clump. He was right. The murders all but confirmed the presence of the Monet.

"Awright," Clump said, turning his beady eyes to me. "I know you've been snoopin' around here and I wanna know just what you found. Chapter and verse."

I didn't know where to start. All I could think about was that picture of Seth Virtunan sitting next to Cricket Koski at Camp Kaleva. But if I mentioned it, Clump would, in his usual heavy-handed fashion, throw Seth into the jail cell with Lars.

Waino, bless his cotton-pickin' heart, came at it from a different angle.

"Who came up with the idea to look for the stolen painting?"

"It was the letter," Elli said. "The letter mentioned a package this young man, Ernst Hautamaki, was planning to send to his aunt."

"But how did you know it was a painting? I mean, it could've been anything, right? It could have been gold. Somebody got you started on a stolen painting."

I thought back to our brainstorming session on Sunday – had that been only three days ago? We'd all been talking about the history of Finland and World War II. Then Elli had found the letter and someone had suggested that Ernst's birthday surprise for his aunt was a missing masterpiece. Who? Had it been Harry, who certainly knew about looted paintings? Seth? He knew about art and he knew about Finland, too.

"Never mind about that," Clump said, after a minute. "What I wanna know is who gave the old lady a sleeping pill?" Once again, no one responded.

The sheriff, once again, eyed Harry Dent.

"What'd she say about it to you then?"

"Not too much," Harry said. "She said she'd come from the B and B and I guess I just assumed she'd gotten the pills from Elli." Clump turned to my cousin who shook her head.

"I don't have any sleeping pills. If I took one I'd sleep for a month."

Clump looked at Waino.

"Doc find sleepin' pills in her blood?" Waino shrugged.

The sheriff folded his forearms over his formidable chest.

"Know what I think? Mrs. P. didn't take no pills cause she didn't have no pills. I think somebody came back from the bait shop and killed her."

This was the time for me to come clean about the stalker-slash-killer and the *karsikko* sign and Mrs. Pike hiding the Hautamaki letter in her corset. But for whatever reason, I couldn't seem to make my lips move.

CHAPTER 30

The snowstorm ended as quickly as it had begun and while it left behind six new inches of powder and a coating of ice, Harry, Jace, Serena, Larry and I were able to skate, slide and stomp our way back to the Queen Anne. I felt a sense of warmth and relief when I stepped into my mother's cheery, green-and-white kitchen. It was good to get away from the stress of the investigation and my own ambivalence about how much to share. I'd only told the locals about R.R. And when I say locals, I don't mean the sheriff and Waino. I had to ask myself if I was keeping that under-cover because there was someone I didn't trust or whether I was hoping to use the clue to find the Monet myself.

In any case, I was looking forward to a little supper and a low-key evening and maybe, just maybe, an encore with my husband.

I'd just put on a fresh pot of coffee and started to thaw some frozen *lihakeitto* or meat and potato stew, when all hell seemed to break loose. Serena Waterfall had seemed perfectly normal if a trifle subdued at the Leaping Deer. Almost the first minute she entered my mother's kitchen she began to shout and swear. Her face turned red and she hurled objects against the wall. I didn't react when she pitched a skein of purple yarn or Larry's rope chew toy, but when she flung a *Sisu* mug onto the linoleum then tried to chase that with one of mom's Bing and Grondahl Christmas plates, I sucked in my breath.

Luckily, Harry Dent handled it better. He trapped the whirling dervish in his arms until she quieted down.

"This tends to happen after she dabbles in the occult," he explained. "She just needs her meds and a good night's sleep. I'm sorry about the mess."

They disappeared up the back stairs and Jace and I looked at each other.

"The artistic temperament," he said. "She seems fairly normal otherwise."

"That's the second time I've seen her lose control. She got upset at the theater and pushed Lydia Saralampi right into the orchestra pit because the woman was flirting with Harry."

Jace lifted his brows.

"I'm surprise she hasn't tried to hurt you in that case."

I didn't pretend to misunderstand.

"I think she knows I'm not a threat. But then, Lydia wasn't a threat, either. Jace, I've been discounting Serena right along. Do you think I'm wrong? Do you think she has the capacity to kill?"

"We all have that. Anyway, most of us, if pushed far enough. In any case, this has been a tough week for everyone involved."

"And, remember, Serena discovered Mrs. Paikkonen's body arranged on the window-seat. That had to throw her seriously off balance."

"To say nothing of the fact that we still haven't identified a murderer."

I shivered. It was almost like we were back at square one.

"Whatever happened to that fishing camp dude?"

"You mean Max Guthrie? He's out of town." I frowned. Where the heck was Max? "Elli said on New Year's Eve he gave Sonya Still-water a lift to the airport so she could get home to Santa Fe."

"Did she say which airport? He could have driven her to New Mexico in four days. Haven't you missed him?"

"In case you haven't noticed, I've been busy. Why do you want to know, anyway?"

"I want to know," he said, moving toward me, "because I'm trying to assess how many guys I'm going to have to challenge to pistols at dawn to get back my wife."

FORTUNATELY, we heard Harry's footsteps on the stairs and by the time he entered the kitchen we were each in our own chairs. Harry, however, was a man of some experience. He looked at me with one eyebrow lifted just so I would know that he knew what we'd been doing.

"Serena will be okay," he said. "She just needs a good night's sleep. This week has been extremely stressful for everybody."

Jace had just expressed the same sentiment but for some reason Harry's comment irritated me. "It was especially stressful for Mrs. Paikkonen and Cricket."

Harry grinned, ruefully and Jace shot me a warning look but his tone was mild.

"Why'd you get mixed up in this romp?"

"As I told the Cupcake, it was a favor to my ex-wife."

Once again, the amusement in his voice rubbed me the wrong way.

"Which ex-wife?"

The laughter was still in his eyes when he looked at me. Life was a joke to Harry Dent.

"You heard about that, did you? Come on, Hatti. You, of all people, know life is full of overlapping circles. The same people cross our paths. Haven't you ever heard the theory that when a man is ready to marry, he looks around at the immediate options and picks the best one?"

"So that's what you did? Twice?"

He leaned back in his chair and regarded me.

"Why is that a cause for contempt? Isn't it what everyone does? Isn't it what your mother did?"

He was right. After my dad left, my mom married Pops, who adopted Sofi and me. Of course, the circumstances were different.

"There's another truism, too," Harry said, reading my mind.

"Not all can mate for life. Both Serena and Helena knew that about me. I did not try to hide it."

His honesty called for a grudging kind of respect and I nodded. Jace appeared to agree with him, too, which took the wind out of my sails.

"Did you know about the stolen painting when you agreed to come up here?" Once again, Jace's question was asked in a pleasant, nonjudgmental tone.

Harry met my eyes with an apologetic look.

"I did mislead you on that, Cupcake. I'd heard some chatter about the Keweenaw in connection with the Waterlilies. Naturally I was curious. I've spent the last number of years trying to track down Nazi loot."

"So you engineered a good excuse to spend some time rummaging around the attics in Red Jacket."

Harry shook his head.

"It was less calculated than that. Vincent and Helena knew Serena – I told you ours is a small world – and they wanted her on the show. Unlike Helena, Serena has never really moved on emotionally from our failed marriage. She got in touch with me and asked if I would participate, too."

"That's a little surprising, isn't it? I mean, Serena was so jealous of Lydia Saralampi that she pushed her into the orchestra pit and yet she didn't mind you spending a week with your other ex-wife?"

Jace said nothing and, once again, Harry smiled at me.

"We're not all romantics like you. Helena and I married quickly and divorced just as quickly. She's no more interested in me than I am in her. Serena knows this. She also knows that I am always moving forward. A woman from my past wouldn't interest me."

A woman from his past.

"Was that what Cricket Koski was? A woman from your past?"

He shook his head.

"You can't make me out to be Prince Charming, Cupcake. I'm much too old and as I've told you, I've never been in the UP before, certainly not at Camp Kaleva ten years ago." He excused himself to check on Serena and, once again, Jace and I were alone. This time we stayed in our separate chairs.

"You're attacking the guy on his personal life. Why are you so offended by it?"

I shrugged. "It just seems so disrespectful. Serena seems to have been so hurt by it."

"Maybe. But that is her business not yours. All we're concerned with here is whether Dent had anything to do with the murders."

"Do you think he did?"

"He knew about the waterlilies. On the other hand, he's not a good candidate for Prince Charming. For one thing, he's too old. And for another, I can't imagine what he'd have been doing at a Finnish youth camp ten summers ago."

We sat in virtual silence, each occupied with our own thoughts, until Harry returned.

"All's well upstairs. She's sound asleep." He smiled at me and then Jace. "Got any more questions or shall we play a few hands of cards?"

After a moment, and somewhat to my surprise, Jace nodded.

"Three-handed euchre?"

I got out the battered deck mom uses to play Solitaire and we played a few rounds. Harry, not surprisingly, was quick and sharp and acquainted with the rules of the somewhat obscure game.

"Got anything to drink in this house, Cupcake? I mean other than coffee?"

I found the only liquor in the house, a liqueur called *Lakka* made of cloudberries. It was thick, cloying and too sweet but both men polished off several glasses. I was contemplating going on up to bed when my phone rang. It was Arvo and he sounded emotional. I braced for more bad news.

"Henrikki, I need you here for an impromptu funeral. It's the oldest inhabitant."

"Who is the oldest inhabitant?" Harry asked, as I stuffed my feet back into my boots.

I had to think about that for a minute. Aarni Tenhunen had held the title for ten years, ever since Pops's mother, Ruth Ann

Lehtinen had died. But Aarni had succumbed last summer at ninety-eight years and the new titleholder, if I remembered correctly, was Sigrid Ahola, who had seemed to be holding strong at ninety-seven. I was sorry she'd had to give up her crown after less than a year. Especially now when, as Aunt Ianthe had pointed out, the ground was frozen and the vault was full.

I threw on my parka and boots and headed out the door.

Engrossed in my personal thoughts, I was surprised when the door to the funeral home was opened by a tall, dark-haired woman wearing a flowing black negligee. I stepped over the threshold.

"Helena?"

"I thought it appropriate to wear black. Come with me."

Aware that I had not taken the time to dress in funeral garb, I followed her into the chapel on the ground floor of the funeral home. A spotlight was focused on the casket at the altar. Two men appeared to be praying over it. Each wore a formal dark suit and, at this distance, they were indistinguishable. It was only when they straightened and the light gleamed off Arvo's blond-white hair and the heavily applied product in Vincent's coiffure, that I distinguished them. The notes of *Abide with Me*, played with a respectful soft pedal, emerged from the piano in the corner.

"You got Miss Irene to come out in this weather," I whispered to Helena. She shook her head.

"It's Seth."

I was touched that three of our visitors had agreed to participate in one of our rituals. There were only two other mourners present, Otto, Mrs. Ahola's octogenarian son wearing a fur-lined cap with ear flaps and a stoop-shouldered elderly lady wearing an ancient pillbox hat with a little black veil and holding a small, gray dog on her lap.

"Isn't that Mrs. Ahola?"

"That's right," Helena said. "She brought Mirri because she believes the dog needs closure. She and Musti had been together their entire lives."

"You mean this is a funeral for a dog?"

"If you don't believe me, check the casket."

Helena Tallmaster gave me a genuine smile for the first time all week. She was obviously sympathetic about the loss of a pet. It made me like her. It also made me realize I'd misjudged her and maybe Harry had, too. She was a total romantic at heart.

Arvo caught my eye and I felt a spring of tears. Holding a funeral for a beloved dog was exactly the kind of thing he would do and I was suddenly flooded with affection for the folks of my hometown.

When I got home, Harry asked about the service and I tried to explain. When I'd finished, both men had held onto their cards but their jaws had dropped.

"Small towns," Harry said. "They always surprise you."

"Speaking of surprises," Jace said, "in light of everything that's happened and out of an abundance of caution, we're going to double up. Dent will sleep in your folks's room with Serena and you and I will share Sofi's old bedroom. Your own room, you'll recall is now a crime scene and I don't want you in the attic."

He didn't say where he did want me, I mean, not explicitly, but a secret smile from Harry made me blush.

As it turned out, we could hear Harry moving around in the room next door and Jace flopped on his back and went to sleep. It felt like déjà vu to turn my head to the right and see his chest rising and falling steadily. It felt safe. Good. Right.

I cushioned my head with my hands, stared at the ceiling and thought back over the evening. I'd been struck by how hard it had been to tell Arvo and Vincent apart in the faint light of the chapel.

I must have dozed off because I awoke with a start and an image and an epiphany. The picture, in my mind's eye, was of two men bent over a coffin and from where I stood, I could not tell which was blond, middle-aged Arvo and which was the much younger man. A phrase from *Moomins in Midwinter* floated in front of me. It was from the wise woman, Too-Ticky, and I couldn't remember the context in the children's book but I knew why it had occurred to me now.

"What's up?"

I jumped. I'd forgotten that Jace can wake up as quickly and completely as he can fall asleep. It almost seems like magic.

"All cats are gray in the dark."

"Profound."

"Sofi stood across the clearing from the cabin on New Year's Eve. She was twenty feet away from the SUV when it pulled up to the cabin. She watched a man get out and help Cricket up to the house. There were no lights and it was snowing so hard she wouldn't have been able to see the color of the vehicle. The man would have worn a parka so his hair wouldn't show. What if the man with Cricket wasn't Lars? What if he was someone else?"

"What time did Sofi see him?"

I thought back to the timeline.

"She said she left Red Jacket around eleven so it would have been eleven twenty or so."

"Then it wasn't Lars. Lars. He told me he'd pulled into the Gas-and-Go to take a twenty-minute power nap. He couldn't have gotten to the cabin until after eleven thirty. I doubt there was a witness. The Mursos close at ten in the summer, eight in the winter, whether it's a holiday or not."

"It doesn't matter. Now that we know it wasn't Lars we can focus on who it was who brought Cricket out to the cabin."

"Prince Charming?"

"Aka the murderer." I said.

CHAPTER 31

The inspiration in the night gave way to another. It felt like the logjam in my brain had broken free. It was exhilarating. I couldn't wait to tell Jace all about it, but when I turned to wake him, he wasn't there.

So what else was new?

I nipped that thought in the bud. Or, tried to. My priority was to follow the leads that Providence had granted me during the night. We all needed to get to the truth about the two murders and I could not afford to let my personal issues get in the way.

As I dressed in an outfit from my mother's closet (a gray tunic featuring a pair of kittens playing with a ball of yarn and black tights), I cast my mind back to Cricket's room on the afternoon of New Year's Eve. Clothing was draped on every surface, jewelry, too, and shoes. She'd spent considerable time choosing just the right outfit for her big date. Wouldn't it make sense that she'd have spent an inordinate amount of time on her make-up and her crowning glory? What was the likelihood she'd visited Copper Harbor's one and only beautician that day?

And, if Cricket had had her hair cut, colored and styled, what was the likelihood she'd have shared her evening plans with the stylist?

I figured the odds at somewhere near a hundred to one.

I HEADED down to the kitchen, fed Larry and made a pot of coffee. If I'd hoped to run into Jace (I had) I was disappointed. Harry Dent, though wandered in, his thick hair ruffled, his tee shirt and sweatpants adorably rumbled. He grinned at me through the engaging stubble on his chin.

"Morning, Cupcake," he surveyed me with sleep-heavy eyes. "That what passes for couture on the Keweenaw?"

"It's what passes for clothing when there's yellow tape sealing off your own closet."

"Oh. Right. Where is, uh, everybody?"

Since he'd just left the room he shared with Serena Waterfall I figured he was talking about Jace. I shrugged.

"He went out early." I told him my idea about the hair stylist.

"Smart," he said, admiringly. "You're turning into a real detective. Mind if I tag along?" He lowered his voice. "Just between you, me and the lamp post, I could use a change of scenery."

There was no reason to refuse and Harry was always good company. Anyway, two heads were better than one, like Pops always said.

Ollie was out with the snow scoop attached to the front of his pickup and Tamarack Street, the main road between Calumet Street and the interstate, was already cleared. At Harry's request I turned down Third Street and took it to Main to stop at the Gas-and-Go. He had returned to the car and handed me a big box of assorted doughnuts and a cup of to-go coffee when my cell phone rang.

"*Hei* Henrikki," said Doc Lahtimaki. "I just got back from the Lunch Box. Vesta tells me your brother-in-law is free. It seems your husband talked to Sheriff Clump."

So that's where Jace had disappeared to this morning. I was amazed he'd been able to convince the stubborn sheriff to let Lars out of jail.

Harry taking the box of doughnuts out of my hand, lifted his eyebrows questioningly. I mouthed the word *Doc*.

"I thought you would want to know that. And there's another thing. You know the letter, yah? I was studying it when Eeva came into the office to let me lick the batter bowl on her shortbread. She reads her Bible in Finnish, you know. When she looked at letter she noticed a phrase *olla koira haudattuna*. Literally translated it means, *I think there is a dog buried in there*."

"I remember you mentioned a dog," I said, although I couldn't imagine how a canine dead for three-quarters of a century could figure into what we needed to know.

"*Joo*," he said, using the Finnish word for yes. "In this case it does not refer to a real dog. It's a figure of speech which means that something is hidden."

My heartbeat kicked into a higher gear.

"Do you think it refers to the stolen painting?"

"That I do not know. He talks about a gift for Bengta and another for the bride and groom."

"Doc, does the letter tell the names of the young couple?"

"*Ei*." This time he used the Finnish word for no. "Just their initials. R.R."

There it was again. The elusive initials. It seemed that, despite the idiom about the dog, they did not refer to a hiding place but to two individuals. R. and R. A couple.

My initial excitement morphed into frustration. I felt like the answer was right there in front of me, handed on a silver plate. All I had to do was figure it out.

More coffee. Harry kept up a stream of small talk as I drove up the two-lane highway to Copper Harbor on autopilot. Names and phrases that began with R. unraveled before me like words on a ticker tape. *Rolls Royce. Reading Railroad. Round-Robin. Rural route. Rough-riders.*

"Do you want the last pink-frosted doughnut?"

I realized, belatedly, he'd asked a question.

"I'm sorry, what?" Harry grinned at me.

"I was pretty sure you weren't listening to me. It's not like you to ignore an invitation for food."

"Maybe later." *Teddy Roosevelt. Respiratory response. Rapid response. Rest and Relaxation. Raunchy rhinos?*

"What are you hoping to learn from the hairdresser?"

Dang. Another question. I forced myself to listen.

"Her name's Pat, right?"

"How do you know that?"

"Man, you sound so suspicious! I googled it while waiting for the doughnut order. There's only one hairdresser in Copper Harbor. Pat's Hair. Very utilitarian name."

"Yoopers are practical," I said.

"And excellent at snow removal. Just look at this highway. It's a clean as a baby's butt."

I laughed at the lame joke and calmed down, which was, I suspected his intention.

"About Pat," he reminded me. "Want me to sit in on the interview?"

"Let's place it by ear."

CHAPTER 32

P at, like Nestor Hyppa, is one of the handful of tradespeople who stay open all winter. Everyone needs peanut butter and milk and most folks, occasionally, need a haircut.

The cross streets are extremely short in Copper Harbor. Pat's Hair, the only structure on Fifth Street, is tucked between the Pit Stop, a convenience store/gas station/post office outlet that faces U.S.-41 and a bicycle rental shop that faces Bernard, an east-west residential street. I had no problem parallel parking in front of the tired-looking, two-story shingled, World War II vintage house, as there were no other vehicles on the street.

Did I mention that Copper Harbor all but closes down during the winter?

"There's no sign to tell you it's Pat's or whether it's open or closed."

"You don't need a sign. Everybody knows what it is and either they'll answer the door or they won't."

He cocked an eyebrow at me.

"You know, Cupcake, I'm starting to understand you. You're a real Yooper."

The observation pleased me.

"A Yooper for life. Come in with me. It's too cold to stay in the Jeep."

My knock was answered, after a short delay, by a heavyset young woman in jeans and a sweatshirt. She wore her lank, dirty blond hair down around her shoulders and a sullen expression on her face. The sound of children squabbling in the background reminded me of our visit to Cloud down in L'Anse. On the surface, both young mothers were the same but poverty and relentless childcare hadn't made the Indian woman discontented, while Pat (or more likely Pat's daughter, I guessed) looked to be enduring a life of quiet desperation. Or, maybe she just hadn't had her coffee yet. In any case, she didn't smile.

"Whatever you're selling," she said, "I don't want any."

"I'm buying," I said, acting on an inspiration I would regret. "I'm here for a haircut."

Apparently she found that believable. She stepped aside and pointed the two fingers holding her cigarette toward a door.

"Just go on down."

I wanted to make friends first.

"I'm Hatti Lehtinen. Are you Pat's daughter?"

"Wanda."

The undercurrent of quarreling got louder and two high piping voices shouted, "I hate you," and "I hate you more." Wanda closed her eyes.

"You know, Wanda," I said, "my friend here, Harry, is an expert at card tricks. Think your kids would like to see some?"

"Okay." She led the way into a shabby living room. A pair of four-year-olds seemed to be rolling around on the floor, attached to one another like a circus tumbling act.

"How did you know I could do card tricks," Harry whispered, as Wanda pulled a battered-looking deck off the top of the television. I grinned at him.

"I think I'm getting to understand you, too."

I left him there and headed down the steep, narrow stairs that led to the cellar which, like most of those in Northern Michigan, ran the length and width of the house. It was dank, composed of stone walls and a concrete floor. The half of the room that contained the washer and dryer, furnace and fruit cellar was separated from the business section by a quilt flung over a clothesline.

The hair salon consisted of a wash bowl and chair, another chair with an egg-shaped hairdryer attached and a plastic chest of drawers in between. Both chairs were occupied, one by a lean, woman with a year-round tan and deep wrinkles and a cap of short salt-and-pepper hair. The legs, in their brown polyester slacks were crossed and she wore a peach-colored sweatshirt that had seen better days. Apparently, she'd seen better days, too, because the shirt proclaimed: I'd rather be bowling.

Next to her, a large, smooth-skinned, pink and white woman sat under the hairdryer, which wasn't turned on. Her hair color was indistinguishable because of the army of pink plastic rollers that marched across her skull. Her sweatshirt was pink, too, with a pink, rhinestone cat and the words, Pussy Galore. It was she who spoke.

"Good morning. I'm Ronnie Kikut. Kikut's Real Estate," she said. She pointed to her companion. "And this is the lady of the hour." The hairdresser studied me with a critical expression on her face. She did not speak or stand or stub out her cigarette.

The anticipated cozy gossip session faded from my imagination. I was going to have to get a haircut. I said as much.

"Piece of advice," Ronnie said, gaily, "don't go for the wet cut. Pat's dryer is on the blink. Your hair'll turn into icicles."

"Dry cut is fine," I said and then told them my name and where I was from while Pat pushed herself up out of her chair and brandished a very worn-looking cape with a Hello Kitty logo.

"Whatcha doin' way up here, hon?" Ronnie asked. "And why does your name sound familiar? Oh, wait just a cotton-pickin' minute. I know who you are! You're the gal that solved that St Lucy murder, aren't you?" She squinted at me. "You here about the dead barmaid?"

There was no reason not to admit it. I nodded.

"I know Cricket had a big date on New Year's Eve and I thought she might have come by to have her hair done. I thought she might have talked to you," I looked at Pat, "about her plans for that night."

Pat's response wasn't very encouraging.

"Nope," she said. "You still wanna haircut?"

"Sure."

I watched in the mirror as Pat attacked my hair. Within seconds she had it standing on end. I looked like the 1950s sunburst clock that Elli's mom had had in her living room. Pat's scissors snipped with quick efficiency.

"I heard that girl was kilt with a knittin' needle," Ronnie said, with unseemly enthusiasm. "And then somebody turned around and did the same to an old lady from Red Jacket. Betty Ann Pritula talked about it on the radio. I heard the killer was some guy from Red Jacket. Lars something."

I knew I should keep my mouth shut but I couldn't.

"Lars Teljo. He's my brother-in-law and he didn't kill Cricket or anybody else."

"Cheated with her though, didn't he?" Pat's contribution to the conversation made me want to leap out of the chair and run out of the room.

"Where there's smoke, there's fire," Ronnie said. "They found the girl at his cabin, didn't they?"

I held onto my temper.

"He was set up."

"Folks are sayin' there was a secret baby," Ronnie continued, "and that's why he killed her."

"Coulda been somebody else was the daddy," Pat said.

"Was the weapon really a knitting needle," Ronnie asked. "Seems like you folks down in Red Jacket get all the excitement."

It occurred to me that I could have stirred their interest even more with an account of Mrs. Paikkonen's knitting needle death but I decided not to. They weren't really ghouls. Murder was exciting when it had nothing to do with you or your loved ones.

A brush was raked through my hair and something highly aromatic sprayed on it. Pat whipped off the cape and handed me a small, oval face mirror. She'd managed to cut it evenly and I now looked kind of fuzzy, like the last stages of an expiring dandelion.

"Thanks," I said, pulling my wallet out of a backpack. "What do I owe you?"

"Twelve bucks," Ronnie said. I handed Pat a twenty.

"Keep the change."

"I seen some gray hairs in there," she said, as her fingers closed around the bill.

"Happy New Year, hon," Ronnie said as I waved and headed for the stairs.

The main floor of the house was disturbingly quiet. I tiptoed into the kitchen where I found Wanda seated at a rickety kitchen table. She was having a cigarette and a cup of coffee.

"Where is everybody?"

"The baby's down for a nap," she said, taking my question literally. I hadn't realized there was a baby. "Harry took the boys down to the market for Twizzlers. He's awesome. Is he married?" I eyed her. I was pretty sure Wanda was younger than I.

"No. Not at the moment. He's with a company of television folks shooting a pilot down in Red Jacket."

She expelled a stream of smoke.

"I'm not surprised. He seems like somebody famous." She squinted at me. "I see mom gave you a scalping."

"It'll grow back. Listen, do you know who Cricket Koski is?"

Wanda nodded.

"You ever talk to her?"

She shook her head. "I seen her around town a few times. Saw her get into a SUV once."

My heart seemed to stop. Lars has a black SUV.

"Did you notice the color?"

Wanda shrugged. "Something dark. There was snow on it."

"Can you remember when it was?"

"Last few days."

I could hardly catch my breath.

"Was it on New Year's Day?"

"Maybe. Days kinda run together. Might have been then. Or before."

I tried to stay calm.

"Wanda, could you see who the man was who was driving the SUV?"

She took a long drag on her cigarette then blew the smoke out in a series of perfect rings. I prayed Harry wouldn't come back with the kids until I'd gotten what I needed from Wanda.

"No. The driver didn't get out." My heart fell. "I could just see a kind of outline from the back, you know?" I nodded. "It stuck up in all directions, like your hair when you got here."

"My hair?" She nodded.

"It coulda been a guy wearing a parka hood, I guess, but, to tell the truth, it looked more like a woman's hat. One of those fancy ones with lots of fur."

I stared at her. A woman's hat? Had we been searching all this time for the wrong gender? Helena Tallmaster had a big, furry hat. On the other hand, Serena Waterfall's hair could look like a furry hat under the right conditions.

I was floored. And confused. How did Prince Charming fit into all of this?

The door opened. Harry, looking like a mother duck followed by a pair of ducklings, stepped through the door.

"Nice hair cut, Cupcake. You look like a baby starfish."

CHAPTER 33

T he snow had started to fall again and when Harry offered to drive, I let him. He made a U-turn on Fifth and a right on the interstate. I glanced at the convenience store.

"A penny for your thoughts, Cupcake," he said.

I wasn't ready to tell him about Wanda's sighting of the SUV. Whether Serena or Helena was implicated in this, that implicated Harry, too. He'd been married to both of them.

"Did you have a good time at the UP version of a Seven-Eleven?"

He grinned. "A great time. The boys got Twizzlers and pop rockets and gummy worms and I got to meet the delightful Mrs. Bjornsen and her dog, Puck. Puck, I have to tell you, was not named after the character in a Midsummer Night's Dream."

"You don't have to tell me that. I'm from the land of hockey, remember."

"What did you learn from Pat?"

"Not much. Pat's not much of a talker and, anyway, Cricket didn't get her hair done on Saturday. So I guess this was a wasted trip."

"Not a bit of it. I got to try a gummy worm and I got to spend time with you." I turned to face him.

"That flirting's just kind of automatic isn't it?"

"Long habit," he admitted, "but I really do like spending time with you, Cupcake. You're so delightfully guileless."

"You mean naïve?" He laughed.

"In a good way. A conversation with you isn't a game of chess. You say what you're thinking. I find it refreshing."

"Thanks."

We drove in silence for a few minutes and then he shocked me.

"Would you go away with me?"

"Away?"

"Somewhere hot and warm, Italy or Brazil. Somewhere we could lie around on the beach and wait for your hair to grow out."

"Geez Louise," I gasped. "You really had me going there for a minute." He didn't laugh.

"It's a real invitation. We'll all be leaving the Keweenaw very soon. I feel the need of some sunshine. I think you could use some, too."

I could, of course. But not with him and he seemed to know it. He let the subject lapse.

We were halfway back to Red Jacket when I spoke again.

"Harry, the murders were committed with a knitting needle, right? Did you ever consider that the killer might be a woman?"

"Because of the choice of weapon? I'm not sure a woman would have the strength to plunge a needle into someone's heart. Maybe so, if she used the element of surprise."

"There was no surprise in Mrs. Paikkonen's case. She knew the killer was after her the whole time she was hiding the letter in her corset, fleeing to the attic and drawing the *karsikko* sign."

"I'd like to think it was Vincent," Harry said, after a moment. "I've never liked the guy and I've come to loathe him. Helena was a fool. But the evidence points elsewhere, Cupcake."

"You're talking about the Camp Kaleva picture."

"That and the fact that he's the right age for Prince Charming. He knows about art and antiques and, perhaps, most importantly, he knew where Mrs. Paikkonen was sleeping that night."

Except, I thought, she wasn't killed during the night. She was killed in the afternoon.

"How many times have you been married?"

"What kind of a question is that?"

"It's a curiosity question. A getting-to-know-you question. You came up to the Keweenaw with a party of five of which there were two women and you were once married to each of them." He chuckled.

"I went through the motions with them because they wanted it. A hippie friend of Serena's did the deed in a backyard and with Helena, it was a justice of the peace. None of that Cinderella wedding followed by happily-ever-after for me."

His comment triggered a twinge of recognition. No Cinderella wedding for him. Ernst Hautamaki had sent his Aunt Bengta a wedding gift for a couple whose names started with the letter R. What if that, like the dog allusion, was a kind of code? What if there hadn't been a wedding gift at all but something meant to look like a wedding gift? What if the wedding gift was the cover?

And as I stared out at the lightly dusted roadway, the bits and chips of information in my mind shook and rattled and settled into a kaleidoscope image and I knew.

Ernst Hautamaki had sent Monet's priceless waterlilies home to his family and asked them to ship it to the U.S. in the perfect disguise; inside a double-knotted rug destined as a wedding gift. A Rya Rug. R.R.

Adrenalin shot through me and I unrolled my window hoping the cold air would take the heat out of my cheeks.

"You getting a fever, Cupcake?"

"Just a little warm."

"Well, since turnabout's fair play and since I know you've only been married once, why don't you tell me how many times you plan to be married?"

"That's a joke, I know, but some folks up here know all that stuff. How many times they'll be married, how many jobs they'll have, how many kids. It's kind of reassuring." Harry made a face.

"If I knew all that in advance, I wouldn't bother to live through it."

The phone interrupted us. It was Elli.

"Hatti! You've got to get back here on the double. All hell is breaking loose. Vincent said Helena was throwing up all night so he called 911 and they're on the way to the hospital now." She paused. "Listen, Seth thinks the Tallmasters killed Mrs. Pike, found the painting and are now escaping."

A picture of Helena Tallmaster driving the SUV with Cricket Koski flashed through my head.

"Wait? They're escaping in an ambulance?"

"They took their luggage. All of it. Anyway, it's not a bad strategy. Who would stop an ambulance? Vincent will probably insist that they airlift them both to a hospital downstate. Then, while she's being attended to, he can slip away and unload the painting. You know, he could put it in a bus locker or, or, mail it to a post office box somewhere."

"You've been watching too much television. For one thing, the hospital isn't going to order a helicopter on Vincent's say-so. For another, there's no reason to think they've got the Monet."

Harry had been driving steadily through the snowflakes, his eyes on the road but when he heard my words he glanced over at me.

"Somebody found the painting?"

I shrugged and then returned to my conversation with Elli.

"Look, just let Jace know what's going on, and Waino. We'll be there shortly. I want to stop at the theater first."

"Don't bother. There's no one there. Vincent canceled the pilot. Big surprise. At least Arvo will be happy when we get rid of the swastikas."

When I hung up I gave Harry the news.

"Hmm," he said. "So it was Vincent all along, with assistance from my former wife. Shocking. Where to now? Back to the Leaping Deer? Looks like there's nothing left but the crying and cleanup. And, of course, lunch."

His lighthearted tone rubbed me the wrong way. We were talking here about major crimes; robbery and the most heinous sin

ANN YOST

of all, murder. I wished I were alone. I wished I could go down to
the opera house by myself to check out my hunch. But I'd let Harry
into the investigation and into my life and now I had him. Life, I
thought, again harkening back to the Moomins, was all about
accommodation and acceptance. *Things are so very uncertain and that's
exactly what makes me feel reassured.*

"I'd like to stop at the opera house."

For once Harry's eyes contained no laughter.

"You gonna tell me why?"

I didn't want to. For one thing, it would entail too much explanation. For another, well, I just felt protective of my idea and Harry
had a tendency to be scathing.

"Tell you what," I said, finally. "I'll show you."

His lips twisted as he looked back out at the road way.

"Sure, Cupcake," he said. "As always, your wish is my
command."

My imagination kicked into overdrive as we stepped into the
theater in which some efficient person (Ollie Rahkunen) had already
turned off the heat. Already the place smelled musty and felt abandoned. And what if the Tallmaster theory was right? What if they'd
already taken off with the Waterlilies? Suddenly, I was glad I hadn't
shared my Rya Rug theory with Harry. A low-wattage stagelight had
been left on and, as we started down the carpeted aisle toward it I
could see the outlines of the curtains and the posters we'd hung of
Rosie the Riveter and G.I. Joe. I could see the shapes of the tables
decorated with Sofi's flower arrangements. In the semi-dark they
looked as curly as the fur on Helena Tallmaster's Russian hat. I was
aware of the presence of a building tension and when I heard
Harry's sharp intake of breath, I realized it was coming from him. I
turned to him.

"What? What is it?"

He pointed a finger at the stage.

"Your rug is gone."

I stared at the spot where the rug had hung. Holy Geez Frickin'
Louise! He was right. The clothesline was still in place. But the rug –
with the sixty-million-dollar painting in it? – had vanished.

Anger galvanized me and I ran up the stage steps to find a pile of white wool that looked as if someone had recently sheared a very small lamb. Whoever took the rug had slashed it open. Of course.

"I'm sorry, Cupcake," Harry said. They were familiar words from him but not a familiar tone. He was breathing hard and sweat had popped out on his face. The tension I'd felt before was suffocating now. "We'll have to report this to Sheriff Andy and Deputy Dawg. Let's go."

The fact is, I wanted to go. Being in the empty theater was giving me the creeps and, I realized, it was less about the rug and more about the heightened mania of the man with me. In silence, we turned to head back up the aisle. That's when I heard a faint moan.

"Harry!" I clutched his arm. "Did you hear that?"

"No."

"There it is again. It's kind of ghostly."

"The ghost is gone, remember? You're imagining things." He took my hand and headed toward the theater doors.

It was the third sound, a kind of muffled thump that made me pull away from him and head back toward the stage. I heard him calling my name but I didn't stop until I'd opened the door to the green room. I froze and stared at the Rya Rug. Someone had slit it open and wrapped it, like pasty dough, around a body. The red hair flaring at one end made a ridiculous picture, like a bulky rocket igniting into the air and finally, *finally,* I understood.

"I'm sorry you had to see this, Cupcake."

It was Harry's voice in my ear. And it was Harry's strong hands that captured mine and bound them, painfully, behind my back.

Of course it was Harry. He was the one with the contacts in the art world. He was the one who coveted the works of Monet. He was the bored soul on a never-ending quest for adventure. He'd undoubtedly had the help of Serena. Had she been complicit or a useful idiot? I guess we'd find out.

Well, somebody would find out. It looked like I was going to be tied up for awhile. A shudder ran down my spine. Who was I kidding? He couldn't afford to let me or Serena live. How was he planning to kill us? Another knitting needle? Maybe someone (Jace) would think to look at the theater. I wished and wished I'd told Elli my plan to come down here. Sooner or later they'd start looking for me but would it be too late?

"Tell me one thing," I said. "How did you know Cricket?"

"Is this a stall tactic or do you really want to know?"

I answered him truthfully.

"Both."

"You know that if I tell you I'll have to kill you." He turned me around to face him. I was pretty sure he intended to kill me anyway, and Serena, too.

"I want to know."

"Sure. I was a guest speaker at the camp. They'd asked for some from the FBI and, since I was in the Detroit office at the time, they sent me. I gave a couple of lectures on crime. Ironic, isn't it?"

"I don't understand why you were interested in a seventeen-year-old."

"C'mon, Cupcake." He sounded bored. "She was tall, blond and all over me. That explain it?"

Was he really that shallow? That much of a sociopath? How had I failed to see any of this?

"Did you really tell her you'd come back to find her after you'd gotten a divorce?"

"It's a bone, you know? Keeps them from hounding you with pleas."

My phone rang and Harry betrayed his tension by digging his fingers into my upper arm.

"Don't answer that."

I didn't bother to point out that with my hands tied behind my back, I'd have had to answer it with my tongue.

When the ringing stopped, he retrieved the phone from the pocket of my jeans and asked for the code to hear the message. The call had been from Seth and he sounded worried.

"*Hei*, Hatti. I was thinking about those days at camp and I remembered that we always had so-called experts in their fields who came to talk to us about possible careers. On a hunch, I borrowed a magnifying glass from your aunt, then found the picture at your house. To tell you the truth, I was looking for Vincent Tallmaster but I found someone else. I guess I owe Vincent an apology. Call me as soon as you get this."

I swallowed hard. If there had been any hope, it was gone now.

"Well, hell," Harry said, softly. "I'd best get a move on. I'll have to take care of Seth, too."

"One last question." My throat was dry with fear and it was hard to talk. "Did you devise this plan because you value a piece of art over human lives or was it because you were bored?"

CHAPTER 34

"A little of this, a little of that. Sorry, Cupcake." He quickly and efficiently hooked his foot under my leg and dropped me to the floor where my head hit hard enough to make me see stars. By the time I'd recovered my focus he was gone and my cellphone, too.

My first thought was that we, Serena and I, would be all right. He'd left us bound but not mortally wounded. Someone would look for us here and find us, but I didn't wait for that to happen. I started to wiggle my wrists to try to free them from the strip of cloth that bound them.

"Is he gone?"

Serena sounded less relieved than heartbroken. At least she was conscious.

"I think so. I conked out for a minute there. He closed the green room door. Don't know if he locked it."

"You can't lock it," she said, dully. "He checked when he retrieved the painting. Just before he knocked me out."

"I'm sorry. Are you all right now?"

She didn't answer but there was no need. She'd adored Harry Dent and he'd abandoned her. She'd never be all right again.

I was so surprised and pleased to be able to wriggle free of the cloth binding my wrists that it didn't occur to me to wonder why

Harry had done such a lackluster job. I should have known that, as usual, there was method in his madness. I staggered to my feet and then to the door where I met a fog of smoke and heard the crackle of flames.

That's when I understood. Harry intended to burn down the theater with Serena and me in it. I beat back the panic that exploded inside me, closed the door and hurried back to Serena. He'd wrapped her as tight as an enchilada in the Rya Rug and I worked, feverishly to loosen the fabric. And to keep the fear out of my voice.

"Can you stand? The theater's on fire."

She didn't answer and things were moving fast. The smoke started to seep under the door and billow into the room in ominous gusts. I tried to make my fingers work faster. All I had to do was free Serena from the rug and dash for the door on the opposite side of the green room – the door that led to the outdoors and safety. The sound of the fire got louder, like a jet taking off overhead but I got the other woman to her feet and, even though she stumbled as the circulation came back, I knew we would make it.

At least until I heard the anguished howl from the stage.

"Geez Louise."

"Harry," Serena said, on a sob.

For an instant (of which I'm not proud) I considered sticking to my plan but five hundred-plus Sundays of being taught to do unto your neighbor as you would yourself kicked in. I let go of her, grabbed what was left of the rug and plowed toward the stage door.

Normally there's little visibility in the scene of a fire and even less when the lights are out. I met the dark plumes of smoke but the stage was lit up like a macabre theater marquee with licks of flame running across and down the curtains. Harry was at center stage flapping wildly at flames that had leapt onto his clothing and skin. I hurried toward him and tried to cover him with the rug, hoping to douse the flames but, as he was whirling and jerking like a man possessed, I wound up swatting at him over and until the fire was subdued. I was gasping for breath and leaning against his kneeling form when a geyser of water slammed into me knocking me onto my back. An instant later I started to kick and struggle as I was scooped up into a pair of strong arms.

"It's me, Umlaut," a voice barked. "Be still and let me get you out of here."

Jace! I slipped my arms around his neck and held on tight. A few seconds later, I remembered I wasn't the only one who needed a knight on a white horse. Or a red fire truck.

"Harry's hurt, and Serena Waterfall is in the green room. I'm not sure she can walk."

"Waino, check the green room," Sir Galahad called out. Strange, his voice sounded deeper and more raspy than usual. "Call Arvo and get the hearse. This man needs the hospital."

He'd carried me to a door on the other side of the stage and I felt a sudden blast of snow and blessed cold air. I looked up into the gray eyes to thank him but they were amber. For a second, I wondered if I was hallucinating, and then I realized my rescuer wasn't Jace, after all. "You're back," I said to Max Guthrie. "Good thing for you," he said. "You just couldn't stay out of trouble, could you?"

Someone must have already called Arvo because we were still crossing the street headed for the fire station when the hearse pulled up and a cluster of fire fighting volunteers rushed into the building to retrieve what was left of Harry Dent.

It didn't occur to me, until an hour later after I'd been pampered, and cleaned up and given a cup of coffee, that the Monet masterpiece had probably been destroyed in the fire.

CHAPTER 35

So we had our murderer. Or, rather, we knew who it was.
Harry Dent, having expired in the hearse on the way to the
hospital, was now en route to *Tuonela*, the Land of the Dead and I
very much doubted he would be leaving a *karsikko* sign.

That evening we gathered in Elli's parlor the way people do
after a cataclysmic event or, in the case of Red Jacket, after church
on Sunday. This time, though, there was no scent of baking
pannukakku or lingonberry syrup. We were there to regroup, to try to
make sense of what had happened to us, to try to see a path
forward. I'd need to do the same with my own life when all this was
finished.

Jace had shown up at the fire house and he'd brought me home
which might seem anticlimactic but actually felt very comforting.
He'd checked me out for injuries, probed the goose egg on the back
of my head and listened to my lungs, for all the world as if he were
a doctor, supervised my shower and told Sofi not to let me go to
sleep any time soon since I probably had a concussion. Then he left.
As usual. And he didn't come back. Not for the smorgasbord supper
or for the gathering.

I sat on Elli's sofa in between Aunt Ianthe and Miss Irene who had finished the pair of socks they'd been working on and were now sitting with their hands folded in their laps. Ronja Laplander, the Hakalas, Mrs. Moilanen, Elli and Arvo and Seth, Sofi, Lars, Max and the Tallmasters were all there.

Much had been made of the role the Rya Rug had played in the afternoon's events.

"The heavens declare the glory of God, and the firmament showeth his handiwork," Miss Irene murmured, not for the first time. "Psalm nineteen."

I exchanged a look with Max Guthrie who stood next to Elli's big, stone fireplace with his arm along the mantelpiece. Tall, lanky with a rugged, unhandsome visage and a shock of salt-and-pepper hair, he was a sight for sore eyes and I felt a little flutter in my heart. My Sir Galahad. I realized I'd missed him. I wanted to ask about Sonya, why she'd gone home to New Mexico and why it had taken him four days to drive her to an airport, but this wasn't the time.

And then the front door opened and I could barely breathe as Jace Night Wind entered the room with the graceful movements of a professional tracker. His gray eyes with the impossibly long, dark lashes found me at once. He stared at me as he took up a pose on the other side of the mantelpiece.

Vince Tallmaster stood and cleared his throat to get everyone's attention. When he had it, he began to speak.

"Our pilot has been bruised and battered but it is not, I think, dead. In fact, not to put too fine a point on it, I think we can see this afternoon's events as a phoenix rising from the ashes." No one replied to the shocking comment. Not even Miss Irene.

"What we have to do now is find that painting. Serena will be able to tell us where he hid it as soon as she's released from the hospital."

I made eye contact with Jace and we communicated silently.
Should I mention that the painting was most likely destroyed in the fire?
No. Don't say anything at the moment.

"I don't think Serena will have too much to add," Seth said, slowly. "My guess is that Harry enlisted her help without giving her any real information. Everything I know about Serena Waterfall indicates she'd never condone the theft of a Monet to say nothing of murder. What do you think, Hatti?"

I thought he was right in general but that, being a guy, he had no idea how badly Serena had wanted to please her ex-husband.

"I think she would have balked at murder. There was no mistaking her shock and distress when she found Mrs. Paikkonen."

Vincent continued as if he hadn't been interrupted.

"This show will have it all," he said, rubbing his palms together. "Everything from grand theft to love and death to Nazi loot. The ratings will be out of sight."

Arvo's deep voice cut through the horrified silence.

"No, I don't think so. This comes to an end now. It would be in bad taste to exploit the tragedy."

"I'm afraid I have to agree," Seth put in. "I really don't think we can continue."

"But my Nazi flowers! I've already paid for my Nazi flowers!"

I realized he hadn't seen the inside of the theater. The red carnations with the swastikas were now toast.

A knock on the front door heralded the arrival of Sheriff Clump and Waino.

"Awright, then," the sheriff said as Elli took his hat and jacket and guided him to an easy chair. "Since you're all together we can cross the t's and dot the i's and get this report sent off to the state." He nodded in response to Elli's offer of refreshments. "Deputy here says that feller that died in the fire, he was the killer. Anybody got any proof of that?"

The beady eyes of our local law enforcer were on me so I tried to gather my thoughts. Did we have any proof? Except for the fact that he'd tried to kill Serena and me by setting the opera house on fire, the answer was no.

"He the one that took the picture?"

"We believe the picture had been hidden inside a double-knotted rug called a Rya. It had been there for three-quarters of a century and we believe that the hiding place was revealed in a letter translated by Mrs. Paikkonen. Harry must have forced the information from her before he killed her. He went down to the opera house with Serena, slit the rug open, took out the Monet, then bound his ex-wife in the Rya Rug."

"Where's that rug at now?"

"It's with the evidence from the fire at the fire house," Max said. "Hatti used the rug to put out the burning man."

The sheriff's beady eyes swung to me.

"I think you better tell me the whole shebang. Chapter and verse. A to Z."

"Soup to nuts," Aunt Ianthe added.

"The whole truth and nothing but the truth," Mrs. Moilanen said.

"And ye shall know the truth, and the truth shall make you free," said Miss Irene. "First John."

Fatigue cascaded down on me like a fall of thundersnow, and, for a minute, I didn't think I'd get through the story. I glanced at Jace and, once again, we communicated without words.

I can't do it.

Yes, you can.

Elli read my thoughts, too, and brought me a cup of coffee. Clump stared at me as he worked his way through a plate of brownie bars.

"The story is that back in 1942, a young Finnish soldier named Ernst Hautamaki who could speak Finnish and German was stationed in Munich as a diplomatic courier of some sort. He came upon this painting by Claude Monet, one of the hundreds of paintings he'd made of his water garden in France. Anyway, we don't know how Ernst got ahold of it but we're pretty sure the painting had been stolen from its original owner by the Nazis. As of now, it is worth some sixty million dollars."

Clump's jaw dropped revealing a mound of chocolate.

We believe that Ernst spirited the Monet out of Germany by mailing it to Finland along with a letter asking his family, probably his mother, to protect it by sending it to the United States to his great aunt who was visiting here at the time. Ernst's mother, who must have been a pretty smart cookie, hid the painting inside the double-knotted Rya Rug and sent it with a note explaining the rug had originally been intended as a wedding gift, but as the wedding was off, she wanted Bengta to hang onto it until Ernst could retrieve it."

"Why?" The question came from Waino. "Was Ernst gettin' married, too?"

"Maybe. In any case, Ernst never came to get it and Bengta Hautamaki never made it home to Finland. They both died that summer. So the Rya Rug with the Monet masterpiece tucked in between the knotted sides, was here all the time. Pops had it in his study for a long time then when we turned the bait shop into a fishing-supplies-slash-knitting supplies shop, I asked if I could hang it on the wall there."

Clump screwed up his face and, for once, his tiny eyes were shrewd.

"How's that letter fit in?"

I nodded. I was feeling better, either because I was nearly finished or because of the caffeine.

"Good question, sheriff. Elli found the letter in a box of memorabilia in her attic. We were all searching our attics because Vincent and his television company wanted to use World War II as a theme for their pilot. As I said, Mrs. Paikkonen offered to translate the letter but she must have realized there was something secret about it and she kept stalling. Finally Harry Dent took the situation into his own hands and forced her to tell what she knew. And then he killed her."

"How's this square away with Cricket Koski," Waino asked.

"Another good question. Harry had met her at a Finnish culture camp ten years ago when she was a camper and he was a visiting speaker. She fell for him and he said he'd be back. I don't suppose he had this missing Monet in mind at the time but he might have, since his business was lost and stolen paintings. Anyway, he got in touch with Cricket to help him figure out which of the houses in Red Jacket might have the painting."

"How in the Sam Hill could she have helped him with that?"

I shrugged. "He told her to hire a private detective to provide background on the Finnish-American families and she hired Lars Teljo, which was exactly what he wanted. Harry Dent was a master strategist. He'd figured everything out ahead of time up to and including the fact that he'd have to kill Cricket and he'd need someone to frame for it and who better than the guy with whom she'd had the one-night stand all those years ago."

"Diabolical," Max muttered. "I can't believe I missed all of this."

"Why now," Aunt Ianthe asked. "The Nazis stole a fifth of the world's art treasures seventy-five years ago. Why did Harry Dent decide to come looking for the Waterlilies now?"

"I believe I can explain that," the Reverend Sorensen said. "In the past number of years there have been several academic studies aimed at finding the contact points between Nazi loot that is still missing and various countries. A study in Finland revealed that there were Finnish diplomats in Germany at the site where the loot was kept. The connection with the Upper Peninsula was noted, too."

"You asked for proof of murder or intent, sheriff," Jace said. "Dent certainly intended for Hatti and Serena to die in that fire."

I smiled at him but I wondered. Harry was nobody's fool. He'd bound Serena closely, but he'd barely tied my hands at all and he must have known there was another exit in the Green Room. I didn't think he'd intended to kill us. He'd just needed time to get away.

"He got caught in a web of his own making," the Reverend Sorensen said.

Naturally, Miss Irene chimed in.

"They hatch cockatrice's eggs, and weave the spider's web: He that eateth of their eggs dieth and that which is crushed breaketh out into a viper. Isaiah."

"Why use a knitting needle to kill Cricket and Mrs. Paikkonen," Waino asked.

"It might have been intended to cast suspicion upon somebody local, since our community is known for knitting," Elli said. "Or, maybe it was just handy the first time and he decided to stick with a theme for consistency when it came to Mrs. Paikkonen."

I felt sick thinking of Mrs. Pike. I should have been able to protect her and I'd failed.

"Here's the sixty-million-dollar question," Clump said, finishing the last brownie and brushing the crumbs off his massive front. "Where in the H-E-double-hockey-sticks is the damn picture?"

For the first time I felt a wave of grief. We'd had the French Impressionist masterpiece here on the Keweenaw and we'd lost it.

"There's one more rabbit to pull out of the hat," Jace said, producing a standard-sized mailing tube. "Hatti, you should do the honors because I found it thanks to your efforts."

I got off the sofa and walked toward him. He'd already cut the tape and the label. All I had to do was pull off the end cap and I did. Then Jace used his long, lean fingers to ease the contents out.

"What is it, Henrikki?" Aunt Ianthe, as usual carried away by the moment, couldn't resist asking.

"If it's not the Monet," Sofi said, drily, "I'm gonna want my money back."

"What money, dearie?"

But Aunt Ianthe's question was forgotten immediately as I carefully unrolled the brittle canvas and held up the small painting, some twenty-four inches by thirty-six inches. The entire surface was water, greens, purples, blues and cream with the sun showing up only as glints in the ripples and on the petals of ballet-pink petals. It was breathtaking.

"An ode," Aunt Ianthe pronounced, "to the majesty of art and nature."

"I will speak of the glorious honor of thy majesty, and of thy wonderous works," Miss Irene said.

"There's no sky," Mrs. Moilanen pointed out. "Just water."

"It's spotted," Ronja Laplander said. "Like a dalmation."

"I've never seen colors like that in Lake Superior," Diane Hakala added.

"This work is titled *A Reflection of Clouds*," I said, reading a penciled note on the back. "Monet was known for his fascination with the effects of light."

"And, remember," Aunt Ianthe said, in her teaching voice, "he was of the Impressionist school. The painting represents his emotions, not what his eye sees."

"And to think it was stolen by the Nazis," Seth said.

"In the morning we'll contact the Art Loss Register in New York," Jace said. "They have a database of missing paintings. But I don't think there's much doubt that it is a legitimate Monet and that it was stolen before or during World War II."

"That's ancient history," Clump said. "What I wanna know is how you came to have it?"

Jace rolled up the painting and handed it to Waino for safekeeping. I was relieved to see the big deputy handle it with care. Jace looked at me.

"After the fire Hatti filled me in on what had happened so far. She told me about the Rya Rug, how it must have been the hiding place for the painting for more than seventy years. We constructed a timeline for Dent and it seemed as if he and Serena Waterfall must have slipped over to the theater during the night, slashed open the rug and removed the painting. He drugged his former wife then tied her up and left her there. That gave him a few hours before anyone else was up and about and it occurred to me that he had few options.

"He could have left it at the theater if he'd planned to come back and collect it and Serena. The fact that he had silenced her but hadn't really hurt her pointed to that possibility. But what if someone came down to the theater? What if Serena was released and there was no way to sneak back in and get the painting? No, I figured someone like Dent would have come up with a better solution. So where else could he hide the Monet?"

"The Lehtinen house?" The suggestion was made by Aunt Ianthe.

Jace nodded. "Possibly but, he risked someone finding it or, more likely, there being people around when he wanted to go. And why didn't he go in the early hours of the morning after he'd retrieved the painting and tied up his ex-wife?'"

"I was wondering that, myself," Elli said. "He could have gotten into Hatti's Jeep and driven to Canada. He could even have left her a note so no one would look for him immediately."

"But we would have looked for him and we would have found him," Waino said. "They have all-points-bulletin in Canada, too, you know."

"And it would have taken a long time," the Reverend Sorensen said. "He'd have had to drive across the UP, cross the Mighty Mac and go down to Detroit to cross into Ontario or he'd have had to drive through Wisconsin and north through Minnesota to cross the border. He couldn't have taken a boat, not at this time of year."

"The fact is he didn't flee," Jace said. "He stuck around and when Hatti said she was driving up to Copper Harbor, he saw his chance. He may have had the painting in his room or he may have stashed it in the back of the Jeep in the middle of the night. I think it was the latter. Then he waited for the perfect set up and he got it when Hatti was talking with the hair stylist and her friend. Dent offered to take the grandchildren to the convenience store-slash-post office. He bought the kids candy and chatted up the postmistress, Mrs. Boykin who packaged it up for him. He sent it to a post office box in New York state."

"Geez Louise," I said, suddenly. "I wonder if he got the idea from Ernst Hautamaki. He used the mail to protect the painting and Harry used the mail to steal it." I looked at him. "How did you know?"

"It was just a suspicion but it seemed likely. How else was he to get it out of town without any questions asked? And this way, it would be waiting for him when he got home."

"How could he have expected to get away with two murders, a kidnapping, arson and the theft of the Monet?" Arvo asked.

I answered him.

"Like Sheriff Clump said, there was no proof that Harry had killed the women. He probably intended to go back to the opera house and burn it down after he mailed off the painting. He'd probably planned to claim that he'd tried to rescue Serena by wrapping her in the rug. I could tell he was reluctant to go to the theater with me. He knew then he'd have to include me in his plans and that may have shaken him enough to throw off his usual impeccable timing in the arson."

"In all that planning," Max said, "he miscalculated on one key thing. The fire department is just across Main Street, twenty feet away from the opera house. That's one big reason the old place has survived this long."

"The Lord works in mysterious ways," Miss Irene said.

The Reverend Sorensen looked at her.

"You know that is not in the Holy Bible," he said, gently. She smiled at him.

"But you have to admit, it fits."

"What will happen to Serena," Sofi asked.

"She'll have to tell her story. I imagine she was an accessory after the fact but she may have been coerced. And then there's the delicacy of the matter. If the U.S. can return this painting to the heirs of the original owners, almost certainly Holocaust survivors, it is a gesture of good faith between countries and strengthens international relations. The crimes can't be hidden but the whole process will be tainted if Serena is prosecuted for murder. I imagine the government will let her go."

More coffee was brought out and more bars, brownies and snickerdoodles. Everyone was talking, asking questions and going over and over the events of the day. It was the way our community always dealt with big events, by coming together and it should have been immensely comforting but I kept seeing Harry with his clothes on fire and I kept hearing Serena's moans and all I wanted to do was go off by myself.

So I did. Larry abandoned his nest in the kitchen and stayed with me in the attic. I didn't expect to sleep but I didn't wake up once. Not even to use the chamber pot.

When I opened my eyes, the daylight was streaming in through the small window and Larry had been replaced by Jace who was sitting on the bed next to me.

"You just slept for twelve hours," he said. "Post traumatic stress event. Very normal. Anyway, I'm glad you're awake. I didn't want to leave without saying goodbye."

He was leaving. I swallowed hard. My instincts had been right, then. He had only come back to help with the investigation. He'd done that twice now and it seemed like this would be the end. Murders were rare on the Keweenaw. It would be years until we'd have another.

"I'm flying to D.C. to talk to the FBI's art theft squad and to turn over the painting. And I'm taking Serena Waterfall with me."

"That's nice."

"Once the paperwork is finished, someone will be appointed to return the painting to the heirs who live in France. The officer in charge asked who should get the honor of being the courier. I suggested a name and he approved it. It was your name, Umlaut."

"My name?"

"If you want to go to Paris."

I stared at him. "You think I want to go to the most romantic city in the world by myself?"

"Not by yourself." He sounded like his usual confident self but his expression was uncertain. "They approved a plus-one. You can take anyone you want. I was hoping you'd view this as your official honeymoon, though, and take your husband."

It was a grand gesture and emotions rose in my throat. But I needed to know whether this plus one was just a one off.

"I want to show you the Eiffel Tower, and Montmartre and the Champs Elysee before the lease starts on my new office. I've rented the space above Hakala's Pharmacy. That way, when times are slow, I can entertain myself by watching you and your knitting circle at Bait and Stitch."

"You want to settle down on the Keweenaw?"

"I want you, Hatti. And if the Keweenaw comes with, I won't complain."

Our goodbye kiss was long and intense and when we finally came up for air, his voice was husky.

He nodded.

"Hell's bells. Pack up a few clothes for the city of lights. I'm going nowhere without you."

That sounded good to me.

The End

Don't miss the recipe for JOULUTORTTU (Christmas Tarts) right after the excerpt for *A Fair Isle Murder*. It's all waiting, just ahead!

A FAIR ISLE MURDER

THE BAIT & STITCH COZY MYSTERY SERIES,
BOOK THREE

A Corpse in a Copse

The bridegroom was late for the shotgun wedding and the bride about to have kittens.

The raw anger on Kensington Hoop's pretty face did not bode well for Chad "the Cad" Cadwallader and I, for one, was okay with that. After breaking my cousin Elli's heart and tricking her out of her family's Bed and Breakfast, the charming snake oil salesman deserved a petulant wife.

Of course, not everybody felt the same way about that.

My Great Aunt Ianthe, for instance, with her soft as melted butter heart.

"My, she's a pretty girl," Ianthe said. "And the dress is so becoming," she added, referring to the Spandex creation that covered Kensington's pregnancy bump.

If Ianthe was reliably kind, her lifelong friend and companion, Miss Irene Suutula, was always Biblical.

"And they twain shall be one flesh," said Miss Irene.

My sister Sofi rolled her eyes and murmured, "One flesh? I think that ship has sailed."

We, my sister, cousin and the older ladies had journeyed from our home on Michigan's Keweenaw Peninsula to spend the weekend on Mackinac Island to help a friend launch a new yarn shop. We had not expected to be uninvited guests at the shotgun wedding between the daughter of the island's fudge king and Elli's erstwhile lover. It was a complete coincidence. Just as (I told myself) that both the bridegroom and Elli were currently Missing in Action.

A feral cry erupted near the rose-bedecked gazebo. It was loud enough to halt the string quartet and halt the buzz of conversations.

"Uh-oh," I said, secretly pleased with the Kensington Hoop's shout. "I think we're going to be treated to a full-out temper tantrum."

Sofi squinted at the gesticulating bride.

"Looks more like labor to me," my sister said. "Call an ambulance."

I scraped my phone out of my pocket and punched in 911. The call went to voicemail.

When I reported that Aunt Ianthe said, philosophically, "well, dearie, it probably doesn't matter. They don't allow motor vehicles on the island, you know. The ambulance is probably a golf cart. She'll have to go to the hospital in the horse-drawn carriage that brought her."

I looked at Sofi. "Do they even have a hospital here?"

My phone buzzed and caller I.D. said it was Elli.

"Hey," I said. "Where the H-E-double-hockey sticks are you?"

"Behind the gazebo in a little copse. There's something wrong with Chad. He isn't moving and I can't feel a pulse. Oh, Hatti! I think I killed him!"

Why was she behind the gazebo? Why was she with Chad? I knew it wasn't the time for a catechism. I could hear the shear panic in her voice.

"You've got to call an ambulance!"

My overactive imagination kicked in and I visualized Kensington Hoop giving birth in the front seat of a golf cart with her comatose and possibly dead fiance laid out next to her. I also (because I am a card-carrying, indoctrinated member of the Lutheran Evangelical Synod) felt a wave of guilt about my earlier wishes for revenge on Chad.) I shook it off. I needed to comfort my cousin.

"It's probably just a panic attack," I said. "Cold feet about the wedding and all. I'll be there in a minute. By the way, El, don't say that to anyone else. Remember, you had no reason to kill him."

"But that's just it," she said, starting to sob. "He asked me to meet him here. He wanted to tell me he'd signed a new Will that benefited me."

"You mean he willed you the Leaping Deer?"

"Not just that. Everything. I'm, I'm his sole heir."

Not good, I thought. Not good at all. My hands were shaking and my heart was in my mouth as I tried a broken field run through the wedding guests. I couldn't believe that murder had tracked me down again, this time in the Disneyworld of the North. And this time the stakes were sky high. This time, it involved my cousin and very best friend.

A FAIR ISLE MURDER
Available in eBook and Print

JOULUTORTTU

CHRISTMAS TARTS

Ingredients:

Pastry:

- 2 sticks (16 Tbsp.) salted butter, softened
- 8 oz. ricotta cheese
- 2 cups unbleached all-purpose flour

(note: ricotta gives pastry a unique melt-in-your-mouth taste but store-bought puff pastry will work, too.)

Filling:

- ½ cup prune jam (recipe below)
- 1 egg, lightly beaten
- Powdered sugar for dusting.

Preparation:

In a large bowl beat with electric hand mixer butter and ricotta cheese. Add flour and mix until dough comes together. It will be soft. Divide dough in half, shape each into a ball, cover with plastic wrap and refrigerate at least 2-3 hours, until firm.

Shape and bake:

- Preheat oven to 425 degrees F.
- Flour countertop and roll out one section of dough to about 1/8 inch thick, about 12x9 inches.
- Cut dough into 3-inch squares. Make cuts in each square from corners about 2/3 of the way toward center. Spoon one tsp. jam in center of each square. Fold every other corner over the jam (to make a pinwheel). Use beaten egg wash to moisten corners to press them over top of the jam. Brush cookies with egg wash.
- Do the same with other half of the dough then transfer cookies to parchment-lined baking sheet and bake for 10-12 minutes. When cool, dust with powdered sugar.

Prune Jam

Place 1 ½ cups roughly chopped prunes, ½ cup sugar and water to cover in small saucepan. Simmer until prunes are jammy. 20-30 minutes. Add more water if necessary. Remove pan from heat and cool before using in Joulutorttu.

ALSO BY ANN YOST

The Bait and Stitch Cozy Mystery Series

A Pattern for Murder

A Double Pointed Murder

A Fair Isle Murder

ABOUT THE AUTHOR

Ann Yost comes from Ann Arbor, Michigan and a writing family whose single greatest accomplishment is excellent spelling.

After six years at the University of Michigan she completed her degree in English literature and spent ten years working as a reporter, copy editor and humor columnist for three daily newspapers. Her most notable story at the Ypsilanti Press involved the tarring and feathering of a high school principal.

When she moved with her Associated Press reporter husband to the Washington D.C. area, she did freelance work for the Washington Post, including first-person humor stories on substitute teaching and little league umpiring.

She did feature writing for the Charles Stewart Mott Foundation on building community in low-income neighborhoods and after-school programs throughout the country.

While her three children were in high school, Ann began to write romantic suspense novels. Later, she turned to the Finnish-American community in Michigan's remote Upper Peninsula for her Hatti Lehtinen mystery series.

She lives in Northern Virginia with her husband and her enterprising mini-goldendoodle, Toby.

CPSIA information can be obtained
at www.ICGtesting.com
Printed in the USA
BVHW071145110319
542310BV00006B/373/P